THE BATTLE OF SEATTLE

Also by Douglas Bond

Mr. Pipes and the British Hymn Makers
Mr. Pipes and Psalms and Hymns of the Reformation
Mr. Pipes Comes to America
The Accidental Voyage

Duncan's War
King's Arrow
Rebel's Keep

Guns of Thunder
Guns of the Lion
Guns of Providence

Hostage Lands
Hand of Vengeance
Hammer of the Huguenots

STAND FAST In the Way of Truth
HOLD FAST In a Broken World

The Betrayal: A Novel on John Calvin
The Thunder: A Novel on John Knox
The Revolt: A Novel in Wycliffe's England

The Mighty Weakness of John Knox
The Poetic Wonder of Isaac Watts

Augustus Toplady: Debtor to Mercy Alone
Girolamo Savonarola: Heart Aflame (with Douglas McComas)

Grace Works! (And Ways We Think It Doesn't)

God's Servant Job

War in the Wasteland

THE BATTLE OF SEATTLE

DOUGLAS BOND

P&R
PUBLISHING
P.O. BOX 817 • PHILLIPSBURG • NEW JERSEY 08865-0817

Printed in the United States of America

Library of Congress Cataloging-in-Publication Data

Names: Bond, Douglas, 1958- author.
Title: The battle of Seattle / Douglas Bond.
Description: Phillipsburg, N.J. : P&R Publishing, [2016] | Series: Heroes & History | Summary: "It's 1855 in the Pacific Northwest. Young William Tidd's courage, friendships, and faith are challenged when he joins a mission with the Rangers to thwart a potentially hostile Indian chief"-- Provided by publisher.
Identifiers: LCCN 2016007197| ISBN 9781596387492 (pbk.) | ISBN 9781596387560 (epub) | ISBN 9781596387577 (mobi)
Subjects: LCSH: Pacific Coast Indians, Wars with, 1847-1865--Juvenile fiction. | CYAC: Pacific Coast Indians, Wars with, 1847-1865--Fiction. | Indians of North America--Washington Territory--Fiction. | Frontier and pioneer life--Washington Territory--Fiction. | Washington Territory--History--19th century--Fiction.
Classification: LCC PZ7.B63665 Bat 2016 | DDC [Fic]--dc23
LC record available at https://lccn.loc.gov/2016007197

For
Gillian, Giles, and Desmond;
Cedric and Ashley;
Rhodric, Tori, Gwenna, and Amelia;
Brittany and Jesse

"When you were born you cried and others rejoiced; live your life so that when you die you rejoice and others cry."

Native American saying

"I have been called to preach to sinners and you are the chief sinners of the territory."

Circuit-riding preacher, Joab Powell, speaking to territorial legislators on the eve of the Indian War in the 1850s

CONTENTS

EXPLANATORY

Historical fiction, an oxymoron to some, ought to provide an authentic lens into the life and times of real people living and often struggling through an-all-too-real historical moment. When done well, historical fiction should give us a more accurate and living perspective on the conflicts and challenges faced by historical figures in a given time—my goal in this historical novel.

William Tidd was a genuine, though lesser-known, historical figure who played a behind-the-scenes role as an express rider carrying dispatches in the Puget Sound Indian War (1855–1856). His equally genuine counterpart among the Indians, Charlie Salitat, was known for his daring and tragic midnight ride warning American settlers of the imminent Indian uprising, a ride that earned him the title, "Paul Revere of Puget Sound."

Woven into the fiction will be an accurate rendering of elements of the history of the Indian War in the Pacific Northwest, including the climactic Battle for Seattle (January, 1856). In the interest of the pace of the story, I have taken literary license by compressing some historical events into a shorter time period. See the timeline on page 305.

While readers will encounter the struggles of various historical figures in this history, I have also taken the liberty of combining some historical characters to create one of my fictional ones in this tale. Noclas (Chinook Jargon for "Black face"), the aging mountain man neighbor of my protagonist, is a combination of three very real figures in PNW history: George Bush (1790–1864), African American freeman settler near Olympia, Washington; George Washington (1818–1905), another black freeman settler and founder of the town of Centralia, Washington; and celebrated mountain man, Jedidiah Smith (1799–1831), called "The Praying Trapper." My amalgamation of Noclas acknowledged, I have, nevertheless, attempted to be authentic in the portrayal of the beliefs, values, and contribution of these three lesser-known figures in PNW history.

1

HOT PURSUIT

His heart thundering in his ears, William Tidd's breath came and went in hot frantic blasts. For an instant the pounding in his ears reminded him of a tribal council seated cross-legged on the floor of a smoky longhouse, war drums thud-thudding ominously. He had some experience of longhouses and of drums.

Moments ago he had been minding his own business making his way silently down a game trail in the Douglas fir forest to the southeast of a prairie more than a mile square, now a Hudson Bay Company field for pasturing sheep. William took some pride in his own ability to move with stealth in the forest, the soles of his deer-hide moccasins making mute contact with the narrow track, cushioned with a layer of dead, mineral-hued fir needles, and spongy moss. Walking softly in the forest, minding his own business.

Then came a tingle at the back of his neck. Vague uneasiness crawled down his spine like bedbugs. There was no mistaking it, the rustling chatter of a ground squirrel—but this was a forest, a forest with squirrels in it. Forests make noises, are never silent. "William Tidd, you're a-letting fear make war on your senses," he told himself aloud, but his throat felt dryer than it ought to. Without needing to tell himself, he quickened his pace, lengthened his stride. The sooner he got back to where he had tethered Prophet, the better.

Then came the knocking hammer of a woodpecker. "And there's red-breasted sapsuckers in a forest," he murmured, nodding as if to reassure himself, "a-hunting for bugs or fixing to attract a mate." Then the snap of a twig. William halted, sucking in his breath, every nerve in his body taut like a drawn bowstring. He swallowed hard and strained to hear. There was no mistaking what he heard next: the mournful hoot-hooting of an owl. William's blood ran cold.

That was no owl. He was being followed. There was no denying it now. Behind him was a sound far more ominous than the beating of his own heart. William had read in books that the noble savage makes no noise when moving in the forest. Not this Indian.

The time for a mere quickening of the pace was over and gone. William bolted, running for what he feared would be his life. Authors who wrote books about Indians and said nonsensical things about how they moved silently in the forest ought to be shot. So William thought as he gasped for air. If they have no intimate experience with the vast timbered nave of the Puget Sound wilderness they should stick with writing stories about polite cabins on tranquil little ponds bordering proper New England villages—but not about red flesh-and-blood Indians! He almost shouted the last.

As he vaulted over a rotten stump, William craned his neck searching the undergrowth for his pursuer, his eyes rolling and wide. Why had he dismounted in the first place? On horseback he could easily elude his pursuer, leave him far behind in the forest. It was too late for that; Prophet was tethered to a low branch on a madrone tree—several hundred yards behind him.

Cutting sharply to the right, William abandoned the game trail and plunged headlong into the dense undergrowth, bracken fern and Oregon grape clawing at his legs. It was no good trying to be silent now.

He lunged down a steep gulch littered with decomposing maple leaves, shaley rock, enshrouded with a layer of damp moss leading precipitously downward to the creek bed. It would be impossible for anyone, sure-footed Indian or otherwise, to move silently on such terrain. This one certainly was not. The Indian in pursuit was clamoring and stumbling, and hitching his breath as his footing gave way beneath him, or as a branch from a slide maple snapped into his face, making at least as much noise as was William.

His heart pounding in his ears, William leapt forward. Wincing as his feet lost contact with the organic rubble beneath him, he landed hard on his back end, glissading on his posterior for several yards. He clenched his teeth, resisting the urge to scream. Suddenly his feet came in contact with a rotten log, and the momentum snapped him upright, his footing precariously regained. William grabbed at branches of salal as the gulch steepened. If only he didn't begin cartwheeling. He had to get away, but cartwheeling could lead to real damage, broken bones, arms or legs—or a broken skull.

On this terrain, he dared not turn back to look at his pursuer. He didn't need to. By the lumbering and skittering behind him, William deduced that he had little more than a few yards' lead, the gap closing fast. And there was a new sound. The hot, steady blasts of air coming from the lungs of his pursuer. Closer, closer came the Indian's breath. As he gulped in air, William felt that he could smell those hot blasts of air—smoked salmon, steamed clams, boiled camus root.

"Boshton!" hollered the Indian. It was the usual name coastal Indians called white men: Boston, a faraway place they had never seen but that had come to represent the mysterious fountainhead of all white men. William desperately wanted to turn and look. The voice sounded familiar somehow. But he needed his full concentration on the steep terrain or else.

"Yow!" The Indian squealed. Behind and above William heard more skittering and the sounds of rock clattering like breaking plates, and the Indian's body plunging and thumping in the moss and rubble, and more hitching of his fishy breath. William figured the sure-footed native had lost his footing on the same obstacle that had nearly overturned him an instant ago.

Leaping downward, William hoped to widen the gap as the Indian stumbled behind him. If only he had his horse, that is, the horse that he wished was his horse. Steep as the gulch was, Prophet would have kept his footing; William knew he would have.

Since arriving in Puget Sound with his pa and sister five years ago, William had taken to horses. It had all been oxen and mules before then. The Indians on Muck Creek knew horses; all the tribes living on the shores of the inland sea were canoe Indians, but the ones who lived on the grasslands and forests watered by the Nisqually River, they were canoe Indians *and* horse Indians. Like no other tribe, the Nisqually knew how to breed horses. Nisqually-bred horses could withstand the perpetual damp and chill of the climate, they could tramp tirelessly through the dense, rugged terrain of the region, and they could plunge in and ford the glacial waters of the rivers that emptied into the numbing cold of Puget Sound. Sure as he was on his own two feet, William had long felt more secure anywhere when riding Prophet.

"Boshton!" There it was again. The Indian had recovered his footing and, by the sounds of it, had made up for lost time. "Boshton!" The Indian was relentless. He was almost on top of him. William's lungs felt like they were aflame. If only he had a Hudson Bay trade musket. He wouldn't be in this predicament if he'd had a primed musket at the ready. Muskets cost too much. Now it would come down to a face-to-face, hand-to-hand (William groped for his bowie knife), a blade-to-blade fight with an Indian.

Worse than the Indian's unflagging pursuit, the clamoring racket of his footfalls coming ever closer, worse than his savage, hot breath, worse than the fear that twitched in William's every nerve, was what he heard next. Laughter. The cackling hilarity of the Indian's laughter was too much. It unhinged William's confidence; his frontier self-reliance shriveled with each outburst.

"Hyuk-hyuk-hyuk!" came the Indian's laughter.

Clamping his hands on his ears to quell panic, William desperately tried to ward off the haunting laughter that seemed to hover on the damp and mist of the forest. Mammoth Douglas firs higher up the gulch had given way to hemlock, then red cedar and alder trees as the floor of the gulch came up to meet him. Woolly green moss blanketed the trunks of alder trees and damp rotting logs and stumps on the forest floor, looking like Fort Nisqually sheep at shearing time after a long winter. The trees, the moss and profuse salal, the huckleberry bushes—all these should have absorbed and muffled sounds, yet the Indian's laughter echoed and reverberated throughout the ravine like the wails of an outcast medicine man.

"Hyuk-hyuk-hyuk!" It sounded maniacal to William's ears. It unnerved and terrified him.

Just ahead, the steep gulch ended in a gravelly streambed. It was time. With a final burst of energy, William flung himself across the creek. He landed on a rotten log, but quickly regained his footing. He spun around and faced his pursuer, feet planted wide, knife at the ready.

For an instant, William heard the Indian, *"Hyuk-hyuk-hyuk!"* but he could not see him, concealed as he was in the dense forest. Any second, the Indian would burst from the undergrowth and be upon him.

William readied himself. He didn't relish a knife fight with an Indian. But he was not one to give up easily. *You may be laughing now,* thought William, planting his feet and gripping his knife more tightly. *But I'll have the last laugh—or take you with me.*

2

SICK TREATY

Suddenly the Indian burst from the undergrowth—in full view. William could see him clearly now, every detail—short, stocky like most coastal Indians, buckskin trousers and leggings, broad chest, muscular arms, shimmering with sweat from exertion, his stringy, raven-black hair tied around his broad forehead with a leather strap.

William's mouth hung open, and his eyes widened as he stared at the man. The Indian's cheeks were broad and sharp, and his skin was glossy, the color of fresh-split cedar wood. His eyes were oily dark and sparkled with merriment, as if he were the guest of honor at an extravagant potlatch. His lips were thin and his mouth was wide. William looked on incredulously. The Indian was grinning at him, a broad, stretching grin—somewhere between friendly and mocking—a grin that revealed two gaps where he had lost upper teeth.

"Charlie Salitat!" cried William, lunging toward the Indian. "If you ever do this again I'll—" William tackled the Indian and for the next several moments there was a scuffle that left both of them red faced and breathing still harder—and covered with mud, bits of moss, fir needles, and dead alder leaves. Straddling the Indian, William pinned his arms to the forest floor. "Say you won't stalk me like that ever again," said William through gritted teeth, "and I'll let you live!"

"Hyuk-hyuk-hyuk!" laughed Charlie, so hysterically he had no strength left to resist. William rolled off the Indian and lay on his back until his breathing returned to normal. He frowned up at the mammoth trunks of the great trees narrowing to a place where he could just make out a bank of gray clouds drifting in the breeze far above the treetops; there an eagle soared on a current of air, its black wings spread wide and motionless, its white head and tail feathers flashing in a momentary shaft of sunlight; and then the clouds recovered themselves and the drab and gloom returned.

"Your face, Bill Tidd—you should've seen it!" said Charlie, his laughter subsiding. "You looked like child lost in Nisqually burial ground on dark night." Clasping his big arms behind his head, he gave off little spurts of merriment at the recollection.

"How you can be a-playing shenanigans like this," said William, rising on an elbow and looking steadily at the Indian, "is beyond me—things being as they are."

Things being as they were. Unrest over treaty signing with the Indians was the talk of the territory, widely reported, and sometimes wildly reported, in the *Pioneer and Democrat* and the *Puget Sound Courier*; William had gotten his facts all about it in the newspapers.

Governor Stevens and his buck-skinned interpreter, Frank Shaw, had called all the tribal chiefs in the Puget Sound region to come to Medicine Creek, called She-Nah-Nam by the Nisqually Indians. Dripping wet and shivering with the December drizzle, Stevens and his white supporters from the settlement in Olympia set up shelters under a giant fir tree on Medicine Creek. In scattered bands, the area Indians paddled to the meeting place in their dugout canoes or rode on horseback, guiding their ponies into the frigid waters as they forded their way across the Nisqually River delta to the treaty tree.

Under that tree, the territorial governor presented a written document to the Indians—Indians who could neither read nor write. It was a treaty and a map that displaced the tribes and put them on reservations, arbitrary ink boundary lines drawn on a piece of paper by Stevens.

"Medicine Creek Treaty?" said Charlie. "Humph! What your Governor Mr. Isaac Stevens did Big Sunday one moon ago—it *bad* medicine, sick treaty, I call it."

William nodded but said nothing. He was forced to agree. It had only been a month ago, Christmas, Big Sunday as Charlie Salitat and the Indians called it. The plot of ground Stevens offered to the Nisquallys in the treaty for their reservation, their new and permanent home, didn't even have access to the Nisqually River, which meant no salmon, the staple food of their diet. Rather than sign with his own hand, Chief Leschi of the Nisqually had trampled the treaty in the mud, and stalked away with his warriors.

"But Charlie Salitat," said William. "You know that ain't but half the story. Bungling as that treaty may be, Stevens done it *for* the Indians. He fears that with all them settlers a-migrating west like waves of geese heading south in October, the Indians won't have nothing left, not enough land for burying the last dead Indian in. At least that there treaty set aside and reserved some land for the tribes."

Charlie grunted. "You give him much credit."

William balanced a soggy fir cone on his thumb and flicked it into the air. It landed in the moss an arm's-length the other side of Charlie. The Indian could be stubborn, so William tried another tactic.

"Then there's the occurrence yonder ways up-sound on the settlement they calls Seattle. And, Charlie, don't you go a-telling me that you done forgot about that little occurrence. Let me help your rememberer. Them Snohomish Indians attacked and viciously murdered an Alki sawmill worker. I read about it in the *Pioneer and Democrat* with my own eyes. Poor fellow just a-minding his own business. *Blam!* They just up and killed him. And it ain't no coincidence that after all this occurred, Mr. Isaac Stevens, hoping to keep the peace in the territory, felt compelled to draft up that treaty."

"Snohomish tribe," said Charlie, "not same as Puyallup or Nisqually tribe."

"Well, there's that, but they *was* Indians, now wasn't they?"

Charlie flicked a fir cone high in the air. It landed inches from William's left foot.

"That were getting mighty close," said William.

"More to story," said Charlie, feeling in the moss for another fir cone. "Seattle sheriff, he hunt down Indian. Kill nine, take two prisoner, and hang by neck—eleven dead Indian."

"There you go again, a-leaving things out of the story," said William. "You've gone and left out the part before all that, the bit about the band of Snohomish—*Indians,* they were—who lay and wait in the forest and picked off three of the Sheriff's men, *Blam, blam, blam!* Shot them right out of their saddles—two they managed to patch up; the other was stone-cold dead."

"Far from here," grunted Charlie, and he flicked another fir cone high in the air. It was carefully lobbed. William watched the falling fir cone, getting rapidly larger as it plummeted straight for his forehead.

"Times like these," said William, batting the fir cone away at the last instant before it landed, "some folks in these here parts might misconstrue an Indian lying in wait, a-chasing down a white man in the forest like you was doing. Shenanigans like that could start something—a thing that might get bloody before it's finished."

William said it almost as a jest. Whatever other troubles there were, real trouble with coastal Indians, warlike trouble, seemed to be the least of their worries.

Back in Kentucky, William's pa, a great lover of books, would read aloud around the firelight on cold stormy nights. One of those books, *The Last of the Mohicans,* it had been called, on the shelf with the other books a stone's throw away back at the Tidd cabin, was all about Indians. There were savages in that tale that had leapt out at William in his sleep—terrifying him with war-painted faces, tomahawks poised over his trembling scalp, keeping him tossing and sweating in his bed at night.

But Mr. James Fenimore Cooper's book Indians were nothing like the real ones his family had encountered when making their way west by covered wagon; these were the real thing: swift, hard, war-whooping horse Indians to freeze the blood. William shuddered at the recollection.

And they were nothing like the easygoing Indian flicking fir cones at his side. William had learned that Puget Sound Indians were different. They had their rivalries and squabbles, but life was mostly easy for coastal tribes: salmon in droves came to them, once a year swimming upstream and, as if it were their all-obliging duty, depositing themselves in great quantity almost on the threshold of the Indian longhouses on the banks of the rivers. Life was easy; food was plentiful. And though most white settlers had their quaint manners and customs, especially predisposed against trading and keeping slaves—at least the Indian way of doing it—and against trading and beating wives, the white man was, on the whole, a benefit. White settlers had brought valuable trade goods: blankets, glass beads, hatchets, buttons, knives, and trade muskets. William had worked it out. He was pretty settled on where troubles came from: The sky might fall, but an Indian uprising—never.

Looking levelly at William, Charlie grunted and became sober. Tucking his knees to his chest, he uncoiled and sprang to his feet. "I go," he said.

"Where?" said William, rising and brushing forest rubbish from his threadbare wool jacket.

"Beaver," said Charlie over his shoulder. "Get horse, then check traps."

Frowning, William watched as the Indian disappeared around a bend in the creek. Musing about his conversation with Charlie, William trotted back to where he had tethered Prophet.

Charlie could be like this. One moment he was playing shenanigans and laughing to bust his guts, and the next he was the stoic Indian, mysterious, stone-faced, and monosyllabic—but surely not dangerous. There were times when William thought of Charlie as if he were a white man, maybe even as a friend. Then there were other times. This was one of those other times. He was never certain where he stood with Charlie. Maybe it was that way with all Indians.

3

TRAPPED

William had learned to be attentive to the myriad of sounds in a forest. He cocked his ear at the *knock-knocking* of a woodpecker echoing through the ravine, and wondered if it was the same one he had heard just before he had sensed he was being followed only a short time ago.

William hesitated. Then he heard it, a soft nickering. Prophet had heard him coming, and somehow knew it was William, and he was blowing a gentle greeting through his nostrils.

Prophet was like that. Their neighbor, Prophet's real owner, Noclas, had given the horse its name because it seemed to have an uncanny ability to anticipate things, know things before they happened. "Don't go a-thinkin' he's clairvoyant or any such nonsense," Noclas had assured William. "He's just more attuned, is he, to what's a-goin' on in the world than most folks is. And if you listen, he'll be a-tellin' you. A little flick of the ears, a slight turnin' of the head, the muscles of the neck goin' taut like, and other signs to tell you what's the matter in the world—that's

Prophet. Ain't no better horse in these parts—maybe anywheres."

"There you are, big fella," said William, stroking the tall animal's velvety nose. Prophet was no specific breed of horse, and the fine horsemen out east and ones from Kentucky where the Tidd family hailed from would probably not have thought much of him. "Let 'em think what they will," said William, patting the horse's neck as he mounted the animal and began retracing the route he had just come on foot.

What swept over him whenever he mounted Prophet was beyond any words William had ever found adequate to describe his feelings. He thought it, though never said as much, that he was no longer just a man or a boy; mounted on Prophet the limitations of mere manhood disappeared. William's imagination flashed back to something his pa liked to recite from one of his books: "My head bathed by the blithe air and uplifted into infinite space, I become a transparent eyeball; I see all; the currents of the Universal Being circulate through me; I am part and parcel of God." Maybe Emerson was thinking of riding a horse when he set down those words.

Mounted high atop Prophet's back, William felt surging in his blood a new sense of power and control, strength and dignity—and speed. There was no faster horse in the region, at least that's what Noclas always maintained. "I'd put him 'longside the best horse the Injuns has got any day of the week. Ride him proper-like, and shore 'nough, Prophet'll come out in the front every time." William believed this, though he was mildly troubled by the fact that he had never actually had opportunity to test the theory.

Prophet was what folks out west called a buckskin horse, but darker than most, the color of aged buckskin, with black mane and tail, and intelligent, oily black eyes that stood out against a resolute face, lighter in color than the rest of him, creamy like butter and soft to the touch.

Lowering his head alongside the horse's strong neck, William dodged a low-lying limb of an old Douglas fir tree reaching out over the sometimes imperceptible game trail. Narrowing his eyes through the trees towering above him at the bland-gray sky, William tried to judge the time of day. He'd seen men with pocket watches, important men like territorial governors, generals or colonels at Fort Steilacoom, or Chief Factors, like Dr. William Tolmie at Fort Nisqually. They could pause and pull out a gold watch, attached to the pocket of their vest with a fine gold chain, and discern the precise time of day. "He has a fine Geneva watch, but he fails of the skill to tell the hour by the sun." William never understood why, but he would have flashes like this, and fragments of things his father had read to him would come out of nowhere, intrude on his thinking. William had no fine Geneva watch—or the sun. Cold gray clouds blocked out the sun. He was forced to guess the time.

It was well into the afternoon, and night comes early to Puget Sound in winter. If he followed Charlie, he'd get nothing else done the rest of the day. There were shakes to split, fences to mend, the chicken coop roof needed repairing, and there was the new paddle he needed to cut and shape for the canoe.

That settled it. "Giddy-up, big fella," he said in Prophet's ear. He'd follow Charlie.

"White man walking in forest," said Charlie, moments later, "loud like ox cart. White man on horseback, loud like railroad train."

"Stalking me back there like you was, you was making heaps of racket yourself," said William, falling in beside Charlie and his speckled pony. "And how do you know what a railroad train sounds like anyway? There's no railroad anywhere near here."

"Yet," said Charlie. "No railroad yet, but I hear stories from James McAllister, other settlers too. Railroad train make big blast, *chug-chug, clatter-clatter, screech-screech,* like Hudson Bay steam ship *Beaver* using loud engine, not whispering sails. Railroad make more big noise—*clatter-clang, clatter-clang*. Noclas tell me about railroad trains coming west. Soon will be here. More white people. No peace, no quiet then."

Charlie was being Indian, so William decided it was time to change the subject. "How does an Indian know where the beaver will be?" he asked.

"Steam ship, *Beaver*?" asked Charlie. "*Clatter, hiss, clatter, bang*."

"Ah, no, Charlie," said William. "Beaver, the real kind, you know, big teeth, thick fur, flappy tail? *Beaver* beaver. How do you know where to find them?"

Charlie narrowed his eyes at William and brought his horse so close their knees jostled against each other. He lowered his voice, as if to keep the mysteries of trapping from the ears of an eavesdropping beaver. Pointing at his eyes with two fingers, he said, "I keep lookout for pond or stream with signs, beaver signs." His voice sounded like he was plotting a conspiracy. He rested his pony's reins on the animal's neck so that he would have both hands free. "Muskrat chew down twigs, but beaver, he chew down full tree anywhere from, yea big around," he encircled an imaginary tree with the fingers of both hands, "to one, yea big," he made a circle with both arms coming together at the finger tips. "Big tree might take him whole night chewing."

"Are beaver nocturnal, then?" asked William. "You know, up and about at night, sleep in the day, noc-turn-al." Sometimes he forgot how well Charlie spoke and understood English. Most Indians if they had to speak to a white man used the local trade jargon, but few spoke English, and none as well as Charlie Salitat.

Charlie looked sideways at William and gave him a chiding frown. "Beaver not noc-turn-al, but beaver do his out-of-pond work at nighttime. Active in water in daytime, building dam, building beaver lodge. Marsh and lowlands like river delta where Nisqually widens, there are marsh reeds chewed down—that is muskrat, not beaver. I want beaver, trade beaver skins, get more better trade. I look for beaver lodge, built from small sticks and big timber. Then I creep close and look for small mud-sliding place, or little stream where beaver drag branch and log."

Glancing left and right, Charlie lowered his voice yet further. "We tie ponies here," he said, dismounting. William followed and did the same; they proceeded softly on foot.

"Beaver always make little mound of mud," continued Charlie, "and he smear oil from scent glands to give message, 'This, my territory. Do not trespass on my dam, on my lodge.' Here is where I set trap. I have two trap set around bend, here on Sequalitchew Creek."

"How do you set traps," said William, "so as to be sure he'll step into it? An iron trap wouldn't fool me if I were a beaver. It don't look like logs and timber trash. I'd know it didn't belong there. I'd see it coming. If I were a beaver, I'd just leave it be and walk around the trap."

"You no beaver," said Charlie, running his eyes over William with a frown. "Beaver better skin. Your skin worth nothing in trade. I trick beaver. I drive stick in water through ring in chain to hold trap," said Charlie. "I anchor trap in shallow muddy water where beaver gets out of water. Then I take willow stick, like this one," Charlie took out his knife, bent low, and cut off a willow growing near the streambed. "I peel it like this, and drive stick in mud by trap." Charlie smiled, almost broke into a laugh. "Then I smear musk oil from different beaver on top of willow stick. This make beaver mad. 'Who marking my territory?' says beaver. 'Who come into my pond, my forest, my trees? Who try steal my dam and lodge?' says beaver. He go to investigate. Snap! Trap close and I have beaver." Charlie clenched a fist and smiled with satisfaction. "I have beaver."

"Wait, where did you get the other beaver's oil?" asked William. "Before iron traps, how did you get the first beaver and his oil to use as bait to catch the second beaver—and every beaver since?"

"Trap is white man's way to catch beaver," said Charlie.

"So how'd you trap them before traps?" asked William.

Charlie didn't answer immediately. "Before Indian had trap," he said, his voice a monotone, "whole tribe tear apart beaver dam or burn down lodge, then when he try to escape, we shoot beaver with arrow or spear or all club him to death."

"So why use traps the white man's way?" asked William.

Charlie frowned deeply and didn't answer immediately. They walked on in silence. "Indian way," he said, choosing his words carefully, "not always best way."

William halted. "Wait, did I hear you right? Because I thought I heard Charlie Salitat say that the Indian way ain't no way always the best way. And I'm surprised to hear an Indian say such a thing."

Charlie too had halted, and the two stood staring at each other. "Is white man's way always best way?" asked Charlie.

Before William could figure out how to reply, Charlie suddenly froze, holding up a hand for silence.

"Sh-sh!" hissed Charlie, grabbing William by the shoulder and pulling him to the ground. They crawled like courting salamanders through the moss and dead leaves blanketing the forest floor. Lying at Charlie's side concealed behind the foliage of a giant sword fern, William peered through the fronds.

This was it. Trees gnawed down on either side of the creek, a mound of forest debris for a lodge, and a dam made of branches, logs, river rocks, and mud, a wide pool held back by the structure. Judging by the wake in the pond, this was a large animal, considerably above average size, and if all went well its pelt would fetch Charlie above average in trade goods at Fort Nisqually. He wondered what Charlie was saving up beaver pelts for; what would he be wanting in trade at the fort?

William sniffed the air. He imagined that he, too, could smell the wild glandular oil that was alluring the beaver into the trap, but it was doubtful. The forest's smells, decomposing leaves along the creek and pond, rotting deadwood that littered the forest floor, his own body's odors—stronger than usual after his mad flight down the gulch fleeing Charlie—still more the Indian's smells made certain William could smell little else, the fish oil all Indians rubbed liberally on their skin and hair to help keep off the rain and drizzle—and bugs and mosquitoes.

But the beaver could smell the oil. The animal slowed to investigate, its wake dissolving gradually into the quiet surface of the little pond. Slowly a dark brown, oily wet mound of fur rose to the surface near the anchoring stake. From where he and Charlie lay, William could see the giant rodent clearly, its small head, its large yellow front teeth, its small black eyes, its black nose, twitching as the alluring scent overpowered the creatures fear.

"Big beaver," mouthed Charlie.

If it could be said that beavers think, William wondered just what the beaver was thinking right at that moment. Its back hunched, yellow teeth poised, William watched as it lifted its nose and interrogated the air.

"What is that smell? Them other beavers down creek smell disgusting. What are they doing in my territory? This is my dam, my lodge, my pond, my trees, and bark, and mud. Who do those foreign beavers think they are? That's it; I've had enough! I'm driving those foul-smelling, tree-gnawing, dam-building beavers off my territory!"

Snap-clank!

The jaws of the trap held fast. Hoping to get away from the iron predator, the fat beaver dove as deep as the chain would let him. The trap didn't need to come up for air—but the beaver did. It was too late.

Dusk was falling fast, but William lingered, watching Charlie gut and then carefully skin the animal. William gave a low whistle. "That's the biggest beaver skin I've seen from around here."

Scraping the animal's flesh from the inside of the thick fur with a two-handed scraping tool, Charlie grinned.

Pleased with his success, his whole manner had changed. He was almost giddy, like a schoolboy. "Hyuk, hyuk, hyuk!" he laughed. "Fetch more big trade money at fort."

He's white again, William thought, breathing a big sigh. He preferred Charlie when he was white. It was like hefting an eighty-pound bale of skins from off his mind to see the Indian laughing and happy with himself again.

"How many skins you got now, Charlie?" asked William. "Must be heaps. And what are you fixing to trade 'em for?"

Charlie paused, blood to his elbows, his knife poised over the carcass of the beaver. William saw and felt the change come over him. His grin had vanished. Charlie was Indian again—all Indian.

"Trade beaver skin," he said, looking deliberately at William, "for powder, ball, and musket."

4

JUNEBUG

It didn't take much for the dark to win out over the damp and gray of a late January evening. Dark was falling fast. William mounted Prophet and high-tailed it for home. Junebug would wonder where he was if he didn't hurry.

So Charlie Salitat wants a musket, thought William. *Whatever in the world does he want a musket for?* It was as close to dark as it gets without actually being so, and William knew that a horse spooked in the near dark by a wild rabbit or a raccoon could bolt or buck and hurt itself—and its rider. But, knowing he was nearing his stable and a supper of oats and alfalfa, Prophet wanted to gallop. And so did William. Speed, wild and free, and stamina—Prophet had it all.

Nearing the Tidd holding and their cabin, William caught a faint whiff of something. He halted, sniffing the air. Wood smoke. He quickened his pace. Wood smoke this time of evening near their cabin could only mean one thing.

Moments later, after taking Prophet's bridle and saddle off and hanging them up in Noclas's log stable, William ran down the path, and leapt onto the front porch of the Tidd cabin, bursting open the door.

"Woof! Woof!" A big dog greeted him at the door, its mouth wide, tongue lolling, its gleaming white fangs clearly visible. On all fours, Wally stood taller than William's knees, and the big animal had to weigh at least twice as much as his sister. Folks in and around Steilacoom referred to the animal as a wolf; encounter him in the muddy streets of the settlement and they would chuckle nervously, their eyes steady on Wally and his charge. Folks always stepped aside to give the little girl and her big dog a wide berth.

Taking a deep breath, William tried to steady his voice. "Junebug, what are you doing?" he said. "Did you build this here fire all by yourself?"

Two handprint smudges of cornmeal on the front of her apron, ten-year-old Junebug beamed proudly at her brother. "Making yummy supper," she said with playful vagueness, skipping his second question. "I heard you coming," she added, turning back to the kettle and resuming her humming.

William wished his sister was not so young; he worried leaving her alone. He worried about her lighting the fire, and preparing food, all on her own. He had been ready to scold her, but he held his tongue. *"Mmm-mm.* And just what's going to be so yummy about it?" he said.

"Well, I reckon you'll just have to wait and see," she said, stirring the kettle with a long wooden spoon.

Absently, William patted the coarse gray fur of Wally's broad head, the animal's tongue lolling as he grinned and fixed his eyes steadily on William's. The beast's pedigree was uncertain, though he may very well be part wolf—almost certainly—but there was more to him than that. William glanced at Wally's eyes and returned the smile.

Wally was odd looking. He was walleyed, as they called it: one eye yellow-green like when a shaft of sunlight passes through a cottonwood leaf in October, and the other the color of the sky after a torrent of April rain and the clouds momentarily scud away in the wind. William glanced again at the dog's eyes—yellow and blue. Walleyed wasn't the only odd thing about him. There was an unaccountable crimp in the dog's tail that made it look like he'd just taken a sharp left turn around a corner, and as if perpetually leaning into the turn, his left ear drooped over, even when the other one was at full alert.

Odd creature that it was, William couldn't help being grateful for the animal. Wally seemed to understand the way things were; from when she was an infant, he'd assumed care of Junebug as if the little girl were his sole responsibility in life. Day or night, he was never more than a few steps from her side.

One thing the events of the last three years had taught William Tidd, there were dangers a-plenty around every bend in the river, and unforeseen hazards up and over every gulch; you never could tell what was going to hit you next. There were a wagonload of other worries in his life, so having Wally, and Junebug safe from any harm—there was at least one thing he felt he could count on.

William stroked the dog's chin and smiled. He worried more about damage the beast would do to other folks than any harm that might come to his sister. There was little to worry about on that score; folks stayed plenty clear of William and June Tidd anyway. They could go wherever they wanted, but folks kept clear of Wally and all those imprinted in the mysterious recesses of his affections and self-imposed obligations. As far as Wally was concerned, there was only so much of him to go around. Everyone else had better steer clear.

Charcoal smudges on her cheeks, Junebug turned and grinned. "Yes-sir, Betsy and me," she nodded toward a rag doll propped up on one of the willow chairs, "we've been making yummy supper for big brother," she said. "Smells good, don't it?"

"*Mmm-mm*," he repeated. He knew what she had been up to. Scanning the interior of the log cabin, William took in the scene. The cabin had only one room, illuminated by sheep-tallow candles flickering warmly and casting jagged shadows against the contours of the log walls. It was furnished with a single bed made of peeled cedar poles, covered with a thin patchwork quilt, two cane rocking chairs made of bent willow, and a fireplace. Scrawny twig that he'd been then, five years ago he'd helped his pa build it, carting armload after armload up from the creek—round and smooth, river rock the size of plump butternut squash, but with the weight of cannonballs. His sweat, and some of his blood, was all over this cabin. So was Pa's.

William stared at the fire; the flames licked over the fuel, spitting and crackling, and hot coals at the base of the fire glowed and winked like creatures from the netherworld. His sister had started the fire with cedar kindling and seasoned windfall branches.

With a moccasined toe, William nudged a stray coal that had popped onto the rough planking back into the confines of the fireplace. Under a high window against the south wall stood a bookshelf, lined with two rows of books. Most everyone in these parts who owned a book, it would be a Bible, and good number would own a copy of *Pilgrim's Progress*, maybe *Scots Worthies, Hymns and Spiritual Songs by Isaac Watts,* and the like. The Tidd bookshelf was different. William's father had had a preference for the newest books, ones by poets and essayists from the east, New England and New York mostly; there were few things Pa would not have traded for one of their kind of books.

In the middle of the room stood a table, the hand-hewn boards polished with use to a knobby sheen. At one end of the table was a little wooden box filled with bits of charcoal. She'd been at her drawing again. William picked up a piece of paper; on it was a charcoal sketch of a horse. Frowning, he glanced from the drawing to his sister and back to the drawing. It didn't seem possible, Junebug's drawing. At times, he even wondered if it was a prank, and Junebug hadn't drawn them at all; surely they had to be pictures somebody else had drawn, somebody who was not ten years old, somebody who was a genuine artist—like Jonathan Trumbull maybe, the artist whose paintings he'd read about George Washington taking such a liking to during the revolution.

William tilted the drawing so that yellow light from the candle illuminated it more clearly. It was a horse, a buckskin, Prophet almost for certain. Somehow she had managed to achieve near perfect proportion between his body and limbs, and his muscles rippled as if they were real, and she had captured something of Prophet's motion and speed. The sketch was unfinished, but what he could make of it left him speechless. There were many ways his sister was not like other children. It crossed his mind that maybe he was seeing more in the drawing because she wasn't like other children, just because she *was* his sister.

He held it at arm's length. It would be remarkable enough if she had drawn a horse standing placidly in a field munching on a mouthful of bunch grass. But this was a drawing of a horse suspended in mid gallop, as if in flight, straining forward, every nerve taut, its mane and tail flying in the wind—how could a child of her years do this?

Clearing his throat, William said, "I, ah—you've gone and made another pretty picture," he said. Gingerly, as if it were a priceless artifact on display at the Smithsonian Institute newly opened in Washington DC, he set it back on the table.

Junebug turned from the kettle and smiled absently. "I was going to put you a-riding on his back, but I needed to cut up potatoes and vegetables for supper."

Looking at the other end of the table, William warmed his fingers over the flame of the candle. He pictured in his mind his sister setting down her charcoal, but, her creative imagination still in full gallop, taking up the knife and starting in on the potatoes. She had been busy. The potatoes she had arranged into various-sized heads; the carrots had become arms and legs, and pieces of squash she had carved into bodies. Next, on a field of dried peas, she then had arranged them into people, shorter ones and taller ones, some with longer hair made from potato peelings, people in various sizes and postures—a family maybe. William couldn't be sure about that.

He swallowed and steadied his voice, "I'm most grateful for yummy supper, but, Junebug, you mustn't carve with the knife all on your own. You're only ten years old. I've told you this before." He was tempted to scold her—frighten her—by asking her what would happen if she sliced off a finger—or worse. But he checked himself. "But it's awful sweet of you, my little Junebug," he said, giving her long pony tail a playful tug. "Where'd you come by the fish?" he asked.

Junebug laughed. "Noclas brung him to me. He said he had plenty and to spare. Noclas, he often says that, don't he?"

William poked at the fire with a stick. She'd built a fire all on her own too. One of these days he feared he'd return home and the cabin would be engulfed in flames. Wiping a hand across his face, he shuddered at the thought. He looked at his sister. Humming a tune he didn't remember hearing before, she balanced a cutting board full of chopped-up potatoes and dumped them into the iron kettle hung over the fire. She was so slight, only a child, far too young for taking on the duties of cook, housekeeper, and mother to her near-grown brother—and to herself. William often worried and was sometimes frantic about just what he should be doing for his little sister, but he was certain he could never forgive himself if anything happened to Junebug.

Wally sniffed at the salmon, though he made no move to help himself. Other dogs would, but Wally would never do that.

"D'you want to know what else Noclas told me today?" asked Junebug, picking up the butcher knife and narrowing her eyes at the salmon.

"I-I'll do that," said William, taking the knife from her. "And just what did Noclas tell you today?" he asked.

Before Junebug could reply, Wally faced the door of the cabin and stiffened. A low growl rumbled from his throat.

William heard nothing, but that was the way of it with Wally. Drooping left ear notwithstanding, Wally heard sounds long before any human heard them, and the dog seemed always to know what those sounds meant. Suddenly Wally's crooked tail began to fan the air, and he gave a cheerful yelp, one single bark. Next a scraping of feet on the cedar boards of the porch, and a light *rap-rap* on the door.

"You can ask him yourself," said Junebug not turning from the kettle. "That'll be him at the door—Noclas hisself, coming for supper and bringing cheese and butter from the fort!"

William lifted the leather latch and opened the door. Standing before him was a stocky man, built like a block of Garry oak with sturdy arms and legs. He was dressed all in buckskin, leather fringe down the outer seam of his trousers and along the arms of his jacket. His broad shoulders were covered with a tightly woven cedar bark cape, the hood pulled back off his head.

It was late January and full dark outside. In the dim firelight of the cabin, all William could see of the man's face were the large whites of his eyes, and a wide row of teeth as white as new-washed wool. It was Noclas, the Chinook Jargon name the Indians had given the man, Noclas—"Black face."

5

BLACK FACE

There was no better cook than Junebug—for a ten-year-old, that is. She did, however, have trouble getting things to finish their cooking at the same time. Hence, meals in the Tidd cabin were drawn out affairs, enjoyed in courses, sometimes with lengthy gaps between, which had the added benefit of allowing the food to settle.

Salmon fillets, loosely woven into willow cooking frames and propped up near the fire, finished first. Junebug had concocted a sauce, "Yummy sauce," she called it, made up of sea salt, a pinch of rosemary, mustard seed, and lots of the melted butter Noclas had brought along from the fort; she dribbled it generously on the fish with a wooden spoon while it baked. Salmon prepared this way, the Indian way with some white-man variations, over an alder fire, was moist and flakey, and best eaten right off the coals. A while later came the potatoes, then the squash, then the vegetables. At the last, while Junebug tended the cornbread baking in the iron Dutch oven over the coals, Noclas pulled a book out of the inside of his buckskin shirt.

"While them delicious smells continues a-floatin' 'bout the room," he said, winking at Junebug, "mind if I reads a spell in the good book?"

William hesitated. Most every settler in these parts owned a Bible; for many, it was a large family Bible, the only book they owned, carted across the continent, shielded from rain and cold, protected from fire and theft, but now sitting on a shelf or stowed away at the bottom of a trunk safe and secure from all alarms under the family quilts. Bibles were for taking out when a baby was born, its birth date duly recorded, for taking out again to record a wedding date, and then at the last pulled down again to record the year, month, day, and cause of someone in the family being taken away in death.

William had no issue with folks having and using a Bible in this fashion; folks needed to keep their family records somewhere; the Tidds had once had just such a Bible, used for just such purposes, that is, until Pa traded it for a new book of essays from out east.

But Noclas was different. Somehow along the way, he had gotten it into his black, woolly head that he was actually supposed to read all the other pages of the Bible. William had long had a suspicion that—without anybody needing to be born, get married, or die—Noclas took it out and read his copy of "the Word of the Lord," as he called it, every single day.

His moccasins rubbing on the planking of the floor, William shuffled his feet uncomfortably. Occasionally he had tried offering to Noclas one of his father's favorite books, a volume of essays, suggesting he read from it instead, or from the latest news from the local Steilacoom newspaper the *Puget Sound Courier*, or the *Pioneer and Democrat*, or, better still, a copy of the *Boston Courier*, brought out west by Pony Express. There were better options.

William turned, about to suggest they read from one of these. But Noclas was looking steadily at William. The black man had a way of looking at a fellow, or was it looking inside a fellow? His head was tilted slightly to the left, his eyes wide with wonder; he was holding his Bible as if it were a pan he'd been panning for gold with all his life, and here it was, at long last, full to the brim with glittering nuggets of pure gold.

"Your golden delicious, finger-licking cornbread 'bout ready, Junebug?" asked William, looking hopefully at his sister.

"It needs cooking a good spell longer," said his sister, winking back at Noclas and flashing a grin at her brother.

William felt trapped. He hitched his eyebrows vaguely and reached for his knife and the cedar plank he had set aside for carving into a new canoe paddle. The old paddle had snapped in half last fall when he was paddling hard against a riptide between Anderson and McNeil Islands. He'd been forced to paddle the four miles back to Steilacoom landing using a length of driftwood he scavenged from the beach, blistered hands to prove it. Nodding vaguely, he squinted down the plank, ran his fingers along the edge, and shaved off a ridge of unwanted cedar with his knife.

Noclas nodded knowingly at William. Then, shifting the willow rocking chair so the light cast by the nearest candle fell across the words, he thumbed the pages of the book. "Ah-huh, ah-huh—ah-ha, here 'tis." And then he cleared his throat and began reading.

Taking another sighting down the plank, William was determined to give his full attention to carving the paddle.

Noclas's voice's had a way about it, almost like music. It rose and fell with feeling as he read about an encounter between a lawyer and the Teacher, the lawyer wanting to know how to inherit eternal life. *Whatever that is,* thought William, cutting a notch in the wood where the handle would be. *I'd settle for a decent life here and now.* To inherit eternal life, the Teacher appeared to be directing the lawyer to do everything written in the law—everything and perfectly.

"Thou shalt love the Lord thy God with all thy heart, and with all thy soul, and with all thy strength, and with all thy mind; and thy neighbor as thyself." To William the words sounded like a father telling his son, "I'll love you if you never ever do anything wrong—if you're perfect." Then like a thunderclap it struck; they were words much like what he'd read in one of his father's books of essays from New England: "Immortality will come to such as are fit for it; and he who would be a great soul in the future must be a great soul now." At the first, words like this felt exhilarating—he could rise above everything and be a great soul, a fit soul—but, the more he reflected on them, the intoxication soon wore off, leaving him dry and empty feeling, empty and anxious. The nagging question always remained: Was it even possible for someone hailing from the Tidd family to be great enough, to be fit enough, for immortality? The answer seemed pretty obvious, and the emptiness got emptier.

Noclas had paused, studying William, his eyebrows arching high. "Inheritin' eternal life only if you're lovin' God and your neighbor perfectly—that there sure is goin' to be hard. Lookin' 'bout at the evils in the world jus' now—more than that, lookin' into the dark places of my own heart, perfect lovin' like that seem nigh on impossible. The lawyer, he may have been thinkin' 'bout the same; he up and tries findin' a way to wiggle out a this here tight spot. He up and pose the question, 'And jus' who is my neighbor?' For an answer, Jesus up and launches into one of his good stories."

Holding the book closer to the candle, Noclas squinted at the page and murmured, "Now jus' where was I? Ah, yes sir, there 'tis," he said, and resumed reading.

"A certain man went down from Jerusalem to Jericho, and fell among thieves, which stripped him of his raiment, and wounded him, and departed, leaving him half dead. And by chance there came down a certain priest that way:

and when he saw him, he passed by on the other side. And likewise a Levite, when he was at the place, came and looked on him, and passed by on the other side. But a certain Samaritan, as he journeyed, came where he was: and when he saw him, he had compassion on him, and went to him, and bound up his wounds, pouring in oil and wine, and set him on his own beast, and brought him to an inn, and took care of him. And on the morrow when he departed, he took out two pence, and gave them to the host, and said unto him, Take care of him; and whatsoever thou spendest more, when I come again, I will repay thee."

"Jesus—that were the Teacher, case you didn't know it," interjected Noclas, "Jesus then posed the question back at the lawyer. 'Which of these three was a neighbor to the man who fell among the thieves?' says he. The lawyer, he sees he can't no way get clear of this one and says, 'The one who showed mercy on him.' And Jesus said back to him, 'Go, and do likewise.'"

William scowled and got his knife into a good bite of cedar wood, the long splinter changing pitch as he shaved it off the handle of the paddle.

"That there Samar'tan, you called him," said Junebug, dribbling a mixture of honey and fresh butter onto the steaming cornbread, "he was the nicest of fellows, seems to me. A-caring for his poor neighbor like that."

"Yes'm, but all the folks Jesus was a-talkin' to," said Noclas, "they would have been thinkin' jus' the opposite way 'round. Samaritan folk back then was like Injuns to most white folk today. They was the worthless ones, the dogs, the ones nobody wants for neighbors, that's who they was."

William looked out of the corner of his eye at Noclas. The old man was scratching Wally's ears and gazing with a look of pity into the fire, the flames glistening warmly in his eyes. But not self-pity, not a hint. It didn't appear to register to the big black man that he was more of an outcast than most of the Indians; at least the Indians had each other.

Setting down the paddle, and wiping the blade of his knife on his buckskin trousers, William cut the cornbread into generous wedges.

"Junebug, you've gone and made another yummy supper," he said. "But it's late. You need to be getting some shut-eye. Finish your cornbread, then it's off to bed with you. I'll be doing the cleaning up. It won't take but a minute."

After his sister had washed her face and hands and readied herself for bed, William gave her a piggyback ride three times around the little room and then deposited her in the trundle bed in the far corner of the cabin, feigning exhaustion at how heavy she had become. He tucked a threadbare quilt up tight around her chin and planted a kiss on her round forehead. "You go on and get some good sleep now, you hear?"

"And for Betsy?" said Junebug, holding the perpetual smiling face of her rag doll up to her brother.

William smiled and kissed the stuffed-rag face. Hugging her doll tightly, Junebug turned on her side. Drawing in a deep breath, she let it out slowly, and lay still.

Adding another log to the fire, William eased himself into the willow chair. He nodded toward where Junebug lay, and held his finger to his lips. "She'll be asleep in no time." He mouthed the words, adding, "Probably is already."

For several minutes, all was quiet, except for the creaking of the rocking chairs and an occasional sigh from Wally. Then, just above a whisper came a high thin voice from the trundle bed. "I sure do like it when someone sings me a song at bedtime. William, he tries to sing for me, but he sings silly songs, ones that make no sense. He tried singing me one about the shores of Gitche Gumee the other night, but it didn't make no sense. He says that's the ones he understands best, though I reckon he's funnin' me when he says it." She hesitated. "Would you sing a real song for me, Noclas?"

If Noclas's reading voice had been difficult for William to ignore, when the old black man sang, his voice was rich and deep, a voice that somehow seemed to transform the one-room log cabin into a vast cavernous sanctuary.

"The Lord's my Shepherd, I'll not want
He makes me down to lie . . ."

William mused that a singing voice like Noclas's—forget the meaning of the words—could start tears of compassion flowing down the cheeks of King Herod.

6

TROUBLE

William frowned long after Noclas's singing faded into the creaking stillness of a wilderness log cabin in midwinter. There were times when Noclas seemed the wisest of men, and then there were others when William simply could not understand anything he said. Why would he sing to a little girl going to sleep about passing through "death's dark vale"? It would terrify her and she'd never get to sleep. Now the part about "fearing no evil," and the Shepherd being a comfort through it all, true or not, that made sense to sing to a little one trying her best to go to sleep, but "death's dark vale"? Singing that nonsense could make her all afeared and anxious, and he was mildly irritated with the old man for having done it.

Getting up, William tiptoed over to the trundle bed where his sister lay on her back, her corn-colored hair spread over the pillow, her arms relaxed and splayed over her head. Her breathing was slow and even, and a slight smile tugged at the corners of her lips. William pulled the quilt up to his sister's chin and tucked her rag doll in close.

"Dead to the world," said William softly as he sat back down in front of the fire. He scowled, wondering who came up with such a metaphor for sleeping.

"Restin' all peaceful-like," said Noclas, his white teeth flashing in the firelight, "storms a-raging all 'bout her, and she's a-restin' just so as she is. Does a body good seein' her so."

William didn't entirely understand why Junebug was like that, peaceful and oblivious to troubles, but he had decided after what happened in '52 that—no matter how much folks talked—he would do his level best to keep her that way.

"Junebug, she says you brung some news," said William, taking up his knife and the cedar board he was trying to turn into a canoe paddle. "But I'm thinking there's more news than the fluff you let on about at supper."

"Yes, sir, there is," said Noclas.

"I doubt that your bones telling you it would be an early spring," continued William, "and that there'd be a bumper crop of trilliums decorating the forest floor, white ones and pink ones—I doubt that was all the news you was bringing us."

"That bit 'bout the flowers, that were for Miss Junebug," said Noclas, "and it's for certain sure, it is." Wally laid his head on Noclas's knee, and the big black man stretched his toes closer to the fire and patted the dog absently. "No sir, it's for sure." He cocked his head to one side. "You listen to that. Wind a-rising like that, we's in for some blusterful times for sure 'nough, then come the cold—perhaps a bit of snow even. Only after all that—then come the early springtime and the pretty flowers I's telling Miss Junebug all 'bout."

"And what else?" said William, poking at the coals, sparks scolding and hissing back, then flying up the chimney.

His smile disappeared. Noclas leaned in closer to William. "I hears things," he said in a raspy whisper.

The black man's skin was etched with crevasses from a harsh existence of exposure to the elements, craggy like the mountains he had hunted and trapped in most of his past life. Noclas had been a mountain man, a solitary fur trapper, emerging once or twice a year to trade his furs, resupply himself with gunpowder and shot, then to vanish back into the remote wilds of the Cascade Mountains.

Abruptly, three years ago something had changed for Noclas. Most trappers, when they'd had enough of trapping, set themselves up as guides for wagon trains coming west, or they took up trading at a trading post somewhere along the route west.

But Noclas was different. After trading two mule-loads of prime beaver skins at Fort Nisqually, Noclas turned his back on his solitary life in the mountains. Instead he traded for enough dried food—peas, corn, and beans—to carry him through to harvest, a plow, a bag of seed, a fine buckskin horse, and the deed to a piece of stubborn part-cultivated land. That's when he had turned up next door to the Tidds—three years ago, now.

Noclas had then set to work, like a beaver racing to beat the onset of winter, felling trees on a claim he had staked out in the mosquito-infested region adjoining the Tidd holding. It had made William tired just watching him, and he had at first hung back and looked on with suspicion, even some hostility: what business did an old trapper have settling down to farming in these parts—and a black one at that? They had more than enough troubles of their own. Others had tried farming the same piece of land but had upped stakes and moved within two seasons; some folks said there were impure eddies and vapors, bad currents and counter-currents polluting the holding. There were times when William felt it was truer than the local gossip. He would have abandoned the miserable plot of ground himself if he'd had anywhere else to go. He hadn't.

After weeks of clearing the land with his mules, Noclas built a tiny cabin, plowed up the soil, and planted potatoes—sweet potatoes. And he planted something else—the

Indians called it White-Man's Foot, but the white men just called it weeds. But Noclas must have known something about that weed that other folks, white or Indian, didn't. Within three months, the mosquitoes had high-tailed it for better feeding ground; with Noclas's steady, tireless ditching and diking he turned his holding into one of the best pieces of farmland in the south Puget Sound region, all the while doing his part to befriend what remained of the Tidd family and share what he was doing with them.

Besides his almost miraculous ability to turn stubborn wilderness into a productive farm, Noclas had more cures and fixes for things than a body could imagine; cuts, scrapes, rashes, headache, bottom ache, bellyache—you name it, Noclas would whip up a White-Man's-Foot poultice or mug of tea, and soon enough things were healed up good as new. Black man and loner that he was, Junebug liked saying that "Noclas, he's in a class all his own." Though William still coddled his suspicions, he couldn't deny that Noclas was the kindest, most generous neighbor any poor settler could ask for.

"I hears things," repeated Noclas, leaning still closer. William could see every ridge and valley in the man's features. Noclas paused, a faraway look in his eyes.

"Go on," said William. "You hear things from the white folks in town?"

Noclas gave a half smile. "Not so much from the white folks," he said. "Mostly from the Injuns." He suddenly became sober.

William knew that Noclas was in a world by himself. The King George men at the Hudson Bay Company fort were happy to trade with him—his furs being some of the very finest quality—but there was a comfortable barrier kept solidly in place. And at the same time, William had heard and seen white American settlers snub the solitary black man, some in open hostility, others in uncertainty or fear. He'd not only seen it; he'd done it the same.

What seemed remarkable to William was that Noclas was a man devoid of the slightest hint of resentment at how he was treated by others. A glance of disdain or of revulsion, an insult or taunt, no matter; Noclas was slave to none of it. Every offense hurled at him dissolved like a rain squall off the oily back of a mallard filling its belly on slugs in the marshy delta of the Nisqually.

But the Indians treated the black man differently. Maybe it was because Noclas spoke their language, not just the cobbled up trade talk: English, French, Salish, and a variety of other Indian language words chopped, diced, shredded, then dumped in the pot and churned into an all-the-world stew. Some claimed there were more than twenty-five Indian languages just among the coastal tribes, forget the horse Indians to the east. Who could know for sure? The five hundred words that made up Chinook Jargon, as the trade language was called, were serviceable for bringing white folks and Indians from throughout the territory together for buying and selling, but wholly inadequate for meaningful understanding and trust.

Though his English sounded odd to some white men's ears, Noclas seemed to have a keen ear for other languages. Understanding very little, William had once sat and listened to Noclas speak for more than an hour to a group of Salish-speaking Indians; he knew they must have been understanding his words because they listened with evident attention, even stopping him and interjecting what seemed to be questions throughout—all in Salish.

"The injuns, they ain't none too happy 'bout that treaty," continued Noclas, "that treaty Governor Stevens drawed up and made 'em all set down a 'X' by their names."

William glanced over at the sleeping form of Junebug. "I've heard the same from Charlie Salitat, just today. What's it mean?"

"I don't pretend to know that for sure," said Noclas, running a thick calloused hand over his black hair, now flecked with little swirls of gray. "But it ain't jus' the coastal Injuns. There's word of the horse Injuns yonder ways over the mountains, the warlike Yakamas. Word is they's fixin' to ride out 'gainst the white folk."

"Are you sure?" William hadn't heard anything about this.

"Pretty sure." Noclas nodded. "It was the Injuns their-selves who told me so."

"What about the Nisquallys and Puyallups? Will they join with the Yakamas?" William studied the black man's face. "Just how do you go about hearing these things?"

"I has my ways," said Noclas with a wink. "Leschi and his brother Quiemuth—they's the Injuns I mostly trade with; that's how I come by Prophet—dead beavers for a 'live horse, that's trading for profit, says I." Noclas chuckled at his own joke. "It do me good to see you a-riding Prophet, it do. Finest horse flesh I ever seen, is Prophet. Most like flyin' when ridin' him. Though I expect he's a bit too much horse for an old trapper like me."

William had often felt the same when riding Prophet, but there were few things that gave him as much pleasure.

"Leschi and the Salish—they're so peaceful and quiet-like," said William. "They wouldn't turn on their white neighbors and fight."

"I'd a said the same, myself," said Noclas, "before that treaty signin'. Ever since, there's been heaps a scowling and grumbling in the grasslands yonder ways 'bout Muck Creek," said Noclas, "where the big Tyee Leschi and his Injuns tends the horses for the Hudson Bay Company."

"But Leschi is a good friend of many of the settlers," said William. "He and James McAllister, everybody knows they're best of friends. Word is, Leschi wanted to make McAllister a member of the tribe. And he manages to get on well enough with Indian agent Simmons, and Acting-Governor Mason down yonder ways in Olympia."

"There is that," said Noclas. "But there's another matter. You know the fella they calls Charles Wren?"

William knew who the man was. Who didn't? "Richest man in these parts, some folks say. Big holding, heaps of cattle and horses, and married into Leschi's tribe."

"There's all a that," said Noclas with a frown, though William thought it looked more like a frown of sadness than dislike.

"Charles Wren—nothing," said William. "Folks call him Charles the Rustler. Word is he deserves the nickname."

"Could be," said Noclas vaguely.

"Could be? Noclas, you know it your own self," said William. "It's about as common a knowledge as drizzle in December. Charles Wren the Rustler earned his name for rustling his neighbors' stock: calves, sheep, goats, even horses. No, he's earned his name, fair and square."

"Well, that's as may be," said Noclas. "But it's for sure that Charles the Rustler's been spending considerable time at Leschi's longhouse up Muck Creek way. I'm loath to be believin' it, but the word is he may be stirrin' the pot with the Injuns. When he's not thievin' his neighbor's stock, it appears he just might be thievin' somethin' far worse. Fuelin' animosity betwixt the white folks and the Injuns, the Rustler may be fixin' on thievin' the peace."

William felt his heart beat faster at the words. "Why would anybody want to go and do that sort of thing?"

"Don't make no sense," agreed Noclas, "but I expect he allows he'll be profitin' someway by it." Then looking levelly at William he continued, "I don't reckon there's much doubt 'bout it now. Whatever the provocation, Leschi and some of the coastal Injuns, they's fixin' to ride out with the Yakamas. Bill Tidd, sooner than later, there's goin' to be trouble."

7

FAINTING FRANK

"What are you reading about?" asked Junebug, looking up from a piece of paper, the squeaking of charcoal halting for an instant.

A week had passed since Noclas had brought the news about Indian troubles heating up in the region. He'd been right about the weather anyway. Warming his hands in front of the fire, William was reluctant to leave the comfort of their little cabin and head out into the frigid cold. Sure, splitting cedar shakes would warm him, but here it came with less effort. So he'd taken to reading that morning.

"About the news," grunted William.

"News about what?"

"Just news, politics, big-people news," said William. "You wouldn't be interested."

"I might be," said Junebug, resuming her sketching. "Read the news to me and find out. Better yet, how about you just tell me it in your own words?"

Taking care to avoid any news that might upset his sister, William proceeded to give her his highlights of what was going on in America and the world, and to give his commentary on it. He felt exhilaration as he found himself selecting and shaping it so that it fit nicely into his hopes and dreams, into what he wanted things to be, what he wanted to believe them to be. But it was not possible to summarize world affairs for long without hitching up alongside troublesome things. Things like slavery. Knowing Junebug, he was pretty certain she would have strong opinions about slavery.

"Since the signing of the Oregon Treaty with Britain in 1846," continued William, "and the ending of hostilities with Mexico in '48, there's been more talk in Washington about the peculiar institution of slavery."

"In Washington?" said Junebug. "I thought we were Washington?"

"No, no, Junebug. The other one. We're just the territory. I mean Washington DC—the one that's our country's capital—you've heard tell of it, a continent away where all the bigwigs have their seats in government, congress and the judges, and President Franklin Pierce living in the White House on the Potomac River. It all happens in the other Washington, not this one."

"What's he like?" asked Junebug, narrowing her eyes at her drawing.

"The president? He's sort of nondescript, looks like he just swallowed a mouthful of apricots and kept the pits in his cheeks for later, unpopular among his own party, is Franklin Pierce. So much so, that one of his old nicknames has resurfaced itself."

"Is it a mean one?" she asked warily.

"You decide. Story is that because he fainted after falling from his horse in the Mexican War, some of his soldiers dubbed their general 'Fainting Frank,' behind his back, of course. It was a nickname his political opponents enjoyed bringing up during his presidential campaign. All the more now."

"That's mean," said Junebug. "It probably really hurt falling off his horse like that. You've taken a tumble or two off Prophet, ain't you, so you ought to know it."

"I have done," agreed William, recalling the raw fear he'd felt that first time he'd found himself heading in another direction than the horse. It wasn't the only time.

"You said he's been talking about slavery?" she continued. "What's he saying about it?"

William fidgeted with the newspaper in front of him and pretended to have something in his eye. Wally lifted his head from William's knee and heaved a sigh that ended in a guttural whine.

"What's he saying about slavery?" repeated Junebug, looking up from her sketch, now becoming a portrait of what she thought a president of the United States of America might look like. She turned the sketch toward her brother. "What do you think?"

"Not much," said William with a shrug.

"You don't like it?" said Junebug, holding her sketch at arm's length and frowning.

"You asked two questions," said William, "again. 'Not much' was me replying to the first one. The president ain't saying much about slavery."

"William Tidd, I always know when you're not telling me the whole story 'bout something or other. I reckon he's my president just as much as yours, so I need to know what he thinks about making people into slaves, buying and selling them, owning them like as if they was pigs or chickens."

Where Junebug got her ideas about such things living out in the middle of nowhere was beyond reckoning to William. What business did a ten-year-old have going and having such strong opinions about politics or anything else, for that matter? But he kept his thoughts to himself.

"President Pierce seems to have gone astray a bit on that one," he said, then added, "depending on whose side you're on, that is. Leastwise, that's what his one-time supporters in the North are all in a dither about."

"Gone astray?" said Junebug. "What do you mean?"

"Well, he's gone and allowed settlers in the new territory of Kansas to make their own decision about whether they'll own slaves or not. Folks are scrambling to Kansas to settle the question, abolitionists to make sure it gets enough of their kind to vote 'no' on slavery, and the proslavery folks determined to make sure it'll someday become a slave-holding and voting state."

"Do you think he has a beard or not?" asked Junebug.

"What?"

"President Pierce, does he have a beard?"

Sometimes Junebug was a puzzle to William. "A beard?" he said. "No, I think he has a crop of unruly hair on top and not a whisker on his face. That's what I think." He was relieved for the change of subject, and pressed on. "Then there's this newly elected federal senator in Illinois, close race it was, Lincoln's the feller's name, Abraham Lincoln—now, *he* has a beard."

Junebug interrupted him. "But what's the news from Kansas? All those folks disagreeing about slavery and living in the same territory, can't be good."

William hesitated. "It's not so good. Though there may be some good in it. Due in part to President Pierce's growing unpopularity, there's been a new party formed."

"A party, like for birthdays?" said Junebug, her eyes sparkling.

"No, silly, said William. "Political party."

"With pie and ice cream, and games and races?"

"Well, there are races," said William. "But no, it's not that kind of party. It's more of a club where things get hashed out, where folks who agree stick together, mostly, and nominate folks they want in office, and vote the same way about things, mostly."

"Things like slavery?"

"And other things."

"And Kansas, what's really going on in Kansas?" asked Junebug. "You can tell me."

William could see there was no getting around it. When Junebug got her teeth in a question she wanted answered, she was worse than a timber wolf lock-jawed on the throat of a frantic old elk. He heaved a sigh and launched in. "Kansas is bleeding. There's been fighting and killing in the territory, and like to be more there and out east. Since the passing of the Fugitive Slave Law in 1850, there's been a rise of books and poetry penned to fire the blood of those who won't stop at anything until they've abolished slavery in every corner of this continent. And the proslavery states won't stand for anyone in Washington DC telling them how to work their farms—or their lives. I'm afeared we're not hearing the end of this anytime soon, not by a long shot."

"Indians have slaves, I know they do," said Junebug pensively. "But it somehow seems worse when white folks does it."

"What do you mean, worse for white folks?" asked William. "A slave's a slave, ain't it?"

"Well, white folks've had more light to see by—every household owning a Bible, and centuries of book learning and refinement. No, slavery's worse for folks who should know better." Junebug cut herself off. "Can you imagine someone *owning* Noclas?"

William wasn't sure what to think about all this. He tossed the newspaper onto the plank table and got up. Cold or no cold, if they were going to eat, it was time he got some work done.

8

SELF-RELIANCE

Hunkering behind the buckboards of the wagon to block the wind, William shivered. The raw, cold breeze made the pages of the book he was attempting to read tremble. Wishing he had a pair of wool gloves, he thumbed his way back to where he had left off reading.

"It is easy to see that a greater self-reliance must work a revolution in all the offices and relations of men." It had been one of his pa's favorite essays.

Nearly an hour ago now, he had reined in Noclas's mules and parked the wagon at the foot of the hill, where the main street of Steilacoom ended and the wharf began. There was no better place close by for peddling a wagon-load of shakes in a hurry, no better place if it weren't for the cold. William blew on his hands and tried rubbing some of the cold from his cheeks. Moaning from the north, the wind whipped the salt water into wavelets that broke into frothy whitecaps that chivied as they broke along the pebbly beach. Noclas's mule team, Molly and Polly, or Mole and Pole, depending on how they were behaving, stamped their hooves against the cold, eager to be on the move.

"Least it's not dumping rain," he called to the mules, "or snow," he added with a shiver. Pulling the collar of his homespun coat up, he craned his neck up the muddy street toward the rows of houses. Surely one of those buildings had a roof leaking every time the rains poured down, a leak that couldn't wait until springtime.

William had read just last week in the *Puget Sound Courier* ("A Weekly Journal—Dedicated to Agriculture, Commerce, Literature, Useful Sciences, Arts, Politics, News, and General Intelligence") that there were now seventy buildings sprawling their way up the hillside from the gravelly shore of Puget Sound in the growing frontier town: many of them houses, mostly log houses, though the newest ones tidy-built from milled lumber sawn by Thomas Chambers at his new mill on the creek just north of town. Houses, a library, a jail, two bowling alleys, a newspaper office, and John De Vore's new church building, and the tall log house he had built for his family just over William's shoulder on the bluff behind where he'd parked the wagon—surely one of these structures needed a load of new cedar roof shingles.

Though the air was brisk, there was no rain falling, and it seemed that more folks than William would have expected—maybe eager for springtime—had braved the cold and were out and about the town and wharf. And William knew most of them by sight. Well, not exactly knew them, but it was impossible to live near a frontier town in Puget Sound and not know about most of the other folks that lived in the region, especially if you read the newspapers.

There were the American settlers Iven Watt, Andrew Byrd, Will Claffin, and the English doctor Matthew Burns—at least he loudly proclaimed himself to be a doctor. They walked along the boardwalk in deep conversation; though he couldn't hear what they said, it looked to William like Dr.

Burns, as he preferred folks to address him, was doing most of the talking, gesticulating like an ensign on a schooner.

And coming along from the direction of Chambers's mill was Andy Burge, a local legend: veteran of the Mexican War, a gold prospector in '49 moved up from California, a tireless mound of energy, who had helped cut a road through the rugged Cascade Mountains at Naches Pass, used now by whites and Indians alike to cross from the coastal drizzle in the west to the arid eastern plains. Burge stopped to converse with Gilmore Hays and Tom Perkins, the latter a man who knew the Indians and was better than most at conversing with them in Chinook Jargon. They were joined by James McAllister and his son George who was two years younger—give or take—than William. Everyone seemed to have something on their minds that needed talking about.

Walking briskly on William's side of the street came a tall, slender man. He wore a black ready-made suit, velvet vest, starched collar, carefully knotted cravat—dressed, William thought, like this was Boston or New York, not the littered street of a ramshackle frontier town thousands of miles and a world away from those places—grand places he had only read about. The man walked like he had forgotten something and was retracing his steps to go fetch it. When he saw William, he hesitated and then, as if an idea had suddenly formed, he stopped.

"Howdy, Bill Tidd," he said. It was James Wiley, editor of the *Pioneer and Democrat,* a Washington territorial newspaper printed every week just south in the territorial capital town of Olympia on Water Street. The newspaperman gave William a quick smile, and then it was gone.

"Howdy to you, Mr. Wiley," said William.

Surveying William and the load of shakes, James Wiley adjusted his gold-rimmed spectacles; he had an odd way of doing it, using the knuckles of a half-clenched fist brought to the bridge of his nose, like a weak salute that never made it all the way to the brim of his hat.

"Bit blustery for lounging out on your buckboard, isn't it?" said the journalist.

"Yes, sir, it sure is."

"You're not fixing to take your sweetheart out for a picnic," said James Wiley, winking and flashing William another smile, gone as quickly as it had appeared, "not on a day like this?"

"No sir." William considered asking the journalist. Maybe he needed new cedar for his roof? But Wiley lived in Olympia. At Mole and Pole's steady clop, that was most of a day's travel, there and back.

Wiley brought his knuckles to his spectacles again, looked left and right, and said, "You know what's in the wind, don't you?" He fingered a black notebook protruding from a pocket in his tailored coat, and leaned in closer. "If you're a man of intelligence who reads the newspapers—and I know that you are. Then you know what's in the wind. Territory needs more men the likes of Bill Tidd. It's your manifest destiny, or as could be. Times like these, noble deeds await the doing by young men the likes of you, Bill Tidd. Mark my words."

With one last salute, James Wiley turned and scurried up toward the main street. Puzzled, William watched as the man grew smaller, pausing here and there to chat with the clusters of people out and about the town that morning.

By the looks of the muddy streets, most of the women-folk were staying indoors, likely to avoid the chilly air, but not Mrs. Longmire. Arm linked in her husband's, James Longmire's, they had halted on the boardwalk to exchange greetings with the town's lawyer William Wallace, and there was the bachelor farmer Frank Goodwin nodding his head but appearing to add nothing to the conversation. Close as they were, William was upwind of them; he could see their mouths moving, but the wind carried their words the other direction. It was like a sideshow at a circus, a pantomime or a charade. William always felt like more of an observer—a spectator—than a participant in the life of the community in which they lived, that is, since '52 he had felt that way.

But his blood quickened as he watched another man approaching. He rode down the street, mounted on a well-groomed Arabian horse. The horse lifted its hooves as if it would do what it was commanded, but it had other things in mind. William smiled. Something about the big animal's manner seemed to convey the clear notion that it would walk for its master, though it would far rather trot; as if it would trot, though it would rather gallop; as if it would gallop, though it would rather fly full tilt, at breakneck speed. A horse like Prophet, William smiled appreciatively.

William studied the rider. He knew this man. It was Charles Eaton. He must have come down from his holding on the prairie a few miles south of town for supplies, or was it to catch up on the latest news? As the man rode nearer, William studied him and his horse with interest. Just two issues ago—or was it three?—James Wiley had reported in the *Pioneer and Democrat* that Eaton had been made captain of a newly formed territorial militia of local volunteers. "Eaton's Rangers" they were being called. Maybe that's what Wiley had been alluding to.

As he came alongside, Eaton touched the brim of his felt hat and nodded at William. William couldn't help liking the man. His features had the leathery toughness that the frontier gives most men who set their arms and backs to shaping a civilization out of such a vast and often hostile wilderness. But Eaton's square jaw, cantilevered forehead, and steady blue eyes had nothing of the exploitive hardness that works into the bone structure of some other men—or perhaps had been there all along.

William had heard that Charles Eaton had fought with valor and distinction in the Mexican War. Noclas knew the man and always spoke well of him, though you couldn't always rely on what Noclas said about other folks; he was always wearing himself out finding something good to say about other folks. The most low-down, good-for-nothing scoundrel might come off sounding more like a patron saint when Noclas was finished with him.

But William believed it about Charles Eaton. He had the respect of his neighbors—white or Indian, including Leschi and the Nisqually village on Muck Creek near his holding. And it was widely known that he was a horseman like few others. William watched Eaton, seated comfortably but ramrod straight in the saddle, his right hand holding the reins, his left resting on his hip, a handbreadth away from a shiny new Colt Sidehammer .28 caliber revolver, protruding from a well-oiled leather holster.

Two men hailed Eaton near the two-story stockade home of John De Vore, the local minister. They were Joseph Miles and Abram Moses, one-time sheriff of Thurston County. Eaton reined in his horse, dismounted, and began conversing with the pair.

The sound of boots scraping hollow on the rough planks of the wharf behind him drew William's attention away from Eaton and his two companions. Four men approached from the wharf. He looked hopefully at them. Maybe he should try being more assertive.

"Shakes—extra heavy?" he called to them. "Been heaps of rain and more's coming. I deliver. And I can fasten them in place for you, if you need the help."

One of the men slowed his pace, eyeing William. He was thickset, his face everything Charles Eaton's had not been: fleshy pocked jowls, with the fiery complexion of maple leaves in October, his skin the texture of a wood rasp. His ears looked like heads of cauliflower, as if he'd spent a good deal of time brawling behind the saloon. The man wore a fine linen shirt, now rumpled as if he'd slept in it for a month, with dribbles of brown tobacco stains running alongside the row of bone buttons.

A sneer contorted the man's lips, one that looked like it never let up. Meeting the man's eye for an instant, William felt a crawling up his neck, like fleas migrating through the straw in a mattress. The eyes, restless ones that never quite met your own, pinched into narrow slits, as if by perpetually squinting the man saved himself needing to blink. William felt like he was being sized up, like the man was taking stock not only of what might be in his pockets—which wasn't nothing—but of his wits, how hard or simple it would be to swindle him.

Spurs jangling on his boot heels, the long spiky rowels like jagged fangs eager to rend the hide of his mount, the man clomped nearer. William felt sorry for the man's horse. Though he'd never met him up close, William decided, it had to be Charles Wren. Noclas said Wren had taken an Indian wife; William shuddered at the plight of any woman married to such a man.

Planting his feet in front of where William sat on the tailgate of the wagon, Wren aimed a brown spurt of tobacco juice at the gravel near William's feet.

"No roof needin' shakin' over my head," growled Wren.

His companions laughed.

"Ya, but there just may be somethin' else," laughed one of his companions, "bein' strung up over Chuck Wren's head one of these here days."

"Shut your cavity!" said the man. He hurled the words at his companion with such violence that it made William's heart skip a beat. Wren aimed another spurt of tobacco juice, this time between William's moccasined feet. "You's that Bill Tidd's boy, ain't you?"

William felt heat rising on his cheeks and a constricting in his throat. He often felt like folks were thinking it, but here was Wren saying it. It was more of an accusation than a question. With a disdainful grunt, Wren planted a last tobacco spurt, this one landing on a worn moccasin. Turning abruptly, his boot heel grinding in the gravel, he strode on into town, his minions fanning out in his wake. Off to the saloon, William figured.

So that's Charles Wren, Charles the Rustler, he thought, wiping his forehead with his sleeve in spite of the cold. He watched the men turn into the main street and disappear around the corner. He'd heard the name—who hadn't?—and he recalled seeing the man before now, but today was the first time he put the name with the face—a cruel face, hard and bitter like a copper penny. William shuddered, but not at the cold.

Swinging his legs to keep the blood circulating, William set down the book he had been reading from and beat his arms against his body. It was cold just sitting still; the sleeves of his old coat had gotten shorter, and the wool was unraveling in places and had grown thinner in all the others. He wasn't sure how much more of this he could stand.

After blowing hot blasts of air into his hands, William took up the book again, found his place, and read on. "Greater self-reliance must work a revolution in all the offices and relations of men, in their religion; in their education; in their pursuits; their modes of living; their association; in their property; in their speculative views.

"We will walk on our own feet; we will work with our own hands; we will speak our own minds. . . . A nation of men will for the first time exist, because each believes himself inspired by the Divine Soul."

William frowned, turning the book in his hands. Judging from the worn cloth of its cover, his pa must have read this over and over. He was pretty sure Noclas wouldn't think much of Emerson's notions about self-reliance.

One of the mules snorted and stamped its hooves, impatient of the cold and eager to be on the move. William looked over his shoulder at the team. "Self-reliance." He voiced the words bitterly. "Humph." Borrowed mule team, borrowed wagon, borrowed horse—there was almost nothing self-reliant about his existence.

"Just the man I am looking for!"

Startled, William looked up. Distracted by his melancholy musings, he hadn't noticed the man approaching. Standing before him was a man in the dark blue uniform of a US Army lieutenant.

"Won't you come with me?" said the officer.

9

SLAUGHTER

Of course William had seen army soldiers before. It was not possible to live so near an army fort, Fort Steilacoom, and not see them about town, on the road, drilling on the parade ground, staggering from the saloon, brawling on the wharf. But he had seldom, if ever, had close conversation with a soldier. And never with an officer.

William stared dumbly at the man, a young man, scarcely much older than himself. He took in the man's uniform, its close-set row of brass buttons polished until they gleamed like gold nuggets; he wore tall black boots, spit-and-polished, and a black wool-felt hat, one side pinned up with a glimmering brass eagle and a French horn medallion decorating the front. William's eyes rested on the black leather belt and holster at his waist; it was a holster with a leather flap that covered the pistol, so he couldn't be sure, but wondered if it, too, was a Colt Sidehammer revolver, like Charles Eaton's. He'd read all about them, new manufactured in Connecticut, the very latest in weaponry, so he'd read. The young man standing before William was clearly an officer newly arrived at nearby Fort Steilacoom.

"Slaughter's the name, William Slaughter," said the man. And then he added, almost apologetically, "Lieutenant William A. Slaughter."

William stared and managed to nod for reply. How could someone have a name like that? He wondered if it was possible to change a name like that one.

"It's lucky I found you, really," continued Lieutenant Slaughter. "The United States Army has good use for this wagonload of fine cedar shakes." He paused, eyeing William. "Up yonder, at the fort. Won't you come with me?"

William recalled hearing or reading in the newspaper—that was it, the newspaper—something vaguely of the man, a young officer from out east, from the military academy at West Point. Most folks, British or American, who ended up in drizzly Puget Sound came on their own, to start a new life, a better life, so they hoped; they came now in droves because for one reason or another they actually wanted to.

It suddenly occurred to William that this young military officer may have been deeply disappointed at his first duty station, a backwater wilderness as far removed from American civilization as it could possibly be, a revoltingly long sea voyage around the Horn, leaving behind New York, Washington DC, Boston, and all the charms of civilization, and leaving behind all prospects for military distinction and promotion—or so he must have thought.

"They are for sale?" continued the lieutenant.

William nodded. "Yes they are," he said, adding, "Sir."

The young officer had pale features, his cheeks sunken as if he never had quite enough to eat; his eyes were dark and eager and were rimmed with black eyebrows. Though his lieutenant's hat concealed most of his hair, the way it sat on his head made William believe he had a higher forehead than most men his age; he wore a sparse black beard that frittered away into an upper lip that seemed to need no shaving at all.

He didn't want to read too much into it, but something about the man's face and posture made William feel that this was a man who had high expectations for himself. Then again, there was something else about his manner that made William wonder if the man had his own secret fears, maybe that he might fall short of those lofty expectations. It was something about his eyes: at one and the same time they had a steely intensity, an eagerness, but they blinked slightly more often than seemed necessary. And there was another mannerism: the way he had of fingering the close row of brass buttons that stood in precise formation up and down the front of his immaculately brushed uniform, toying with them as if to make sure they were all there, each in its place, still lined up in two neatly ordered rows.

"Yes, Sir," said William again.

"Well, then, I am certain we can come to reasonable terms," said the young lieutenant. "My paymaster is at his desk this very moment. We pay in kind or in gold coins, as you prefer."

William slammed the book closed and hopped off the tailgate of the wagon. He nearly collapsed. While he'd been reading, his legs had gone numb, tiny swords poking and pricking into his flesh. He hopped on the leg that had slightly more feeling and stability in it.

"Sir, I am at your service," William managed to say, wincing at the thousand man-eating ants that seemed to be devouring his legs.

"Follow me, then," said Lieutenant Slaughter.

10

FEARFUL ODDS

But the paymaster was not in, and the fort did not pay in gold, only in script, an official-looking, though far too thin, piece of paper that was supposed to represent money, flimsy paper payment for the privilege of being of service to the US Army at Fort Steilacoom.

"I am disconsolate," said Lieutenant Slaughter, a set to his jaw. "I am a man of honor; I will make this up to you. You have my word."

Though he had read that the young man had completed his military training at West Point, in the state of New York, William thought he detected a hint of an inflection that reminded him of the way his people talked back in Kentucky. Maybe military discipline and officer training had that effect: not only changing the way a man carried himself, but changing the way a man formed his words.

William didn't blame him, and the young officer seemed genuinely apologetic. Maybe intended to be his way of making things right with William, Lieutenant Slaughter made a point of introducing William to several of the ranking officers at the fort. One he saluted and called "Colonel Casey, Sir!" and another he saluted and called "Captain Picket, Sir!" And another he addressed as Captain William Wallace. Still another he addressed with somewhat less formality, "My friend, August Kautz, Lieutenant Kautz."

William began to realize, that day, that eking out a living on the stony ground of his little farm was a very different life from that of the soldiers living on a frontier military fort far from their homes.

It had taken dozens of sweaty hours, plus the slivers and blisters, to split those shakes. He reckoned only government could get away with doing a thing like this, print something up and call it money. He could have used the money—the real money—but he had no other prospects for selling his shakes, so William did as he was told; he agreed and took the paper money—such as it was.

Disappointed, William began unloading the cedar shakes where they instructed him to do so: behind a lean-to supply shed on the west end of the fort grounds behind a hand-hewn log officers' quarters. Spicy whiffs of aromatic cedar filled his nose and perfumed his hands as he worked.

From where he had reined in the mules and set the brake on the buckboard, he had a clear view of the activities on the muddy parade grounds encircled by a scattering of other log structures. Maybe Noclas was right after all. The military fort was astir with activity, though there seemed to be few men in actual uniform present. As he worked, he overheard snatches of a conversation, one that would trouble him considerably in the weeks to come.

"There's only 1,200 soldiers in the entire vast region," said a man who didn't appear to be an actual soldier. William thought he recognized the fellow; he could be the frontiersman Edgar who used to work for Fort Nisqually, word was, and who had settled a few miles south near Olympia. Though the man was now here at the fort, by his casual attire, buckskins held up by black suspenders over a dingy undershirt, buttons missing and stained down the front with tobacco juice, and by his backwoods manner, maybe he'd been retained as a scout.

From where the man lounged on a barrel smoking a pipe, he continued. "From Canada to California, and from the Rockies to the Pacific Ocean—you've got but a lousy 1,200 soldiers!"

"What's worse," said his companion, knocking the heels of his boots against the barrel he was seated on, "is we've only got about 200 of those fellers here at Fort Steilacoom, you me and 198 others. That's it! Edgar, if the Injuns decide to put up a fight, we'll beat the savages in the end, won't we? Sure we will. But the odds of doing it—I'm thinkin' they ain't so good."

"Addisom Parham, you'll be outnumbered five to one, easy," said Edgar. "If it were gamblin', I'd fold up at them stakes every time, would I. I know when I'm licked."

"But shucks, Edgar, we're way better equipped, ain't we?" said Parham. His voice was pitched more like a girl's, so it sounded to William. Parham continued as if listing things on his fingers. "We gots more muskets, more powder, more lead—and we've got artillery, them Napoleon cannons right there. Nothing can't stop them."

"You're new 'round here, ain't you?" said Edgar, blowing a blue spout of smoke into the cool air from his pipe. "The only way them Napoleons could help you if it comes to war with the Injuns, is if the Injuns walked up to the fort and had the good breeding to present themselves in front of the barrel of one of those." He nodded toward a brass cannon mounted on a caisson, its mouth gaping in William's direction. "And you'd have to encourage them to hold real still while you blast 'em with it."

Moving slowly and methodically, William set down each bundle of shakes with care so he could listen in. And from where the buckboard sat he had a clear view of the parade ground, half a dozen soldiers mounted on horses lining up for what looked like some kind of training.

"Have you strolled into the forest yonder?" continued Edgar, pointing with the stem of his clay pipe. "And that's nothing compared to where this war'll be—if it comes to war, which I'm not saying it will—but the terrain around here, it's wilderness—dark, dangerous wilderness, the real kind. This here's a-every-soldier's-nightmare wilderness: bushwacking through underbrush so dense the rain can't reach the ground, white waterfalls, cascades, and river crossings, sheer rock cliffs and glaciers, mountains and ravines, gulches—gulches everywhere a feller turns, and there's nothing you could call a proper road, not of any account. In this territory, thinking cannons'll help you against Injuns slinking behind every tree and boulder, it's danged crazy. Like thinking ole Davey Crocket could have held off Santa Ana with one hand in his buckskin britches. Danged fool craziness."

"But there's heaps of settlers here abouts," said Parham. "Region's thick with 'em."

"Who'll be 'bout as much help as field mice 'gainst mountain lions," said Edgar, thumping his knuckles on the staves of the barrel for emphasis.

William dropped a bundle of shingles with a clatter.

"Sure there's heaps of 'em," continued Edgar. "But except for a few fellers like me, they's mostly farmers, not soldiers, and fewer than one man in five even owns a gun of any kind, that's what Colonel Casey reckons; heard him say so himself. Shucks, a farmer can't protect his own family without a gun; how's he going to fight Injuns? Parham, don't you go expecting no help from the locals."

"What about the territorial militia?" said Parham, his voice cracking on the word "militia" like a boy's.

"The territorial *what*?" said Edgar, with a snort.

Parham laughed, but William thought it sounded like a dry laugh close to catching in the young private's throat.

From the parade ground a bugle signal rang out. "Right about!" called a cavalry officer. William paused at the buckboard, watching the mounted soldiers in their precise maneuvers. Another bugle call and the command, "Left about!"

"Imagine territorial militia," said Edgar with a laugh, "trying to do that." He gestured toward the cavalry with his pipe. "At best the militia in these parts is disorganized, undisciplined, and ill-equipped. And that's the best part."

"But they know the territory," pressed Parham, "the ones who've been around awhile do. And they know the ways of the Injuns."

"That ain't no help!" said Edgar, slapping the side of the barrel, making a gonging noise like a kettle drum.

Another bugle call pierced the cold air, interrupting the two privates' conversation. William looked on.

"Right cut against cavalry!" barked the officer in charge. With a metallic shying of blades and scabbards, the cavalry drew their sabers. Brandishing them in the air, they spurred their horses to a gallop and charged at the enemy, straw-filled dummies propped against stakes. William looked on with fascination. Amidst the thundering of hooves and the cries of defiance, the cavalry slashed at the enemy infantry. All but two of the enemy soldiers had their heads severed by the whirling sabers.

At a signal the mounted troop reformed, sabers at the ready. "Left cut against cavalry!" barked the officer in charge. Swiftly and efficiently, they did it again, more straw-filled heads rolling onto the parade ground.

"Knowing the territory, and the ways of the Injuns," said Edgar, "that ain't no help. Fact is, that there's the real problem. They know it too blamed well. Some of them's married into the tribe, gone and taken Injun wives, they have. Now, on that score, Injun womenfolk, they're good looking enough, but they do smell to tarnation, fish oil smeared over every square inch of their bodies, so I'm told.

How you going to trust a local settler—it don't matter if he emigrated from Washington DC itself—how you going to trust him if he's gone and married into the tribe? You answer me that."

He spat brown tobacco juice in the mud at his feet, and nodded toward the horse and men re-forming in rank. "Image the bloodshed if some territorial rough tried his hand at doing cavalry maneuvers with a sabre."

There was another bugle call. An instant of silence, then the officer yelled, "Front *moulinet!*" Suddenly, men and horses spurred into a charge, hooves thundering on the hard ground, leather harnesses creaking. Sabers forward, the cavalry bore down on another row of straw-filled enemy.

Spitting philosophically, Edgar said, "Your own trained cavalry sometimes kills a horse doing the front *moulinet*. Now and then, one of them boys lops the head of his own horse clean off."

"I once saw a feller take his horse's tail clean off with the rear *moulinet*," said Parham. "Mangled its rump so bad they had to put the beast down. Made it into stew meat for the soldiers' mess. Good eating is horse meat, when victuals is low."

Edgar thumped his barrel with his knuckles. "There you have it. There ain't no help from no militia around here."

"How many Injuns you reckon there are," asked Parham, "hostile ones, that is?"

"No way of knowing for sure," said Edgar. "A few thousand, I reckon. Depends on how all painted-red and riled up they get. And how organized, and how many of the Yakamas over the mountains they can get to join in the killing."

Parham didn't reply, but William heard rapid clunking against a barrel and reckoned it was the young soldier's boot heels.

"The Injuns know every rock," continued Edgar, "and every Wapato root, every clump of bunch grass, every salal bush and backwater, every gulch, every slab of granite. Not only are there heaps more of them than there is of us—." He paused for effect, his pipe making a wide arc of the countryside. "This here's *all* their territory." He stretched out the word "all" for effect.

"So what do you reckon'll happen?" asked Parham, a tremor in his voice and more heel knocking on his barrel.

"Who knows?" said Edgar.

"Sure wish this fort had a stockade," said Parham. "Shucks, can you imagine an army fort unprotected by fortification? Seems downright crazy to me, calling it a fort when it ain't got no *fort*-ification."

Edgar grunted in reply. They smoked in silence for a few moments. William's frown deepened as he put the last of the shakes onto the pile. He closed the tailgate of the buckboard.

"Sure glad I ain't got no kin folk in these parts," said Parham with feeling.

"There's that, for sure," agreed Edgar. "When they gets riled up, Injuns don't much care who they kill, and that's a fact. Womenfolk, little boys, little girls, babies. Killing's, killing—it don't make no blame difference to savages who they do it to."

11

FORT NISQUALLY

Noclas was right about the weather. Within a week, the wind shifted from the southwest and blew steadily from the north, an arctic blast that felt like it was going to blow the skin off your face.

"Do you think it'll snow?" asked Junebug, her face crammed against the window pane. "I think it will. I love it when it snows. Don't you, William? Everything covered in a fluffy blanket, like goose feathers sprinkled over the whole countryside. Or maybe it's more like thick frosting on a birthday cake, or a weddin' cake. Which do you think it looks most like, William? Goose feathers or frosting on a cake? It looks so delicious when it snows, and you can't eat goose feathers. I think it must be more like frosting, like frosting on a cake, a weddin' cake."

William smiled and nodded. He had learned not to try and answer his sister when she was like this. Nor did he want to dampen her enthusiasm by reminding her how cold it would be, how he would have to break the ice to get at the water in the rain barrel, how much more work it would be to feed the chickens and ducks, and do the other chores.

Mount Rainier rising high over Puget Sound was never free of snow and ice. On a clear day even in summer, sunlight shimmered on the many glaciers that flowed from its summit down to where its lower slopes met the evergreen forests. But those glaciers turned into rushing rivers that snaked their way through miles of forest and into the tidelands and estuaries where the rivers emptied into the salty waters of the inland sea. Here, on the shores of Puget Sound, snow only fell a few times a winter. William joined Junebug at the window. The clouds looked thicker than they had been at first light, and they seemed to be pressing down lower than before; it did look like this would be one of those times.

"I'd best go to the fort," said William, his breath fogging the window as he spoke. "If snow's a-coming, we'll be needing more cornmeal and peas."

"And chocolate!" squealed Junebug. "Can I come?" Her eyes were wide and hopeful. "There's ever so much going on at the fort. Folks to see and talk to. Maybe we'll see Mrs. Tolmie and her sister Letitia Work, wearing their lovely hoop-skirt dresses, and maybe we'll get to see her two little boys—one's barely walking. You know she's expecting another baby? Oh, William, don't look like that; surely you knew. *Everybody* knows she's having another baby soon. Oh, please, William, can I come along?"

William smiled at his sister and tugged her ponytail. "Why not? But you'll need to bundle up nice and cozy for the ride."

An hour later William and Junebug, riding double on Prophet, came near Fort Nisqually, Wally loping along beside. When first the wolf-dog and horse had met, there were rolling wide eyes and a quivering of every nerve and muscle in the horse's body. That was more than two years ago. But once Wally got it clear in his mind that Prophet was part of his responsibility, like Junebug, he was done with bristling and sniffing. Soon enough, the horse came to accept the odd companionship of a dog-wolf, like a lamb willingly curling up between the protective claws of a lion.

From the smoke of a dozen fires drifting into the gray skies, they could see the trading fort coming into view when it was still a ways off. Wide grasslands surrounded the fort, a prairie with sparse clusters of gnarly oak trees, their bare branches rimmed and glowing with yellow lichen, a murder of crows cawing and circling over the upper branches. A flock of a hundred or more sheep cropped away at the bunch grass in a large split-cedar-rail enclosure west of the fort.

Prophet snorted, impatient with mere trotting. "Prophet looks like a dragon," said Junebug, peering around her brother's arm. She clung to the side seams of his coat under his arms; William pressed his arms tightly to his sides to keep the warmth in her bare hands.

"Look at all the people!" she added with a squeal. Pressed hard against her brother's back, her body trembled with excitement.

Clearly, with the threat of snowfall, William and Junebug were not the only ones converging to stock up on supplies at the fort that day. As they came closer, they heard a rumble of activity, settlers on horseback, in farm carts drawn by mules or a yoke of oxen, some on foot, and Indians wrapped in Hudson Bay blankets from the chill, mostly riding sleek white-on-black horses like Charlie Salitat's, but some walking alongside dogs dragging a wood-framed travois loaded with skins or dried salmon or baskets for trading at the fort.

Rising on a ridge flanked by a small lake on its east side was Fort Nisqually. The fort was made entirely of logs and timber, surrounded by palisades ten feet tall, with each log cut to a point. It wasn't intended to be a military fort, but as the only trading fort between the Columbia River and Canada, it drew people from a diverse range, from the Sandwich Islands, French Canada, local Indians from a variety of tribes, roving trappers, and settlers from all corners of the eastern and Midwestern United States as far as three thousand miles away. Chief Trader William Tolmie and the Hudson Bay Company seemed to believe that an amply fortified trading post was a prudent deterrent to trouble. More than once that belief had been tested, and the fortification had proven its worth.

"We're going to have some weather!" shouted one settler to a friend. "How's that new young'un getting along?" called another. "Growing plump, pink, and juicy like a feeder pig," came the reply. There was a carnival atmosphere, with a clamor of calling and greeting, as people dismounted and tethered their animals.

William swung Junebug down off Prophet then dismounted himself and tied the horse up at a hitching rail. William glanced at the faces in the crowd. He recognized most all of them, even nodded at folks he knew slightly more than the others.

"Charlie Salitat!" he called, catching sight of the Indian.

On either side of Charlie and his horse rode two Indians; one of them—taller than most, with strong heavy shoulders, and a face more slender than other coastal Indians—leaned in close and seemed to have been speaking to Charlie as they neared the gate of the fort. Charlie had rigged a travois on his horse loaded with beaver skins. When he heard his name called out he looked blankly in William's direction.

"Shucks, he's being Indian," murmured William.

"He's with other Indians," said Junebug, as if that was a satisfactory explanation. "When he stops and talks with Noclas, like he's been doing more of these days," she paused, nuzzling Wally's nose with her own, "he's just people, like Noclas is. He probably thinks you're being white."

William craned his neck in wonder at his sister. What does she know about it? He was about to say, but said, "Maybe so," instead.

Tying a half-hitch in Prophet's reins to the hitching post, he searched the dozens of faces passing through the gate into the inner precinct of the fort. Stroking Prophet's neck he looked for one man in particular—Charles Wren. From what he'd heard of the man, and after his brief encounter with him in Steilacoom, he didn't trust leaving Prophet unattended—not for long. He hesitated. Maybe he should put Wally on guard. The dog would stay put, and nobody would dare get near either horse or dog when Wally was on duty.

Wally looked up at William, as if awaiting instructions. "Stay put, Wally," said William, sharply, pointing to the ground in front of Prophet. Glancing for an instant at Junebug, Wally settled on his haunches and grinned up at William. "Good boy," said William. Taking Junebug's hand firmly in his own, William led her through the timber gateway into the fort.

It was like entering another world, a world in a flurry of business and activity. William drew in a deep breath. The maddening aroma of fresh baking bread drifted from the kitchen to their left, mingling with the smells of alder wood smoke and bacon, with a hint of burning coal. Entwined with the rich oily smell of cured beaver pelts, and a hint of roasted coffee, was the sweet piney scent of new lumber.

Everywhere there were people and a jumble of voices, talking, arguing, bartering, and shouting, and children laughing and squealing as they played together.

Farther into the fort compound, to their left, stood a wagon laden with fresh-cut milled lumber, the harnessed mules resting each with one hind leg on the tip of the hoof. Two men in buckskin trousers and point-blanket hooded capotes were sitting on the tailgate of the wagon, apparently awaiting instructions for unloading the lumber. There was more shouting and laughter of children trundling with a hoop-and-stick behind the blacksmith shop and the granary. Junebug laughed with them as she caught glimpses of them scurrying between the two buildings. Tongues lolling, two or three dogs, barking and yapping, joined in the fun.

"There she is!" cried Junebug, pointing at a tall woman, a child on each hip and another clinging to her wide hoop skirts. Judging from the thickness in her middle area, another child would be coming along in a few short months, word was, before another winter set in.

At her side was a broad-shouldered man wearing a store-made black suit and tall beaver hat. William leaned down near Junebug's ear and nodded toward the couple. "There's Dr. William Tolmie," he said. "He's Chief Trader of the fort, and word is he's soon to be promoted to Chief Factor, a very important man."

His sister narrowed her eyes, studying the man.

"He's a man of many talents, so I've heard," continued William. "Besides being a man of business, he's a doctor, a botanist—"

"What's a botanist?" asked Junebug.

"Someone who studies nature: plants, trees, bushes, flowers, you know, a botanist. They say he has discovered new plant species in the region, star-tulips, onions, saxifrage, even a unique bird species, a kind of warbler—all unknown elsewhere in the world. And he's a great friend of the Indians in these parts."

"I like him," announced Junebug, watching Tolmie holding the plank door for his wife and sons as they entered their small hewn-log house near the flagpole at the center of the fort grounds. Then Dr. Tolmie strode purposefully across the courtyard toward a group of men.

"And the Tolmies are soon to be living there," continued William, pointing to a house under construction adjoining the Tolmie's rough cabin, the men with the wagon now unloading the milled lumber and stacking it next to the stick-framed house.

"It will be much bigger," said Junebug, "I think," she added uncertainly.

"It will be," agreed William, mentally measuring the wooden skeleton being formed into a new home for the soon-to-be Chief Factor. It appeared to be more than three times the size of the Tolmie's current home, and with a wide veranda encircling three sides of the house, a far more comfortable one. More than a dozen men worked cutting and shaping timber for the various parts of the new house.

"And it will need shakes," said William, calculating the hours of labor it would take him to cut and split the vast number of cedar shakes such a house would require. "Lots of shakes," he added.

"I've never seen a house that big," said Junebug, awe in her voice.

William agreed. "You could put our cabin inside it five or six times and have room to spare."

People were everywhere, in small clusters, talking and laughing, the vapor of their breath hovering over them like protective clouds. And there was James Wiley, the newspaperman from Olympia. He had cornered the Chief Trader, Dr. Tolmie, and they were engaged in a lively conversation near the Hudson Bay Company flagpole in the middle of the fort compound. William led his sister closer.

"It's a new world emerging, Mr. Wiley," said Dr. Tolmie.

William watched the Hudson Bay trader as he spoke. He was no rough frontiersmen. Wiley and Tolmie stood out amidst the blanketed Indians, buckskin-clad trappers, and the scruffy homespun garb of the farmers and settlers. They both wore black ready-made suits, vest, starched collar, cravat, tall beaver hat, though it seemed to William that Dr. Tolmie's costume was more precise and accessorized than Wiley's. He spoke with a Scots cadence, and with an operatic roll to his Rs. "This fort is a monument to free enterprise, a market economy, freedom of exchange without a king or parliament telling us what's what."

"How can that work?" said James Wiley. "Someone or something has got to guide the market. What about the poor, the worker? You'll have nothing but chaos and exploitation. I propose that government—"

"—The Invisible Hand," interjected Dr. Tolmie. "Adam Smith, my kinsman, don't you ken him? *Wealth of Nations,*

1776—Och, aye, surely you ken him. *Laissez-faire* economy; it's the only thing that works. When left alone to be regulated only by the legitimate wants and needs of your neighbors, the free market—what you see working before your very eyes at this moment—will produce the goods and services that your neighbors want, need, and are willing to purchase without being coerced, that is, without being hog-tied and forced to buy or sell this or that by some king or MP—or by a bigwig president or congressman.

"Hence, my friend, you may purchase or trade here for everything from ostrich plumes to trade muskets: coffee from the Sandwich Islands, biscuits, sugar, flour, candles, candlesticks, kettles, lamps, oil, brooms, dried fish, blankets, iron nails, hammers and tools, trade guns, shot, gunpowder, tobacco, bolts of cloth from the four corners of the world, and ready-made clothes and hats. Here in this backwater wilderness there are things to purchase from Boston, New York, London, Hawaii, South America, Jakarta, and beyond. Nobody is forced to buy; anyone may participate—it is truly a free market, open to all."

"Sounds far too risky, to my way of thinking," said Wiley, hiking his glasses up on his nose. "Trapping beaver, that's risky in itself. It could cost a man his skin."

"Skin for skin," said Tolmie. "*Pro Pelle Cutem*, it's the Hudson Bay motto. Everything worth doing in life has risks. Your journalism, my friend, now there's a trade with risks. In my business it all begins with trappers who risk their skins—for skins."

"What if someone has nothing of value to trade with?" asked the journalist. "The poor have nothing with which to trade. What of them? Who's to provide for them?"

"Ah, if he needs a product badly enough," said the Scot, "the free market invites him and motivates him to participate; while his hunger motivates him, free enterprise invites him to create a trade good that his neighbor needs and for which he is willing to make a free exchange, and by which the poor man's hunger is assuaged and his dignity is maintained."

"What if someone has no capital," said James Wiley, "nothing whatsoever with which to trade? What then? Who's to take care of him then?"

"Man, there are trees aplenty, and fish, and small game to trap or snare!" said Tolmie, excitement in his voice. "Many of the poorest settlers, all they can bring for trade is cedar shakes, split with a borrowed tool from a windfall cedar tree downed by Providence. But in this climate so replete with moisture, everyone needs to keep the rain off his head, and so will make willing exchange for the poor man's shakes."

Though the man's words came as no surprise, they mildly troubled William, and he hurried Junebug toward the blacksmith's shop, the Trader and Mr. Wiley's voices fading behind them. As they passed in front of the granary, a boy was visible through the arched doorway upending a wheel barrow loaded with sacks of flour, a white mist hovering about the building.

William's attention was drawn to snatches of another conversation nearby.

"There's simply no hope for them," said a man whose accent sounded like a frontiersman speaking uppity British talk. "They're a condemned and worthless race. And I say we stop pandering to them with these ridiculous treaties. Leave them to their own. They'll die off in a generation, and good riddance, says I."

It was Matthew Burns, Dr. Burns, as he called himself, or Surgeon Burns. William never quite trusted the man.

"And what of the war?" asked Tom Perkins.

"War?" said Burns. "Bring it on, says I. The Indians don't stand a chance against white folks. Let's give them their little war. It'll be over and done within a week. If we're lucky, there won't be an Indian left standing. Bring on an Indian war, says I. Nothing would be better for all of us. Them too. Be done with the lot of 'em, the welcome end of a miserable race!"

12

MISERABLE RACE

"Be done with the lot of 'em," said the Englishman who called himself Dr. Burns, "the welcome end of a miserable race!"

William glanced down at his sister. Her cheerful countenance had disappeared; her tiny fingers gripped her brother's hand so tightly it almost hurt.

"What's the matter with my Junebug?" asked William.

There was an uncharacteristic set to her jaw, and she seemed to be searching for words. "Is it wrong not to like some folks?" she said at last.

"Depends, I suppose," said William. "Let's go watch the blacksmith," he added, hoping to change the subject. "You'll like the blacksmith."

"Well, I don't like that man," continued Junebug, glancing back over her shoulder in the direction of Dr. Burns. "Anyone who says things like that about the Indians, I don't like them. Is that bad of me?"

Sometimes William wished that Junebug could be more like other children. This was one of those times. He looked around the fort for a diversion. "Junebug, look at this placard. There was one on the main gate when we came in. It says, 'Horse racing—open to all comers,' and it's this afternoon."

Junebug brightened. "You could ride Prophet!" she said. "How beautiful Prophet would look running with other beautiful horses!"

William looked at his sister. "It's a race, Junebug," he said. "A race isn't about how beautiful the horses look. Besides, if I enter, I don't plan to be riding Prophet *with* the other horses, however beautiful they may be. They can ride together; that's fine by me, but I don't plan to be riding *with* them."

Junebug laughed. "What do you mean?"

"I'll show you this afternoon," he said.

Sniffing the air, William inhaled the sharp scent of the blacksmith's coke, and heard the bright clanging of his hammer shaping molten iron on his anvil. Squeezing Junebug's hand more tightly, he tried to pull her with him toward the blacksmith's hearth.

But Junebug tugged against her brother's hand.

There was so much to see at the fort, and her attention had been caught by someone. On a split-log bench in front of the granary sat a young woman, covered from head to toe in black. William looked at her and frowned. A nun, one of Father Blanchet's, no doubt, her figure enshrouded in a stern black habit, from her wimpled head to the thick black soles of her shoes. All kinds came to the fort, William mused, and for various objectives. "Come along, Junebug," he said.

Tugging against her brother, Junebug smiled at the nun. "Excuse me, madam, but what are you making?" she asked.

"She's knitting," said William shortly, "and knitting, I'm told, takes concentration; she doesn't want to be troubled. Let's see what the blacksmith's up to." He applied firmer pressure on his sister's hand. But Junebug was enchanted. Her eyes riveted on the nun's fingers, she listened with fascination to the woody percussion of the needles click-clicking like music hammered out on a mountain dulcimer.

Junebug giggled. "I can see she's knitting. I am sorry to interrupt you, madam. But just what are you making?"

The nun glanced up and smiled. "They will be mittens," she said, "for keeping fingers and hands warm from the cold." Without missing a beat, the young woman looked more closely at Junebug and smiled. "Do you like knitting?"

"I don't know," said Junebug, squirming in her brother's grip; she tried stepping closer to the nun. "I like watching knitting."

The nun smiled. "Well, then, you must come sit with me. Watch me knit."

With a little twist, Junebug let go of William, and planted herself on the split-log bench next to the nun. In moments they were lost in conversation, as if they were lifelong friends, so it seemed to William. He never would understand women.

"I will demonstrate how it is done," said the nun.

William felt his cheeks grow hot as he listened to Junebug and the young nun. His sister sat so close that folds from the woman's black habit partially enveloped the young girl. As he listened in to their chatter—it sounded like mere womenfolk chatter to him—William detected the hint of an accent to the nun's precise English, not an American manner of speaking, and neither English nor Scots.

He slouched up against the sturdy hand-hewn log wall of the granary. In spite of his irritation at the woman, he smiled. Singling out something unusual about a person's way of speaking in Puget Sound was like being astonished to discover that there are no two pebbles alike on the seashore. With such a multifarious array of English, Scots, Irish, Indian, Sandwich Islander, French Canadian, and American accents—American settlers hailing from Princeton to Pahokee, Tallahassee to Toledo—there were barely two people alike in the territory who spoke in the same fashion.

The nun must have said something funny, for Junebug threw her head back and laughed, one of her infectious giggles that seemed to erupt from deep within, bubbling over with the guileless enthusiasm of her childish good humor. Scowling, William turned on his heel and strode back to reread the placard about the horse racing. "Prize for the worthiest horse and rider," it promised.

"My dear, you are a ready learner." The crisp air carried the nun's voice to his ears. It was something about the way the accents landed, late in the words, tardy and lingering apologetically as if to make up for not landing earlier. Her speech reminded him of how the French Canadian voyageurs spoke. Only the young nun's words were softer, delicate like eider down, and sweet, like the delicate frosting his mother used to spread in swirls and wavelets on her oatmeal apple cake. Three years ago.

"And then you cross the wool over the needle," the nun said, demonstrating the stitch, "just so, and then again, only this time . . ."

An accent that sounded like a mother singing a lullaby, thought William, *or like talking in cursive.*

Bewildered and more than a little angry at his thoughts, William stepped close and planted his feet in the packed earth beside the bench. He had had enough of this. "Let's go." He said it more shortly than he intended to. His sister looked up, surprise and disappointment on her face.

The nun looked up at William too. Though her wimple obscured some of her features, there was enough of her visible to make William still more irritated—with her, or was it with himself? She was young, maybe not yet twenty, William concluded. Her face was slender, and her nose was long and narrow. He drew in his breath sharply. It was impossible not to observe that the skin on her face had not developed the crevasses so common to a frontier woman's complexion.

That won't last, he humphed to himself. It was only a matter of time before her face looked like most other women's—like the sole of a well-stomped moccasin. But it was her eyes that caught his attention. They were wide and observant, unique like her voice, a warm, translucent amber, not unlike the eyes of a newborn heifer, William thought, and rimmed with the same long delicate lashes of a young heifer.

All of this William took in when her eyes were open. Which was not for long. She glanced at him, and then hooded her eyes like a great horned owl. But with a flutter, or was it more of a shudder? It mildly disturbed William; she had not done that when talking with his sister. It looked like it was a habit, a disconcerting habit of looking at someone but with her eyes shuttered, closed off—or closing the other person off. There was an occasional flutter and then that long closing, as if she was looking within for the fortitude to endure patiently the presence of someone who required all the longsuffering she could muster from her inner self.

Since the nun had not looked that way at Junebug, William decided it must be the look she reserved for others, for men, insufferable men with whom she was forced to dredge up the greatest forbearance.

"Where is your mother and father?" asked the nun, looking past William and at the busy clusters of settlers, Indians, and Hudson Bay employees going about their business in the compound of the fort.

Junebug smiled back at the nun but said nothing. Before William could stammer a reply, which was going to be along the lines of, "It's none of your business," he heard shouts coming from the central commons of the fort.

A man strode by, half walking, half running. "What's happening?" asked William.

"Racing," said the man over his shoulder.

A Scots employee of the fort appeared in the doorway and came down the steps of the granary. William recognized the man and said, "Mr. McPhail, sir, what kind of racing will there be and when?"

"There's to be a bit of the horse race," said McPhail, pulling out a shiny gold pocket watch and opening it with a flourish, "at precisely half past the next hour."

"I read about it on the placard," said William. "Where?"

"At Round Plain," said McPhail, "hard by and just south of the fort."

"It is an open race, so said the placard?"

"Aye, laddie, it'll be out in the open! What did you think, they'll be racing horses in the bachelors' quarters?" He laughed uproariously. The slap he gave William on the back felt like he had just won the approval of a jovial grizzly bear.

"I-I mean," began William.

"I ken what you be meaning, laddie," said the trader. "I was just having a wee bit of fun with you. Open race it is, for any man with a horse." He paused, eyeing William critically. "Indians included—any man with the skill to stay bestride his beast at breakneck speed." He narrowed his eyes at William. "Does that be you then, laddie?"

Trying to look confident, William smiled and nodded. "And the prize?" he asked. "It says there's to be one. What prize for the winner?"

McPhail narrowed his eyes. "Now there's the rub. If you're asking me, it's an unwise prize, indeed, says I, given the tenor of the times at the present."

"What is it?" said William. "And is it the same for Indian as for white?"

"Enter the list," called McPhail over his shoulder. "You'll find out what the prize is—and you'll be right proud if you win it."

13

THE PRIZE

"Prophet, let's trot around the course," said William, leaning close to the horse's right ear. "Giddy up."

The cold snap in the weather made the ground hard, a faster course for racing horses—and harder ground to fall on if you came off your mount. His face numb from the cold wind as they trotted the course, William was hopeful. Sure, he had never been in a horse race before, not an official one, with a prize for the winner. But he was a good rider, and Noclas always said Prophet was the fastest animal in the region. "You can do it," said William, clearing his throat and patting the horse's neck.

Though he'd been loath to ask for the nun's assistance, he had not wanted to leave his sister alone with Wally while he rode Prophet in the race. She'd have been safe enough. There was no fear of that with Wally. But Junebug liked being with people, and clearly she liked the nun, so he asked. Sister Marguerite, the name she used for herself, had hooded her eyes when he asked, and without actually looking at him, had replied, "I would be enchanted." Junebug had giggled.

Not only did the Hudson Bay Company employees take pleasure from horse racing, the crews of the supply ships that serviced the region, the *Cormorant,* the *Fisgard,* and the *Beaver,* enjoyed placing their bets on the horses, some of them entering the races themselves, on borrowed mounts. But no one got more enjoyment from the races than the horse Indians on Puget Sound, especially the Nisquallys. Nothing was so likely to turn a stoic, unsmiling Indian into a wild screaming fanatic than a horse race. Shrouded in buckskins and point-blankets against the chill air, dozens of Indians lined the race course outside the palisades of the fort. William noticed that some of the Indians were passing crockery bottles around and drinking deeply of the contents.

Some of the whites were doing the same. It wasn't only Indians that liked a good horse race in these parts. Lining the track, there were plenty of men in buckskins and coarse homespun clothing, and some in ready-made suits, white collars, and top hats. In and among them, there were a few women folk, some wearing ready-made calico hoop dresses, fine tailored wool cloaks and bonnets. They were folks he knew of, had seen in town, at the fort, in buckboards on the military road. He felt their stares, the smart of their whispers; it was the stigma, he'd heard James Wiley call it. Maybe winning a horse race, getting the prize, maybe this was the way to shake it off—that is, if he could win.

The likeliest champion for the Hudson Bay Company was Edward Huggins, trader at the fort, who had recently acquired a new saddle horse in a trade with Quiemuth, brother to Leschi, of the Nisqually tribe; that was the word, if rumors could be trusted. Huggins had put his name down and was trying out his new steed in the race.

The least likely champion for the company was a French Canadian voyageur who had somehow been persuaded to enter the race. Likely on a dare backed by money—or liquor. Roaring with delight, the crowd hissed and stomped as the novice rider bounced and jostled around the course in a practice lap. It was clear that the poor fellow would need far more practice riding than that lap could give him. He sat his horse as if he would far rather be kneeling in a canoe, and William half expected the man to try and propel the beast forward with a canoe paddle.

Seated ramrod in the saddle, Charles Eaton nodded and tipped his hat at William as he rode toward the start line. There were others: James McAllister, William Connell, and from Fort Steilacoom William thought he recognized several of the cavalrymen he had seen training the day he sold his shakes to Lieutenant Slaughter. And there was another settler, a solitary fellow known as Abram Moses, Abram Benton Moses, a man who kept to himself, a man given almost as wide a berth by folks around here as they gave Noclas. And there was Charles Wren. Though not making any move to enter the race, he appeared to William to be studying the horses far more closely than was appropriate for a mere onlooker drawn for casual diversion.

William was reining in Prophet near the start line when he saw him. Mounted bareback, Charlie Salitat rode his white-on-black Arabian like they were one and the same; so complete was their harmony, that where the horse ended and the rider began was difficult if not impossible to discern. Walking, trotting, cantering, or galloping, it made no difference. Watching his friend take one last practice lap around the course before the race began, William's blood slowed like a watercourse in midwinter. And it wasn't just the effect of the sharp cold air.

Charlie knew his horse, and he knew how to ride. William had seen it all before, in the forest, over the wide-open spaces at Bush Prairie or the grasslands along Muck Creek, he'd seen Charlie ride like the wind. And Charlie was being Indian. He must have seen him, but he didn't so much as glance William's direction as he readied himself and his horse for the race.

"Ridin' Prophet's most like flyin'," William recollected what Noclas always said. Feigning unconcern, he looked without turning his head as Charlie dismounted and squatted, inspecting his horse's hooves and ankles. William glanced down at Prophet's hooves then back at Charlie; he wondered if he ought to do the same.

Huddled in their blankets, several Indians stood close by, talking in guarded tones with Charlie. Unhurried but deliberate, one of the Indians strode up to a sleek Arabian; in a single fluid motion, the Indian leapt onto its back, reined the animal around with a jerk, and trotted it to the start line. William recognized the man; it was the same tall Indian he had seen Charlie entering the fort with earlier. He was a powerful looking man, with the bearing of a chief, a tyee, as the Indians called their leaders.

"Gentlemen, take your posts!" called a man designated as the race official.

"Prophet, are you ready?" whispered William in the ear of the animal. He had never been more afraid. What was he doing? He had never raced before in his life. And against such a formidable lineup of competition. These were horsemen of the first rank, Indians, trained cavalrymen, each one of them—except the voyageur—far more experienced at riding than he. Being born in Kentucky wasn't likely to help against these odds. His eyes darting down the line of horses and men, William felt like a black bear was sitting on his chest. A lurching wave passed through his stomach; for an instant he was afraid he might unswallow his breakfast. "Prophet, I need you to go fast, really, really fast," he stammered softly in Prophet's right ear.

Holding a pistol aloft, the race official yelled, "On the pistol crack, and not a second before!"

It was as if the world suddenly ground down to a slow crawl, the sun, moon, and stars moving ponderously, more imperceptibly than was usual, and everything standing out in fresh-cut detail. William observed that the official's pistol was a Colt Sidehammer, like Charles Eaton's, like Lieutenant William Slaughter's, and he wondered which caliber version it was. He was fascinated by the eruptions of vapor emitting from the flaring nostrils of the dozen horses pawing the earth at the starting line, and the smaller puffs of hot air showing like tiny clouds from the nostrils of the men on their backs. And the mute crowd, bundled in their capotes, or buckskins, or pelt coats, standing watching like statues, silent and unmoving, or so it seemed. And there was Junebug and Wally, grinning in his direction, and that nun at their side, still knitting, her eyes shuttered, as if the activity of horse racing was too beneath her dignity to unfurl her eyes and lift them from her needles and twisted wool.

"Crack!"

With that pistol retort, the muted, stalled world—creeping along under the smothering weight of William's fear—suddenly hurtled itself into motion. Prophet, launching himself like a fury, nearly unhorsed his rider.

In the mysterious workings of his instincts, Prophet was unencumbered by the need to make a choice. For a horse who loves to run, to fly if he could, there was no choice to be had, no energy to be expended in weighing options. Hooves thundering on the frozen ground, mane and tail flying behind, Prophet hurled himself forward, lunging with every fiber of his powerful being toward the prize—massive heart pounding, the mighty twin bellows of his lungs gulping in air, fueling every sinew of his body with new stores of energy, every muscle straining far beyond the boundaries of past endeavors—Prophet galloped like hot wind in a hurricane.

But there was a catch. Though in furious motion, somehow Prophet seemed to know that no matter how fast he galloped, without a human on his back at the finish line, he could not win; some other horse would take the prize. Hence, when it was obvious to the horse that his human was incapable of doing this or anything else on his own, he instinctively did all he could to remain under the rider on his back. How Prophet managed to keep William astride his great body, lunging forward at terrifying speed, would never be clear to the animal—or to William. Perhaps the horse kept his rider in place by expending power that would otherwise have been converted to forward thrust. This was the catch—imperceptible to none but the most discerning horseman—this was the catch in Prophet's giddy up.

William's first conscious recollections of that race came in his ears, the staccato thundering of hooves, the chattering of straining harness, the heaving and blowing of air, and the flurry of bodies, the bodies of both men and horses—his and Prophet's among them, but his nearly launching from the saddle. Perhaps it was the hurtling imbalance of that instant, and the ensuing terror, that acted as a jolt to bring him to his senses. Out of the corner of his eye, he saw the French voyageur rounding a turn, more than a dozen lengths behind the main body of riders. Angling into the turn, the voyageur's horse put on a burst of speed. Suddenly, the novice rider seemed to take flight. Arms and legs flaying the chill air, man and horse parted ways, a guttural scream piercing through the clamor of hooves.

The voyageur plunged headlong into a mound of straw bordering the turn. William caught glimpses, flicking rapidly past, of guffawing hilarity on the features of white and Indian alike.

Something surged inside of him. William did not want to finish the race that way, nor did he want to be the last one to cross the finish line. This desire acted like an icy plunge into the frigid waters of Puget Sound. His mind and body were suddenly alert. He wanted desperately to win.

"Giddy up, Boy!" he yelled in Prophet's ear.

His breath short and his chest tight, William assessed his position. How it was so, he could not explain it. He and Prophet were far from last, the credit due entirely, he knew, to horse not rider. Yet five men—or was it six?—and their mounts, their tails flying and their hooves churning up clods of frozen earth and sod, were ahead of him. A mere hundred yards remained, the britches of five men and the muscular rumps and streaming tails of five horses rising and falling in front of him. At this speed, the race would be over in moments.

Could he do it? William buried his heels in Prophet's flanks, urging the animal forward. Cheeks numb with the frigid air, he clenched his teeth. There was so little time. Ahead of him were five men—yes, it was five, not six. One was Charles Eaton, in first or second position, he could not tell. Another, by his blue uniform, was clearly a soldier from Fort Steilacoom. Both of these rode with skill and ease. Another looked like he might be the loner Abram Moses; for a fleeting instant William wondered if Moses were to win the race might it help folks get past their prejudice against the man for his name and heritage. An idle speculation, if William had anything to say about it. The other two horsemen out in front of him, their long black hair streaming behind, were clearly Indians. There could be no mistake. One was Charlie Salitat.

"Faster! Faster!" screamed William. "We need this, Prophet!"

The only thing louder than the thundering of hooves was the pounding of William's heart. He had narrowed the gap, and Prophet's head was now alongside Charlie Salitat's right leg. As the reek of sweat filled his lungs, flecks of spittle from the mouths of the horses ahead of him peppered his face, smarted in his eyes. Like a flash, Charlie glanced back; for a split second, William's eyes met the big Indian's. William felt he just might have the momentum; he could overtake the Indian in two strides—surely he could. After that, maybe, just maybe, he could overtake the others and win.

Then it happened. The lunging, straining, hurtling-forward rhythm abruptly ended. A horse was down. William looked in wonder as the boots and blue-striped uniform trousers of the soldier lifted off his saddle, pointing into the gray sky above. For an instant, the man's legs remained in the u-shape of the horse he had been riding, but now inverted, horse down; the man's feet and heels aloft as if he were standing on his head in the saddle—but only for an instant.

The tight knot of men and horses nearing the finish line suddenly fell into a mangle of stumbling disorder. Hide and flesh, hooves and boots, tangled arms and legs and bodies crashing onto the frozen turf in a heap.

Folks would talk about what happened in the last instant of that race for months to come—some for years. William would later describe it as dominoes, what Junebug liked to do with the tiles, stand them up in a line, then push one over, the others tumbling after.

Miraculously, no one—man or horse—was seriously injured. Charles Eaton, though he lost his hat, managed to stay on his mount. Charlie Salitat did too. William knew all this for a certainty because he watched both of them cross the finish line—before his very eyes, ahead of him. He and Prophet had lost.

14

CHARLIE'S MUSKET

William lost that race. But in the confusion and chaos of the finish—who was the clear winner? It was too close to call, at least that's what the official at the finish line claimed. When at last the tangle of arms and legs, and horse and harness, was disengaged, Dr. Tolmie spoke through a bullhorn.

"Fine riding, fine riding, indeed!" The Chief Trader paused, deliberating with battered Huggins, his left eye nearly swollen shut but otherwise unhurt. William looked on as the men deliberated. Haggling seemed more like what they were doing. Several more men, mostly Hudson Bay employees, joined in the deliberations. And it was taking a while. The Indians scowled, and a stout, broad-faced matriarchal Indian called Mother Steilacoom by everyone in the region, stood close, her ear cocked to the deliberations, her arms straight at her ample sides.

At one point, Huggins' voice rose louder than the others, William just catching snatches of his words. "He done it, fair and square, he done it."

Meanwhile, Charlie Salitat had dismounted and was

checking his horse's hooves and forelegs, feigning indifference. He didn't join in with the other Indians who were grumbling and casting dark looks toward Huggins and Tolmie and the rest.

"Fine riding, Charlie," said William. "Whatever the outcome, it were fine riding on your part."

Charlie hesitated, looking first at William and then at Charles Eaton. Still on his horse's back, Eaton had slung a leg up by the saddle horn and was leaning forward on his arms, easy-like. Was he being that way because he was so certain of the outcome? Or was it genuine unconcern, as if there was nothing at stake, as if the outcome mattered very little to him. William wondered which it was.

Charlie Salitat's eyes met William's. For an instant it looked as if the Indian was about to cross a boundary, about to break into a grin, about to relinquish his reserve and reply to William. But Dr. Tolmie's voice boomed above the din, and the instant passed.

"We have determined the winner," he announced. "A close race, it was, and no mistake. But the officials are settled." He hesitated. All eyes were on him. No one spoke, though an eagle being chased by two crows screeched and reeled overhead. "The prize goes to—Charles Eaton!"

Mother Steilacoom stepped closer to Dr. Tolmie and placed her hands on her hips. Like carved wooden masks worn at a potlatch or a funeral, the faces of the other Indians showed no reaction to the Chief Trader's words.

William glanced at his friend Charlie Salitat. Like his kind, the Indian showed not so much as a whisker of emotion at the announcement. "I really can't say who it was that won," said William. "I know this much. You beat me. And you rode like the wind."

For the first time that day, Charlie's features softened. The hard line of his mouth curved first into a slight upward arch, then he broke into a full grin, two teeth agape, and slapped William on the back.

"Thanks to you," he said.

"And the prize for the winner," continued Dr. Tolmie. He said no more but held aloft over his head with both hands a long, lean, shiny-new trade musket.

William swallowed hard and tried to quell the envy he felt clogging up his insides. Huggins held aloft a powder horn with silver fittings on both ends and a leather pouch bulging with lead ball. Gesturing for Eaton to remove his slouch hat, he slung these over the man's head.

"Well, if they're awarding such fine weaponry for prize," growled a voice, "we can all be most grateful to our lucky stars no Indian won this fine contest today." It was Dr. Burns, and several grunted their approval.

Whenever William heard the pompous accents of Dr. Burns's bigotry, he wondered if the man had not been planted by the British to create tension between the Indians and the American settlers. It would probably work. When the dust settled, the American settlers would all be wiped out by the Indians, and the territory would be open again for British trading with no rival American claims getting in the way.

Eaton, who had remounted his horse, turned and rode toward where William and Charlie Salitat stood. Swinging easily out of his saddle, he touched the brim of his hat and nodded at them.

"At the finish line, I do believe I saw out of the corner of my eye a bit more of you, Charlie Salitat, than I ought to have been seeing if I was out ahead of you and the clear winner. Mind you, I'm not faulting Dr. Tolmie for his judgment, no sir." He paused, taking the powder horn and pouch from his shoulders. "With all respect to the good folks at the Hudson Bay Company, nevertheless, I believe—I firmly believe—these belong to you."

Charlie Salitat stood rigid like a carved cedar totem pole, without moving, without saying a word for fully a minute.

"Take them, friend. And my congratulations to you," said Eaton, thrusting the gun and its equipment into Charlie Salitat's hands.

Speechless, Charlie weighed the trade musket in his hands then ran his hand over the polished hardwood stock, then his fingers over the firing mechanism and down the well-oiled barrel.

"You won it in good faith," said Eaton, looking steadily at Charlie Salitat. "I remain confident you will use it in good faith."

William studied Eaton's face as he spoke. There was no shifting of his eyes, nor was there a hint of condescension, or rebuke. It was the honest face of one man, looking with regard at another man, and believing the best about him.

And then Eaton turned deliberately and studied William, his eyes taking him in, from his worn moccasins, buckskin trousers, threadbare coat, to his limp felt hat with a worn hole in its point. "Fine horse you have there," he said, now turning his attention to Prophet and stroking the big animal's neck. "What's more," he continued, glancing back at William, "It were fine riding, at least it were fine riding in the home stretch." He paused. Then looking levelly at William, he said, "Were it your first race, I'm thinking?"

William felt his cheeks turn hot in spite of the cold. He thought of a retort—"It's none of your business," or of making up an excuse—"Prophet don't start out so well, but he finishes strong," or some way of explaining things so he wouldn't gape wide like the fool he feared he was.

But when his eyes met Eaton's, there didn't seem to be anything else to say but the truth. "Yes, Sir," said William. "It were my first."

Meanwhile, a small band of disapproving hecklers, who did not share Eaton's opinion of Charlie Salitat, pressed closer, their voices loud so as to be heard clearly.

"I'd a thought Eaton had more horse sense than to do a danged fool thing like that," said one.

“Giving an Injun a trade musket—” snarled one burly onlooker, “Shucks, might as well be putting a bullet in your own back.”

“Go the whole danged way,” said another, grabbing a fistful of his own hair and gesturing as if with a knife at his forehead. “Save ’em the trouble. Give ’em your own scalp while you’re at it.”

15

MOUNTAIN DEVILS

As predicted, snowflakes fell thick and furious the night after the horse race. William and Junebug awoke to a fresh new world deliciously covered over in a blanket of downy white.

"Just like Noclas said!" squealed Junebug, her breath fogging the windowpane.

But it didn't last. It was as if the fury of winter snow had spent itself high up on the craggy summits of the Cascade Mountains, and all the snow that remained for the lowlands was timorous stuff, temperate in disposition, incapable of staying around long enough to make for a lasting winter wonderland. By early afternoon, the wind hesitated, slackened, swirled about aimlessly for a bit, and grew calm. And then decided to puff warmly, more gently out of the southwest. The air temperature rose noticeably; within twenty-four hours the snow had vanished.

Noclas really had been right about the weather, William was forced to admit. Next day he left the cabin in his shirtsleeves, took up his axe and splitter, and set to on bolts of cedar waiting for splitting.

Within a week, springtime broke suddenly and with exuberant splendor throughout the region. Goldfinches, flitting from branch to branch, their bright yellow plumage glittering brilliantly in the morning sunlight, chirruped their enthusiasm about the change. Robin redbreasts trilled their delight, and swallows, and warblers, and jays joined in the chorus.

"It sounds like the trees are alive with them," said Junebug.

Junebug made it her duty to report all the latest wonders to her brother. She left no detail out.

She told him about the pink and white trillium that had pushed their way up through the carpet of dead oak leaves, spongy moss, and fir needles that blanketed the forest floor, unfolding their delicate stems and flowers.

"I think I can actually see them sprouting and turning into flowers," said Junebug with wonder, "before my very eyes! Come see!"

And overnight, bare seemingly lifeless willow branches along the path suddenly sprouted furry little catkins of new life.

"Pussy willows!" cried Junebug. "They make me think of little bunnies hopping in the bunch grass, their fluffy tails bouncing like these pussy willows trembling in the breeze."

Along the wetlands that rimmed the southeast boundary of the Tidd holding, the bare branches of alder trees suddenly sprouted new curly green leaves that shied and swayed softly in the breeze.

"On the pond, yonderways, there's ducklings already," announced Junebug one morning, "heaps of fuzzy gray ducklings! Whole families of them. Oh, William, don't you just love springtime? Who wouldn't? And then comes summer! Ain't it wonderful?"

William nodded and smiled absently in Junebug's direction. He had no interest in discouraging her, and wasn't about to dampen her enthusiasm. But he knew what was coming. Sure some brilliant days of springtime, and a few gorgeous days of summer, but only a few. It would always disappoint him, the weather in these parts. The good weather never lasting, and the gray and drizzle never ending, so it seemed to him. He wasn't alone. A traveler from out east once quipped, "The nicest winter I ever spent was a summer in Seattle."

William had learned not to put too much hope in the weather. Foul or fair, whatever the weather, there was always work to be done.

"Hold your place, Molly, and you too, Polly!" said William as he harnessed the mule pair to his plow. "None of your flouncing about. We've got some work to do."

After he'd hitched the animals to the plow, he looped the reins over his neck and shoulder, gripped the plow handles, and narrowed his eyes at the twisted madrone tree at the east end of the field. With a click of his tongue, the mules bent to their tresses, the plow lurched forward, slicing into the earth. At first the sod rolled aside smooth as waves breaking on a gravelly seashore.

Breathing deeply, William savored the earthy smell of the fresh-turned earth, the steamy richness of it. Then came scraping that ended in *Clunck!* The plowshare struck rock, a big glacial rock the size of a watermelon. And with the striking, the reins burned against William's neck and shoulder.

"Whoa there, girls," he called to the mules.

"I can get it," called Junebug. She had been walking along beside the field, plucking a bouquet of tiny blue and yellow flowers that sprouted in the bunch grass of their own initiative. But now she set down her flowers and was on the run, her skirts tucked up. Dropping to her knees she looked more closely at the rock. "Well, maybe with help I can get it," she said.

"This one's mine, little sister," said William. "But I need your help. You see if Molly and Polly are getting on just so.

I can't plow with disgruntled mules." Grunting, he hefted the rock end-for-end out of the furrow.

"Walk on, girls," he said, snapping the reins on the mules' rumps. He wondered if he ought to call neutered creatures like mules "girls" or "boys" or just "it"?

"Just get the ones that fit in your hand," he called over his shoulder to his sister. "There's plenty of them kind 'round here. No sense in growing another crop of stones this season. Give 'em a good heave off on the side. I'm fixin' to turn them into a wall or something."

Rounding up on the west end of the field, there was an unobstructed panorama of Mount Rainier—*Tacoma,* "Mother of Waters" to the Indians, so Charlie called it. William was not the best at farming and he knew it, and though plowing required all his attention, he couldn't help gazing at the glacial precipices of the volcano dominating the eastern horizon, looming vast and high above the trees—high above everything. William halted in his plowing and squinted up at the mysterious ridges and crevasses of the grand mountain. Sunlight glistened on its crags and glaciers. Following the southwest ridge with his eyes, William imagined what it might be like to ascend the massive peak. From up there, a fellow might have a view of everything, the whole continent—maybe even see in advance the painted Yakamas skulking over the mountain range, joining up with the coastal tribes to fall on the white settlers in their sleep. He shuddered at the thought and resumed plowing.

As he plowed the next furrow facing east and the mountain, he glanced up often, the furrow making a dogleg every time he did. Rimmed in morning sunlight, Junebug was stooping low to pick more flowers, the bouquet growing larger in her arm. Beyond her, the mountain seemed, at the moment, like a pristine world of its own, hoary-white and glittering like gemstones in the sunlight. The Indians, however, made no secret of their fear of it. If what Charlie said about it was true, saying they feared the mountain wasn't near strong enough; it was more like terror.

Charlie had once told him, "On warm days in summer, mountain not happy; it hurl down great ice stones, bigger than longhouse, and ice cascade down like waterfall on river. Other times mountain send hot smoke high in clouds; it grumble and moan like old man sick of life. Other times, it send great blast of wind, break forest and rocks. Long ago, elders tell of fire river from mountain, and great river of mud flowing down, destroy Indian village, bury much people alive."

But Charlie had become still more sober when he had described "Mountain Devils," he called them, "giant hairy Indians with big feet who descend mountain at night, steal women, sometime children. *Tacoma* alive," Charlie had insisted, "mountain have power, great spirit power. All tribes fear mountain, give mountain big space when passing."

Musing on these things, it was not entirely surprising that William would react the way he did at what next occurred. Hot and sweaty from plowing, William had rounded the far northwest side of the field, farthest from the Tidd cabin, with a full view of the great white *Tacoma*, sunlight in his eyes and backlighting partially blinding him. There, silhouetted against the shimmering waters of the wetland pond, was the outline of someone or something, a creature, tall, wide at the shoulders, its hair long, its legs wide apart.

Like a hooked salmon flailing on the wharf, William felt his heart flop against his ribcage. Junebug stood still as a stone. She had seen the creature too.

With a violent jerking of the tresses, William halted the team and dropped the reins. Grabbing up a fist-sized rock in each hand, he bolted toward the creature, letting off a scream like he had done only one other time in his life. Planting corn nearby, Noclas later said William's racket was so fierce and terrifying, "The very marrow in my old bones turned to glacier ice."

16

KILLING HOSTILITY

What was you thinkin' 'bout, Bill Tidd?" asked Noclas, a few minutes later. "Why, you let off such a racket, I thought you'd come face to face with your own ghost. Carrying on like that, you make a cougar sound like a kitten."

"Here, drink this," said Junebug, handing her brother a mug of cool tea. "I was afeared you'd gone and chopped your foot off with the plow or something worse."

"Bill Tidd make growling bear sound like bumblebee."

It was Charlie Salitat, his musket cradled in his arms; he was grinning so wide it looked like his lips would split apart in the middle.

William scowled at the Indian over his mug.

"It were only Charlie," said Noclas. "What did you think you was seeing?"

"Nothing." It sure hadn't looked like Charlie, or anybody else of normal size. Must have been the shimmering of the sun reflecting on the pond behind him, making him glow bigger, look creepy and sinister. Or it may have just been William's imagination, thinking about man-beasts and mountain devil legends. "It were nothing," he repeated, trying to make his voice match the words. "Just stretching my lungs a bit."

"After that holler," said Junebug, "you need more Noclas tea, and some smoked salmon and yummy corn bread—Charlie brung some honey. All that plowing—maybe you've gone and overworked yourself. Food and drink'll do you wonders."

"It sure 'nough will do," agreed Noclas.

Junebug set the food out on a narrow plank table; as they ate, conversation was about the weather, plowing, fishing, repairs needed after the winter. But William was careful to try and steer the conversation away from trouble with the Indians.

Sunlight slanted across the southwest edge of the little porch, leaving most of it in the cool shade. Noclas was sitting in the bent-willow rocking chair he had steamed, bent, and lashed together for William and Junebug, mostly for Junebug. But she always insisted that Noclas sit in it when he joined them on their lean-to porch. A wedge of sunlight in the southwest corner came over Noclas's shoulder, rim lighting his graying curls.

When the midday meal was nearly finished, Junebug asked Noclas, "Would you read that part you was reading to me yesterday." She was trimming the ends of the armful of forget-me-nots she had gathered that morning. "That part about busting down walls and making peace." She looked eagerly at Noclas, her eyes sparkling as if the old trapper had given her a pan full of gold nuggets or the sweetest honey from the comb, and she wanted more of it. William couldn't figure why his little sister put up with Noclas's nonsense. Probably just being nice to an old black man for pity's sake.

"For he himself is our peace," read Noclas. The wedge of sunlight coming over his shoulder shone full on the white pages of the Bible he was reading, and reflected a warm glow back onto the man's features.

As the old man's voice rose and fell with the reading, Charlie Salitat sat cross-legged in the shady part of the porch, his elbows resting on his knees, his eyes staring unblinking at a trail of ants carrying tidbits back to their hole. William couldn't help noticing that the Indian occasionally stole a glance at the doorframe, where he had propped his musket, ready to hand. It seemed to William that Charlie looked at his musket like he was afraid it wasn't real, or if it was real, it was about to be snatched away from him.

William was mildly troubled by the fact that Charlie never went anywhere without his new trade musket: checking his beaver traps, there was his musket; paddling his canoe, there was his musket; walking the streets in Steilacoom, there was his musket; riding his horse in the forest, there was his musket; coming around at dinner time for a free meal, there was his musket; spooking William while he was plowing and pretty nearly giving him the fright of his life—there cradled in his arms like a newborn was the Indian's infernal musket.

"Who hath made both one," continued Noclas, his voice rich and resonant; the reflected sunlight off the white pages of the Bible intensified, glowing off his black skin like polished old-growth cedar wood. "Who hath made both one, and hath broken down the middle wall of partition between us; having abolished in his flesh the enmity, even the law of commandments contained in ordinances; for to make in himself of twain one new man, so making peace; and that he might reconcile both unto God in one body by the cross, having slain the enmity thereby."

Slaying the enmity, William mused to himself, *making peace?* His knife poised over the cedar paddle he had been carving, William blurted out, "Who in the Sam Hill is it talking about?"

Noclas eyed William before replying. "You mean who is the 'he' in 'he made us both one'? The one who's squared off with the dividing wall setting folks 'gainst each other and busted it all to pieces? The one who's done gone and 'bolished the enmity, done killed dead the hostility?"

"That'd be it," said William. "That's the one. What the Sam Hill is it?"

"It's not an 'it,' a thing," said Junebug. "Don't be silly William. It's Jesus! Who else could do it, could tear down the dividing wall, bust to pieces the hostility? Don't be silly! Sister Marguerite, she'd say the same thing."

What the nun had to do with it was beyond William's reckoning. He racked his brain for a reply. There was something he knew he had read in Emerson. Something about this Jesus that went something like this: "Historical Christianity has fallen into the error that corrupts all attempts to communicate religion . . . It has dwelt, it dwells, with noxious exaggeration about the person of Jesus."

There's the whole blamed problem, thought William, scowling at Noclas and his sister—and he was feeling none too pleased with Charlie Salitat, sitting there Indian-style, leaning in and listening as attentive as if Noclas was something special, some learned orator, a senator or industrialist, or President Franklin Pierce his self. And here they were doing it, getting themselves all hot and fired up about some long-dead Jewish carpenter fellow. Emerson was right. "As men's prayers are a disease of the will, so are their creeds a disease of the intellect." *Shucks, who's being silly?*

For all intents and purposes, it was finished, the paddle William had been carving all winter. He'd been trying to make it as good as any coastal Indian's canoe paddle, even trying to decorate it with Indian designs, eagles and the like. It was final details he was whittling on at the moment, but his fright that morning had made him irritable, distracted and irritable.

Readying himself to straighten them out with some Emerson, while shaving off the last slivers of cedar here and there, suddenly his knife blade slipped.

Now William took considerable pride in keeping his knife honed sharp—sharp like a razor. The blade went to the bone. The knuckle of the index finger of his left hand stared up at him with a cruel smile-shaped gash. Blackberry-red blood began coming. He clenched his teeth at the pain.

This was too much. Hoping nobody had noticed, and pressing hard on the wound with his left thumb, William thunked his knife blade into the floorboards between his feet. "Will one of you tell me how this Jesus you keep yammering about, will one of you tell me just how it is a long-dead revolutionary—Jewish one at that—how it is he's going to bring about peace in our day, 'specially considering the fact that he stirred up a hornets' nest of trouble in his own day? Peace between Injuns and white folks—?" William halted, glancing at Noclas's black face. "A-and others. I'm thinking there's more wisdom in Emerson. 'Nothing can bring you peace but yourself,' said he. That there makes a heap more sense to me." Stealing a peek at his cut, he pressed hard on it again with his thumb, and reached for the handle of his knife.

Noclas nodded slowly, stroking his chin in thought. "I don't see no problem with this feller goin' and sayin' them there words; it's a free country," said the black man. "Let him speak his mind. But then it's up to us to do some hard thinkin' 'bout what he said. We've got to decide if them words is true ones."

Taking a quick look at the black man, William tried to juggle the paddle with the three unoccupied fingers of his left hand and keep whittling. He felt shy of the blade and over cautious. Some of his blood was on the handle of the paddle where he had been carving, and a drip or three had already stained his buckskin trousers.

"Court is in session," said Noclas, making his voice sound like what he imagined a lawyer or a judge would sound like. "Are Mr. Emerson's words true or are they false? Can't be both." Noclas never argued; even in this imaginary courtroom, he never seemed to care two hoots about winning an argument itself. He was always that way. It's what made William fidget, wondering what he was up to. You never could tell with Noclas.

Charlie Salitat, who hadn't said a word for over an hour, just squatting there in the shadows listening in on every word, rose slowly to his feet and said, "How we know if true?"

"Course they're true," snapped William, though his voice cracked on the words as he said them.

Noclas nodded approvingly, and then repeated the words William had recited. "'Nothing can bring you peace but yourself,' them's the words this feller said. Well, a sure-fire way of tellin' if it's true, is askin' if things is workin' out that way." Noclas turned and looked earnestly at William. "How does that be workin' for you, William Tidd, this conjurin' up peace from within your own self?"

The black man steepled his fingers and resumed rocking. "How's that be workin' for the white folks? Charlie, how's that be workin' for the Injuns?" Then he fell silent.

"No peace," said Charlie at last, his arms crossed on his broad chest.

"Everybody looking within," said Noclas. "Yet, there ain't a whole heap of peace coming from within most folks, not 'round these here parts right at the moment, it don't seem to me."

William threw a dark look Noclas's direction and tried again to keep whittling.

"No sir," continued Noclas. "If everybody keeps looking within, the evidence don't point nowhere near to peace."

"Trouble," said Charlie. "Governor Stevens and peace treaties—bring no peace. Only more trouble."

"More trouble for sure," said Noclas, "unless there's someone who can bust down the wall and kill the enmity."

The black man stopped rocking and leaned closer to William, squinting critically at his finger. "Now, you just let old Noclas plug up that there hole in your finger before you empty out all your blood on your buckskins."

17

RUMORS OF WAR

"There's sure to be trouble—sooner than later, I'm afeard." That's what Noclas had been warning for months now. It would be lying for William to say he was not worried by Noclas's words. As always, Junebug slept that night like there was not a sinister particle in the universe, but William was feeling out of sorts with sleeping. He had tossed and turned on the straw-filled mattress until his back felt like someone had been laying into him with a bull whip.

The old black man was not given to exaggeration. He was not given to any kind of intentional misrepresentation. And few white folks were on as intimate of terms with the Indians as the black man. There was good reason to be deeply troubled at the latest rumors. The slice in his finger had throbbed in the night, and William had dutifully spent much of the night awake feeling his own pain and being deeply troubled.

But it wasn't just rumors about Yakama and Nisqually uprisings. William had read more about it in the *Puget Sound Courier*. Not a good thing to read just before hitting the sack.

It sounded like war with Indians around the country was as common as bracken fern in a bog, salmon in the Sound, smoke in a Salish longhouse. He reached down and scratched Wally's big head—maybe as common as fleas on a dog.

It wasn't just here; if the newspapers could be trusted, it was happening from Oklahoma to Montana, Illinois to Georgia. He read all about other Indian wars and conflicts; he couldn't help himself. All the way back to Andrew Jackson and the Indian Removal Act, and the Cherokee trail of tears—and dead Indians. In the wars, the US Army was often, though not always, victorious, but there was nothing glamorous about it: sure, there were pitched battles, soldiers lining up and meeting Indians on the plains whooping it up and slugging it out till the dust settled and the bodies were counted and a winner proclaimed. But that was in places where there actually *was* a US Army, thousands of trained soldiers, experienced at fighting—at fighting Indians.

With effort William swallowed the lump that had formed in his throat. It felt the size of a spring duck egg. He recalled what he had heard that winter at Fort Steilacoom. It was common knowledge. Two hundred soldiers, at best, against perhaps thousands of angry Northwest Indians. War with the Indians in Puget Sound—barring a miracle, and William was pretty settled about his disbelief in that kind of intervention—would be a disaster, that is, a disaster for the white folks.

Seeing stealth attacks in his mind's eye brought a cold sweat to William's brow. Night raids that started innocent enough: the soft hooting of an owl, the *knock-knocking* of a woodpecker, the nervous whinny of a horse, the low growl of the family dog—then painted savages splintering the door with their tomahawks, the howling and burning, the plundering and pillaging, the scalping and killing, the screams of terror—worse yet, were the ones who didn't get their selves killed on the spot—women and children taken prisoner, used as slaves at the warrior's whim.

"My giant goes with me wherever I go." William wiped his brow with a sleeve. Sunny though it had been that day, there was seldom enough warmth in Puget Sound nighttime air to account for sweat. Maybe Emerson was right about this much. William felt that, no matter how much his circumstances changed, there were things that always came with him, his fears, mostly, fears he would be ashamed for anyone to know, fear that haunted him from the past, fear of the unknown future, fear of all that might happen to his sister—to himself.

"Have the courage not to adopt another's courage." It was confounded Emerson again, or was it the ghost of his father coming to torment him? "There is scope and cause and resistance enough for us in our proper work and circumstance."

William wiped his hand across his forehead and down his face, wincing at the pain in his finger. In the essayist's world, it sounded like not only was he required to find peace within himself, but that he was supposed to go the whole hog and find courage there too. William was haunted by another inner torment: what would his father have thought of him if he knew him, deep down inside of him? If he knew what was not there? William drew in a deep breath and sighed.

What was his proper work, his proper work under the present circumstances? He wished he knew. Was joining up to resist an Indian uprising, was that it? Was that his duty?

Ever vigilant, Wally whined and nuzzled his face, his cockeyed tail thudding softly against the pine poles of the bed frame. Absently William reached over to finger the animal's down-turned ear; he winced again and switched hands. This funny-looking old dog had more courage than he had.

18

DEATH WAIL

"You look like you been up taking on the whole world's troubles all the night long," said Junebug next morning. "This'll help," she said, setting a plateful of fried eggs and five strips of crunchy bacon on the plank table. "Just the way you like it. And Noclas's brew to wash it down with. How's your finger?"

William flexed the fingers of his left hand, taking care to keep his bandaged index finger still, and assured her it was nothing.

Good as it smelled, William picked at his breakfast and only managed to force it down so as not to hurt his sister's feelings. After swallowing the mug of White-Man's-Foot tea, he filled a water skin with the rest of it. Pushing his chair from the table, he got up and put on his frayed wool coat.

"I'm fixing to take care of some business," he told his sister. He hesitated. He felt it was necessary to form a plan, a strategy of defense should it come to trouble. But how was he to go about preparing her without alarming her? "Should the Indians come 'round with their tomahawks fixin' to split your pretty head open and lift your scalp off, don't be afeard. Just be nice. Serve them up some eggs and bacon, and some White-Man's-Foot tea. Not to worry. They'll head off and burn and murder about some other folks' homestead. Leastwise, you'll be safe."

It couldn't be done that way, not without worrying Junebug. It occurred to him that nobody gets things right all the time. Maybe Noclas was telling stretchers about the Indians and their plans. But he knew it wasn't just Noclas. He'd read it all in the newspapers. Everybody in the region who could read and whose ears still worked knew what was coming. And they were doing their best to get ready for it.

William knew he had to do the same. He just wished he knew what it was. He grabbed up the new canoe paddle, turned up his collar, and opened the cabin door. "Be back before dinner time," he called over his shoulder. "Keep Wally nearby—as always."

He made it sound like he had business to attend to, like he was important enough to be needed somewhere, as if he had a plan. But in reality he had left the cabin to be alone, to be alone and do some serious thinking.

His first impulse was to saddle up Prophet and go out for a long ride. Invigorated by the exercise and the speed, he could think while riding. Weighing the canoe paddle in his hands, however, he hesitated. It was as good as finished—sure, he might add a few more Indian designs, but those could wait till next winter. There was his canoe down at Sequalitchew Creek, below the fort, near the landing where the *HMS Beaver* loaded furs and unloaded supplies and trade goods for Fort Nisqually. *His* canoe. It was actually not his. It was Charlie's but the Indian had always before let him use it anytime he pleased. He eyed the near-cloudless sky above the tree line. Fair weather and a day gunkholing along the Sound, maybe a fresh salmon or two, a prize drift log for splitting into shakes. That settled it.

It was funny to William as he walked through the forest to the village alongside the landing. Even with rumors of

Indian troubles on everyone's lips, he had absolutely no thought of fear from the Sequalitchews living peacefully in their cedar longhouses where their creek emptied into Puget Sound. There were Indians and then there were Indians. Maybe it was their dependence on the Hudson Bay fort and the benefit they derived from trading with the white man just up the gulch. Maybe they just had too much invested in peace to be joining up with hostile Indians and making war. Why shoot themselves in the foot?

As he neared the village, William sniffed the air. It was always the odors that let you know a village was nearby, and in five years he had yet to get entirely accustomed to the stench. It was a terrific mingling of aromas, not all bad, but far from all good either. Prominent in the air at that moment was the stench of rotting fish, decomposing game, human waste, and wet dog hair, though he was less certain of the precise origin of the latter; it could be just wet hair generally, combined with clay, dirt, and feathers soaked in rancid fish oil.

This panoply of stench would have been unbearable, securing for the Indians their most potent defense against intrusion from outsiders, were it not for the pleasant aromas swirling and mingling and sometimes overpowering the former. There was the spicy scent of fresh-split cedar planks and shavings, the incense of smoke rising from their alder wood cooking fires, and the mouth-watering scent of salmon fillets baking slowly over the coals. These tantalizing smells, combined with the piney scent of the forest and the off-shore salt breezes, tempered the reflex to disgorge one's breakfast, leaving in its place an oddly compelling aroma of humanity.

Then came the sounds of the Indian village. The slow rapping of the carver's mallet as he chiseled tribal legend in the sometimes frightening and grotesque cedar totem poles guarding the longhouses; the yapping of dogs, the laughter and squeals of children, the sounds of adult conversations, murmuring like the wings of hummingbirds on a summer day; the scraping of a dugout canoe being launched into the saltwater from the gravelly beach.

William suddenly halted, straining to hear another sound that filtered through the labyrinth of fir columns to his ears. Or was it merely the anticipation of another sound? He narrowed his eyes through the trees. The village was just visible, blue smoke hovering over five or six cedar longhouses, a naked boy or girl—it was not possible to tell which—running near the shoreline with a scrawny dog nipping at his heels, steam rising from the open belly of a cedar log being shaped into a canoe, a woman squatting near a tangle of rubbish, a man making water on the roots of a madrone tree. For an instant, it was as if the orchestra of sounds made by all this activity abruptly halted, became like a mime, motion but with the suspension of sound, like a flicker of calm before the storm.

Then it came. An eerie moaning and chanting, a rising and falling in grief. William had heard it before—the death wail—but it was impossible merely to hear the death wail. The death wail was meant to be felt, and William felt it resonating deeply with his own fears. The gnawing anguish, the keening despair, the hopeless emptiness, the paralyzing horror.

Swallowing hard, William considered turning and high-tailing it back up the gulch, leaving behind the haunting wail and what it conjured up in his own mind. But through the trees the water looked smooth and inviting. *Indians die too*, he tried reassuring himself, *like the rest of us*. He wondered for an instant who it was who had died, an old man or woman, a hunter torn by the claws of a black bear or wolf, a child caught in a riptide and drowned, a woman straining at the birthing rope, the newborn baby she had just delivered—or both. William decided to be discreet, to leave the Indians to go about their own grieving in their own way. He'd flank softly around the village to where Charlie kept his canoe pulled up on the beach and launch away.

The stench grew stronger. William glanced at the painted cedar planks and pointed gables of the longhouse village. Nearing the most prominent totem, he caught sight of Charlie's canoe—no more than twenty yards of beach, littered with a mound of decomposing carcasses—one looked like it had been a seal or a small sea lion, flies hovering drunkenly over the mound, fragments of old baskets, and a heap of clam shells. Twenty filthy yards and he'd be there.

Another keening wail rose from the largest of the longhouses. William glanced at the elongated hole carved in the cedar entrance. Several dozen Indians had gathered around the painted figure that surrounded the entrance hole, a painting that looked like a terrified coyote, its front paws raised as if to fend off something evil, and its hind legs splayed as if it was about to be cut open and have its bowels torn out. But it was the giant face of the carved figure at his eye level on the totem pole that, combined with the death wail, sent a chill up his spine. Its eyes were rimmed with blue paint and goggled with terror, its flaring nostrils were painted iron red ochre, but it was the mouth that was the worst. Its black lips stretched wide across the creature's face, with two white walls of teeth clenched in horror, its fore claws held up as if to fend off the torments of some fiend boring down on it. A crawling sensation ran up William's spine; he shivered and made to turn away.

But just as he did, something odd caught his attention at the longhouse. He halted. It had been all Indians in their daily attire—or lack thereof—women wearing cedar-bark woven skirts, men in buckskin trousers or blankets, children in a state of nature, scrawny, flea-bitten dogs slinking in and among the rest.

But what William witnessed next set an ice flow loose in his veins. For an instant he thought it was a Sasquatch emerging through the longhouse entrance hole—maybe the skookum man-beast legends were true after all. But this was no legendary beast of the mountains. It was real, a terrifying creature shrouded in a bearskin robe, a carved wooden eagle for a hat, painted in red ochre and black, its hooked beak extending almost an arm's length over the man's face. His long, oily hair was decorated with white feathers that extended onto the bearskin robe, making it difficult to tell where the man's hair ended and the bear's began.

As the medicine man stooped to exit the longhouse, there must have been a downdraft of wood smoke from within that followed him, swirling and hallowing the shaman as he stood upright. Beating a hand drum, slowly, ominously, with a bone for a drumstick, he walked toward the beach—and William. Staring wide-eyed as the shaman drew closer, William's eyes fastened on the man's neckwear, a buckskin strap with three skulls for ornament—human skulls. Rattling his drumstick across the skulls, he strode nearer.

Just when William was about to turn and bolt in terror, another figure bent and stepped through the opening. Terrifying as the shaman was, the second figure halted William dead in his tracks.

This was no Indian. Covered from head to toe in a wide-flowing black robe, bending low through the carved entrance hole, the bowels of the painted coyote doorway, and blinking at the sunlight was Sister Marguerite. The Indians parted on either side of the young woman to let her pass as if she were a princess. William stared in amazement, the shaman almost forgotten. As the medicine man passed, he halted, looking squarely at William.

"You my witness," he said, his voice hollow, reverberating from under the carved eagle headdress. "They should call me first. White-Man priestess no power to heal sick tyee. He dead. Sequalitchew people must call me first. But now—too late. Dead. Not my fault. You my witness."

William nodded. It sounded as if the man was covering his tracks, making sure he didn't get blamed for the death.

Pin it on the White Man, on the nun, but not on him. William had heard stories, a shaman killed by family members when the medicine man treated their loved one but who died anyway. They'd done it to white doctors, too. Indians seemed to have an unwritten code about their sick and those who tried to heal them; if the sick person died, the healer must have been responsible. He shuddered at the recollection.

Sister Marguerite put the back of her hand to her mouth and coughed; she walked slowly, deliberately, as if she were in a trance. She looked like she might collapse. William felt a surge of satisfaction at the sight of the once-proud, confident nun, now ashen, halting, and about to lose her balance. Hard on the heels of his smugness was a twinge of remorse—but only a twinge.

"I need air," she murmured. Her face, what little of it was visible under her wimple, was drawn and ashen, and her eyes stared unblinking at the open water beyond the village. William took her arm and helped her over a drift log.

"Take some of this," he said, holding up his water skin.

Sister Marguerite took a sip and then a long drink. "Ah, Noclas's tea. I do hope he's right about it." She took another drink and handed the skin back. "But nothing could have saved the tyee."

William scowled. "But isn't that what you do? Save people? Isn't that what your religion claims to do?"

No sooner had he said the words—more of a taunt—than he wished he could take them back. He expected for reply that sustained look of condescension he'd experienced before, the unseeing hooding of her eyes. Instead, she continued to look out at the blue water of the Sound, nodded slowly, but saying nothing.

"What on earth were you doing in there?" persisted William. "There's trouble enough with the Indians these days. I'm sure you meant well, but it can't be a good idea for you to be going to an Indian village and—and doing whatever it is nuns do. You saw the medicine man. He was none too happy about you being here—being here before he was, at that."

William looked around them. The shaman had disappeared. Others had taken up the death wail. Several men had started rolling a canoe up the beach on poles toward the longhouse; the tyee would have a canoe burial, reserved for the important people in a tribe, his corpse laid out in his favorite canoe, suspended in the crook of a tree in the burial grounds on the ridge just northeast of the gulch.

"I was summoned," replied Sister Marguerite simply.

"Summoned? You? By who?" said William, wishing as he heard himself that he'd asked it differently.

"By the tyee, by his wives," said the nun, "and others in the village who have come to follow the teachings of Mother Church."

Follow them over a cliff, thought William, though part of him was glad he hadn't said the words aloud.

"The shaman, dressed up all heathen like, with the skull necklace—I take it he's not with you? One of the followers?"

"No," she replied slowly.

The confident, condescending nun he had met with Junebug at the fort that day, the haughty, knitting nun, was gone; she was like a hide float he'd seen the Indians use in their whale hunts, a shriveled up one, punctured and deflated. In her place was a young woman shrouded in a black robe, weary, vulnerable, frightened, perhaps even doubting things of which she had before seemed so certain. William leaned over slightly, trying to see her eyes; she turned and he followed her gaze out onto the calm inland sea. A mad idea suddenly struck him.

"I-I sometimes find paddling on the sea, on the Sound, just here, helps me think, clears my head."

No reply.

"In fact, I was coming to do just that," he continued, holding up his paddle awkwardly, doing his best to conceal his bandaged finger. "Fixing to go paddle on the sea, just this morning, I was, when this happened." His gesture took in the longhouse and the Indians mourning their dead. "Sometimes helps." He hesitated, then, in a careless tone, he added, "Might do for you."

As if extracting herself from a trance, Sister Marguerite turned slowly toward William. "You need more than a new-carved paddle to paddle on the water." Then she did it. Veiled her eyes and spoke unseeing, as if by memory, or wishing to block out a memory.

William felt the heat rise in his cheeks and he was on the verge of withdrawing his suggestion. Why did she do it, this infuriating gesture; was it pride, or fear? There was that persistent thought that she had some notion of the stunning effect her amber eyes had on men, at least on some men, and had developed the seemingly pompous habit of sparing men the wonder of her eyes. Then again, it may be that she was sparing her eyes from the barbarism of men, of the wilderness, the cruelty of the frontier. It was hard to tell which it was. Perhaps it was both, switched from one to the other.

Sister Marguerite was a nun, after all, though William had to admit he had little notion of what that actually meant. Perhaps when she was brought over by Father Blanchet in 1847, leastwise, that's what the *Pioneer and Democrat* had reported—she must have been only a young girl in those days—she may have been carefully instructed to divert her gaze. With eyes so alluring it would be a mercy to others; with eyes such as hers, men would be inflamed with lust and women enraged with envy. William imagined Mother Joseph scolding her for having such beautiful eyes. "Sister Marguerite, the less the world sees of those seductress's eyes the better."

Glancing at the nun, William wanted to believe this. She hooded her eyes as a mercy, and out of obedience to her mother superior. The heat returned; either way, he concluded, it was an infuriating habit. Drawing in breath, he was about to tell her as much.

"You have the paddle," she said, "and do you have some craft to paddle?"

William was irritated at the question, though he was disarmed by the inquiring lilt she so often used at the end of her words. Of course he would have some craft to paddle. Who would carve a paddle all winter—with slivers aplenty, and now this cut that would leave a scar, to prove it—and have nothing to use it in, nothing to paddle? He nodded toward Charlie's canoe, about to reply.

But before he could get the words out, from behind him came, "He has canoe," in a clipped monotone.

William spun on his heel. So Charlie could move with stealth when he wanted to after all—or when he needed to.

19

EAGLES DARE

Kneeling in the bow, William bent his back, his paddle poised, then he plunged the blade of the paddle into the sea. He chose to ignore the salt sting in his finger as water seeped into the bandage. Surging forward, Charlie's canoe glided through the calm water like an eagle in flight, silently, effortlessly—or so it seemed. Recalling his first time in a coastal canoe, William smiled ruefully. It felt like wrestling with a buffalo, hogging back and forth and tipping precariously every time he tried to put his paddle in the water. The canoe won out that first day on the Sound, and William got a frigid drenching for his efforts.

Again and again, William drove his paddle into the sea, and with each stroke the canoe shot forward, faster and faster. It had taken time and practice—and several more wettings—but with Charlie's patient guidance, he had eventually become more proficient than the average white settler in the region. Charlie had said as much.

Pointed entry, blade tapered on both edges, sturdy shaft, comfortable hand grip—his new paddle was good. Sea breezes cooling his face, William drew in a deep satisfied breath; the momentum of the canoe sluicing through the frigid salt water of Puget Sound sent a shiver of exhilaration throughout his frame.

"Paddle, good." Charlie's voice rose above the gurgling of the wooden dugout craft and the breeze. "I teach you good," he added. And then he threw his head back and laughed, one of his white-man laughs—so William termed them—uninhibited and companionable, like a carefree child, *Hyuk-hyuk-hyuk!*

Charlie was feeling it too. Out here, on the vast expanse of the Sound, troubles melted away like the snow pack in May on Naches Pass; troubles dissipated like smoke in the wind—at least for the time being.

"We'll follow the shoreline to the wharf at Steilacoom," William called over his shoulder. "Then cut across to Fox Island, just there," he signaled with a nod, but kept his pace.

"You boss," said Charlie with a laugh.

When the first heaving breathlessness of exertion had passed, William began to feel that he and Charlie, paddling in coordinated effort like they were, could keep this up for hours, maybe days. He felt this, though he knew from experience it was not so. Everything was in balance, the boat, the paddles, the sea swells—everything. It felt effortless, unresisting, without obstruction or hindrance, nobody to stop them or tell them to slow their pace or turn here or there. Freedom, that's what it felt like, freedom.

Out of the corner of his eye, William spotted the oily wet head of a speckled seal as it slid to the surface on their starboard bow. Whiskers dripping water, nostrils flaring, it inspected them warily with its eyes. He could hear the blast of its breath as they came nearer, skimming through the water; then too near for comfort. Startled, the seal's wide body arched and dove, disappearing below the surface with a departing flourish of defiance from its flippers.

Then William heard a sound from above. Honking as

they passed overhead, a flock of geese from Canada flew in perfect formation; V-shaped, like the trailing wake of a well-navigated canoe; each bird's long black neck straining southward. William stole a glance at the shoreline where here and there wisps of smoke from settlers' cabins or Indian villages rose lazily into the evergreen branches of the vast forests. And there, rising high above the rest, was an ancient Douglas fir. William wondered at the centuries of stories that tree could tell.

Suddenly, from the gnarly upper branches of the tree, a dark shadow took shape—an eagle spreading its great black wings. In moments, the raptor was so close above them, William could see the penetrating eyes staring wide and menacing from its hoary head as it bore in on its unsuspecting prey.

"Indian good fisherman," said Charlie, resting his paddle on his lap. "But eagle more better fisherman."

William rested his paddle, water dribbling from its blade. He wiped his brow with his sleeve and positioned the brim of his hat to shield his eyes from the sun. Behind him the steady clicking rhythm of knitting suddenly fell silent. William stole a glance over his shoulder. In the end, Sister Marguerite had accepted his invitation, if that's what it had been. Even she would keep her eyes wide open at what was about to happen.

Circling ominously, the eagle gave off a chilling screech, then tucked its wings and dropped like a stone toward the surface of the water. At the very instant that William thought the bird could not possibly avoid crashing into the icy waters of the Sound, and no more than two canoe lengths in front of their bow, it spread its vast wings. As wide as a grown man's reach, the bird's great wings acted like feathered brakes. In the same instant, the eagle, its talons spread wide, snatched up a salmon. Then, lifting itself with several powerful sweeps of its wings, it carried its prey with ease back toward its ancient fir tree perch.

Though William and Charlie had seen this spectacular display at other times, they both knelt in the canoe, their paddles poised and motionless, gazing in open-mouthed wonder. Though the eagle performed this feat with detachment and nonchalance, the fish had clearly been unwilling and unprepared, writhing and straining, its silvery scales flashing in the sunlight, desperate for its life to be free of the winged demon preying from the sky. But that would not be. The eagle had won.

"'You shall mount up with wings as eagles.'" Marguerite's voice was hushed and awestruck. William stole another glance behind him. It appeared, by her voice, her upturned face, wide with wonder, that she had never seen anything like this before today.

"That from Book of Books," said Charlie.

William frowned. Why did they have to wreck this moment with the Bible? It flashed into his mind—on his next stroke, with the flick of his wrist—he could douse the nun with a shower of icy saltwater. He couldn't help grinning as he thought of her gasping for breath at the cold and wet. *Try quoting Bible at me while choking on a mouthful of saltwater.*

"Noclas say Bible, 'Book of Books,'" repeated Charlie.

William had to admit it: he had read more *about* the Bible than *from* the Bible itself. And most of what he had read about it had not been overly impressed with it. Taking a clean stroke with his paddle, William felt more than heard Charlie's paddle enter the water at the same instant. This time William set a more leisurely pace, a stroke pace he could maintain and think at the same time.

Something he had read from Emerson came to mind. To the rhythm of their stroke, he tried recalling the precise words. It went something like this: "The stationariness of religion; the assumption that the age of inspiration is past, that the Bible is closed; the fear of degrading the character of Jesus by representing him as a man; indicate with sufficient clearness the falsehood of Christian theology."

Sister Marguerite had started it, quoting from the Bible like she had done. Turning his head for the benefit of Charlie and the nun, he quoted Emerson out loud. To his ears, it sounded so much more sophisticated than the tidbit Marguerite had managed to dredge up from the moldy old pages of the Bible. He drove his paddle into the sea with the renewed vigor of conquest. Let them chew on that one for a while.

After several moments of silence, Charlie spoke from the stern of the canoe. It always mildly bothered William that Charlie never sounded winded when he spoke, or so it seemed.

"'Sta-tion-ari-ness . . . ,'" the Indian paused. "'Inspiration past, Bible closed.' Jesus is only man, falsehood of what Christians believe. This Emerson man you quote like talking raven, Charlie think he not much like Book of Books and Jesus."

"And with good reason," said William. "Don't you see his point? Christians say the Bible is everything. And Jesus is everything, not just a man but God, so they say. That nothing changes, that there's no new inspiration, Bible closed, no new truth to be added, end of discussion." He was warming to the debate. "Isn't that what you Christians say?"

William took pleasure in imagining Sister Marguerite scowling at his challenge. Her knitting needles had been idle for several minutes. As for Charlie, well Charlie was an Indian; he didn't know enough about things to do much arguing. This discussion would do the nun some good, help get her mind off seeing the old tyee in the longhouse trembling in his death throes—and get her mind off the shaman. He shuddered himself at the recollection.

"So what do you think?" he persisted. "Is the Bible true, the whole story, and nothing else?"

"Well, yes and no," she said.

William glanced over his shoulder. Her eyes were tight shut, but this was different than the condescending hooding of her eyes. Her brow was lined and she was scowling as if trying to work it out. "I realize you will think that a—how do you say it—a wishy-washy answer."

"Blamed tooting, it sounds wishy-washy," said William, smiling broadly. This was easier than he had thought it would be. "Let me rephrase. Do you or do you not believe that the Bible is closed, done for, no more new ideas to be added? That it's true and your sole authority in everything, 'faith and practice,' Isn't that how you say it?"

William could not help himself. He had to see her reaction. Sister Marguerite cocked her head to one side and became engrossed in her knitting, the needles clicking together like a drummer at the head of an army.

"Well, do you?" persisted William, absently stroking the water with his paddle, contemplating the flick of his wrist and the wetting he could give the nun at that moment, if he chose to. He could claim it was an accident.

"Not exactly," she said at last. "There's other things for Catholics. The Bible, yes. But Popes and councils, and the magisterium. Together these are our authority."

"*Magis*-what-*ium*?" said William.

"Ma-gis-ter-i-um," said Marguerite, her tone like a school dame's to a dull-witted pupil. "The collected teachings of Mother Church, that's the magisterium."

"So the Bible, it's just sort of along for the ride, then?" said William. He was enjoying the argument, though he felt vaguely uncomfortable, like he was a beaver being lured into a trap but wasn't sure where it was staked—or how much it would hurt when he sprung the trap and the jaws bit deep into his flesh and bones.

"The Bible is important to Catholics," repeated the nun. But William thought he detected a hint of hesitation in her voice, the slight quavering of doubt in her tone. "But so are the traditions of Mother Church."

This was a new tack for William. He paddled silently for a few moments before it struck. "So that'd be 'No,' then.

The Bible *can* have new ideas added, the ideas cobbled up and added in by some Pope or council, right?"

"Well, if you put it that way, yes," said Sister Marguerite, her voice flat. "I suppose so."

"Aha!" said William. "Reminds me of one of our modern poets—read a poem of his in the *Puget Sound Courier,* just a few weeks back. Goes like this. 'They must upward still and onward, who would keep abreast of truth.' That makes more sense to my way of thinking."

"Noclas say," said Charlie. "He say, 'If a thing's true, it's true.' No matter what pope say, no matter what council say, no matter what magisterium say, no matter what new poet say, no matter what man Emerson say. 'If a thing's true, it's true.'"

William rolled his eyes, glad his back was to them.

"Bible true," continued Charlie. "Jesus true. Change what true—it become false, become error, become untruth."

Sister Marguerite's needles had been still. William had been readying his reply, not really listening to the Indian, thinking how primitive and ignorant Charlie could be at times.

"But what is true?" said William. His voice cracked as he asked it. "What is truth?" he tried again. He had meant it to be a gauntlet, an ultimate question too clever for some wilderness nun or backwater savage to answer. But a gust caught at his words; they came out with less force than he had intended.

"'And ye shall know the truth,'" recited the nun to the rhythm of her needles, "'and the truth shall make you free.'"

There she goes again. "Humph, that's not saying much," said William. "Doesn't really answer my question, now, does it?"

The clicking of the knitting needles slowed then stopped altogether. "*Au contraire, monsieur.* The words of Jesus himself tell you much: firstly, that there is an answer to the question—for the honest questioner: you *can* know truth, and when you know truth you will be free. That, I think, is saying very much, indeed."

"But you've already argued against truth being closed," said William. "It was you saying that the Bible by itself ain't your sole authority, that it ain't the single inalterable way to truth. Them's your words. So how can you know truth?" William swallowed hard. His own question bothered him, and he wished he hadn't asked it. He worried that he might be nearing the place in the mud where the beaver trap was staked.

"Jesus' words," said the nun lamely, "seem pretty clear, though."

They paddled on in silence, silence except for the steady stroke of their paddles, the gliding of the canoe on the sea, and the slow clicking of knitting needles. Except for the straightness of the path of the canoe through the water, William might have forgotten Charlie was there. Charlie had added little or nothing to the debate, so William had decided to believe.

But it was Charlie who broke the silence. "Noclas show me in 'Book of Books,'" he said at last. "Jesus give answer to question, what is truth. Jesus say, 'I am the way, the truth, and the life. No one cometh to the Father, but by me.'"

William took several strokes before attempting a reply. "Well, yes, but what does his answer mean?"

"You ask Noclas," said Charlie. "But I'm pretty sure it mean, Jesus himself, he the truth. He the answer."

Again William rolled his eyes. Truth can't be a person, he thought, Jesus or anyone else. Wasn't truth just ideas folks decide to agree about?

Readying a guffaw at Charlie's words, William opened his mouth. At the same instant, from dead ahead, came a long hot blast from a steam horn.

20

INDIAN ISLAND INTERNMENT

Another sharp blast from the steam horn screamed across the surface of the water. The sublime was over. The peace and tranquility they had felt paddling Charlie's canoe so freely on Puget Sound ended there—and so did the debate about truth.

Another sharp blast. Crossing their starboard bow was the *Beaver,* Hudson Bay Company steamship, smoke belching above its raked stack, leaving behind a choking column of steam clouds.

Back paddling to avoid the unsettling wake of the steamer, William and Charlie maneuvered the high bow of the canoe to slice through the approaching mounds of water that would soon descend on them from the steamer's wash.

"Did you know it takes ten men," said William, resting on his paddle, "chopping wood all day long to supply wood to feed the hungry boiler of the steam engine on the *Beaver*?

Forty cords a day, she consumes, so James Wiley told me. Looks like she's heading to Fox Island. Wonder what for? There's not much there."

Charlie grunted. "I hear," he said, his voice monotone.

"What'd you hear?" asked William.

"*Beaver* take Indians to island," said Charlie.

"They're doing it, then?" said William. "The *Courier* reported something about plans for doing it. Word is, Acting-Governor Mason, while Governor Isaac Stevens is busy drafting more treaties with tribes in Wyoming and Montana, far east from here, Mason has ordered that Indians be relocated and put in camps, the non-hostile ones, that is."

"That doesn't seem very kind," said Sister Marguerite, "putting them on an island in a camp like that."

William took his eyes off the steamer and glanced over his shoulder. "You saw what they live in ordinarily," he said. "Why not? Can't be much worse than their own camps. Besides, it's for their own protection. Keep them from being attacked by the hostile ones—if it comes to that."

"But isn't doing this kind of thing—" she pointed at the *Beaver*. "Isn't taking them from their land and homes, just like this, isn't that what changed them from friendly Indians into hostile ones in the first place?"

Charlie grunted approvingly but did not speak.

"That's as may be," said William. "But what's to do now that they've done gone and become hostile ones, now that they're fixing to join up with the Yakamas and make war on the rest of us? What's to do, you answer me that?"

"But the Sequalitchews, they're not hostile Indians," said Marguerite. "They're peaceful folk. But they're still living in their longhouses in their village at the mouth of the creek. Nobody's put them on an island—for their own protection, as you say."

"Yet," said William. "Their time's coming. If you can trust the newspaper, Agent Gosnell's sending them—for their own good—to Squaxin Island, off around Devil's Head, for their protection. For their own good. To keep them safe from the hostile kind."

Charlie had not said a word.

"Hey, Charlie," William called over his shoulder. "Any of your people on board making their way to internment on Fox Island?"

"Yes."

"Well, that's good," continued William. "Because that means they're not hostile ones. Everything'll be okay for them, then. Indian Agent Simmons's just following governor's orders: all non-hostile Indians to be removed to islands in the Sound designated for the safe internment of friendly Indians in the various tribes. They'll be safe on Fox Island, out of the fray. Plus, there's good hunting, lots of deer, on the islands, and fish on all sides."

"But not home." Charlie grunted. "Not free to go home—maybe ever."

"There you go, Charlie, sounding Indian again," said William.

"Who decides which ones are hostile Indians?" asked the nun. "Or non-hostile Indians?"

"That's easy," said William. "I reckon the Indians have to make their choice."

"Well, of course," said Sister Marguerite, a hint of impatience in her tone. "But how does Acting-Governor Mason do it, identify which ones are which?"

"Ask Charlie, maybe he knows," said William. "Hey Charlie, how do they decide?"

Charlie shrugged his shoulders. "They have ways," he said and fell silent again.

"I was at Fort Nisqually only yesterday," said Sister Marguerite. "They haven't hauled off Indian Steilacoom and his wife, fiery-tempered Mother Steilacoom, or Indian Bob, or any of the other Indians that work at the fort—some for many years now."

"Just you tell me why that would be?" said William. "Some folks is saying that the British might be behind all this, stirring up war with the Indians in hopes of driving out American settlers. Scheming to get their land and fur trade back, they are."

"I think not," said the nun. "Dr. Tolmie and his family, they are the best of people, peace-loving folks. They would not stir up war, even if there was something to be gained for Britain. But consider: trade works best in times of peace; war with the Indians means no trade with the Indians. It would be silliness. If not for purely humanitarian motives, they'll do what's right for commercial motives; Britain is not going to stir up a war and ruin their own trade. Mark my words, neither Britain nor the Hudson Bay Company are—how do you say it—'stirring the pot.' They are not the cause of unrest, of that I am certain."

William glanced at the nun. He had not heard her speak as many words together, and, he was forced to admit, casting about as he was for a retort, nothing was coming ready to hand.

"The governor in Olympia," said William, changing the subject instead, "he's calling for volunteers."

"That is true," said Sister Marguerite. "And I have done so."

"What? You've done volunteered?" said William with a laugh. "You, to fight Indians? Hey, Charlie. What do you think of our chances now that we have Sister Marguerite on our side, defending us from the savages?"

Charlie did not reply.

"I haven't said on whose side I volunteered," said the nun with a smile. His back was to her, but William could hear it in her tone, and in the disarming lilt that so often was in her voice.

After their encounter with the *Beaver,* they had turned the canoe around and paddled back toward Steilacoom and Sequalitchew Creek. As Charlie steered the canoe onto the beach with his paddle from the stern, William stepped into the shallows, the bottom of the dugout scraping on the gravelly beach.

There was an awkward moment, the nun still seated amidships in the canoe, William and Charlie ready to heave the vessel fully out of the water and up higher above the tide line. "Ah, you'll be needing a hand," said William, extending his. Sister Marguerite hesitated, then took his hand, hiked up her habit, and leapt onto the beach. It was a soft, delicate hand, but with a firm grip; William dropped it the instant she landed.

"You was saying?" said William through clenched teeth, straining as he and Charlie heaved the canoe.

"About what?" said the nun.

"About volunteering—whose side you fixing to do it on?"

Sister Marguerite laughed. "I have some training in nursing," she said, "and experience. That's what brought me to the village today, in fact. I aim to volunteer so as to be useful in restoring peace and healing to both sides."

Turning toward the village, William murmured under his breath, "What in tarnation! She's sounds like another Elizabeth Cady Stanton."

Activity around the cluster of smoky longhouses had returned to normal, no death wail, no ominous drum beating, no terrifying shaman. Children played. A group of women gutted fish, and a cluster of men sat cross-legged in a circle in front of the longhouse, tossing stones into a ring, laughing, shouting—gambling, no doubt; it was one of their favorite pastimes.

"And you?" said the nun. "Will you volunteer?"

William pretended not to hear her at first. It was the big question he tried to avoid. What would happen to Junebug if he enlisted in the militia? Who would care for her, protect her from harm? It was the duty of other men to volunteer in the militia and fight Indians.

"I'll do my duty," he said shortly.

After they tidied up the canoe, bailing water that had sloshed in while they paddled, Charlie, took up his musket, powder horn, and shot pouch.

Heading up the wagon road from the village, William turned to the Indian. "You've been awful quiet." He looked sideways at Charlie. "You fixing to volunteer?"

Charlie met his eye, and nodded.

Suddenly William felt a tightening in his gut. "Wait a second, Charlie," he said slowly. "You're a friendly Indian—everybody knows that." He hesitated. "How come they haven't come to take you yourself off to the island?"

Charlie made no reply.

21

CALL TO ARMS

"Well now, lookie here!" called one fellow, hitching up his trousers and giving a low whistle. "This here poster says the governor is calling for volunteers. 'Washington Territorial Militia needs you!'"

"Well, I'll be dang busted!"

"Then it's to be war with the Injuns after all." It was a man they called Tom Perkins.

"Looks like it."

"Won't amount to much," said Tom.

"Oh sure 'nough, it may at the first," said a man called George Bright. "The Injuns'll come on a-thumpin' on their ole drums and a-whoopin' and hollerin', but when it comes down to real fightin', there ain't nothin' to worry 'bout from no Injuns 'round here."

"Too lazy to get riled up 'nough for any real fightin'," said a man they called Andrew Laws, spitting tobacco juice on the boardwalk for emphasis. "Them's our Injuns 'round here, just too danged lazy."

"Oh, make no mistake about it, gentlemen," said a voice William thought sounded familiar. "They'll make a show of it at the outset. But when it comes to firing their muskets—that is, *if* they fire them at all—simply dashed miserable shooting it will be."

It was Dr. Burns—William could tell from his English-sounding intonations.

"You see, the Indians' real problem—that is, if one can narrow it down merely to one problem—is that they are in the habit of employing entirely too light a charge. Bewilderment on their visage, they pull the trigger and the lead ball fitfully meanders its way out the barrel and in the general direction they have pointed the weapon. In the very unlikely event that the lead manages to strike its intended mark, have no fear, there shall be little harm done. Little harm, indeed. A contusion, perhaps a scratch, nothing more. We must not fear them any more than we would fear an attack by—"

Dr. Burns broke off, stammering theatrically as if casting about in search of a sufficiently proportionate metaphor. "—One must not fear the Indians any more than one would fear an attack by a local family of polecats. Oh surely, as with skunk, there may be a bit of unpleasant stench—there will certainly be that—but there'll be no harm done, not in the least. No harm, indeed. Mark my words."

Stroking the barrel of his musket, Andrew Laws agreed. "We could be a-sending out half our militia—the untrained, untried, untested half—and it won't be more'n a few days, weeks at the most, and the Injuns'll be squealing, 'Uncle! 'Nough, 'nough! Leave off! Hold your fire! We've done gone and had 'nough!' That's what it'll be sounding like around here in an Injun war."

"War? History won't call any skirmish with the Injuns in Puget Sound a war," said Tom. "Not a real one."

William smiled. He hoped the men idling about the wharf in Steilacoom were right.

"My only regret," said George Bright, his arms folded like he was pouting. "Is that when we mount up to take the

Injuns on, the painted heathens'll not stand their ground and fight. They'll turn tail and clear off, no fightin' to be done. That there's my only regret."

"If I might add one more important observation," said Dr. Burns. "Tragic as the cowardice of the enemy will render any war with them; nevertheless, there is always great good that comes from war. In the conflict of arms, young men are schooled in the art of courage. Regardless of the disproportion of our enemy, all true-blooded young men will know and feel it their duty to enlist and fight."

"Enlist, go on, then," quipped an old fellow, trailing a hook from the wharf. "Enlist, for sure, but they'll be precious little real fighting to be done."

"More's the pity," said Dr. Burns, his voice like a bishop's pronouncing the benediction.

William had heard enough. Stuffing his hands in his pockets, he spun on his heel and shuffled back to where he had tethered Prophet. Courage—he wasn't really sure what courage was. There were those who thought the Tidds were on more intimate terms with its counterpart. He'd overheard folks in town gossiping about their pa, that what he had done was the height of cowardice. With a quick jerk of his head, he tried pushing the memory away.

William didn't care much for Dr. Burns—and he knew that Junebug strongly disliked the man—but he wondered if the Englishman might not be partially right about a conflict of arms being a training ground for teaching young men how to be courageous.

He had gathered the reins and was just putting his foot in the stirrup, when he heard a voice he recognized.

"Bill Tidd! Hold up a minute, there, young fellow!"

William turned. It was James Wiley. As if in salute, the journalist hiked up his spectacles with the knuckle of his index finger. "So you've no doubt heard the news," he said, tapping a fountain pen on a notepad and narrowing his eyes at William. The man was never without pen and paper.

"There's a general call to enlist. Washington Territorial Militia needs able-bodied volunteers."

The journalist paused, scanning William from the soles of his worn moccasins to the topmost hole in his felt hat. "Men like Bill Tidd, that is, especially men who can ride like Bill Tidd. There aren't been men who can ride like William Tidd since the days of Paul Revere, and that's a fact."

William wondered, as he retied Prophet's reins to the hitching post, if all journalists were given to exaggeration, or just Wiley. "I saw the poster yonder on the wharf," he said. "So it's come to war, then, for sure?"

"Well, now, do not quote me stirring up war fever by saying such a thing." Wiley smoothed his waistcoat and adjusted his cravat. There was a nervous eagerness about the man. The journalist seemed excited about mounting tensions with the Indians. William knew James Wiley well enough not to think too ill of him for it. It came with the territory; the man was a journalist; getting excited about bad news was what he did; one had to make allowances.

"Though Acting-Governor Mason is doing his best to negotiate with Indian leaders," said Wiley, scribbling in his notepad as he spoke. "The prudent thing is to prepare for the worst. The US Army at Fort Steilacoom is short-handed. That's being kind. Two hundred soldiers will not prove sufficient, should the Nisquallys and Puyallups form an alliance with the Yakamas over the mountains. Which could very well happen—may have done already. Mason and Agent Simmons, they're doing all they can, calling for Leschi and other hostile Indian leaders to set down their arms and come to Olympia for talks, a powwow with the great white chief."

"Will they come?" asked William, giving Prophet a lump of sugar he had been saving in his pocket.

"I do not know," said Wiley, taking his spectacles off and eyeing through the lenses toward the sun. "But it is a gesture the acting governor must make before making any declaration of war on them." With a huff, he breathed on his glasses and wiped them on his handkerchief. "Meanwhile, the US Government sends its aid. As we speak, Bill Tidd, the US sloop-of-war *Decatur* is en route from Hawaii here to Puget Sound. With a fair wind, she'll be here soon."

"What for?"

"Well, my friend, if it comes to war with the Indians, it is imperative that we have superior firepower to our enemy. They are likely to have superior numbers, almost assuredly so, though it is impossible to get fully accurate counts of who is with them and who is not. The *Decatur* has guns, big ones, cannons that fire exploding shells, and her crew is not shy about using them. We'll need something to tip the scale in our favor."

William thought of his earlier conversation with Sister Marguerite and Charlie. He decided Wiley might know the answer.

"Who decides which ones are hostile and which ones are not?" he asked.

Wiley shrugged, fitting his spectacles back onto the bridge of his nose. "The Indians themselves make their choices. But things can change. The littlest thing could make an Indian who was friends with white folks one day, their direst enemy on the next. A perceived slight, a business transaction gone bad, a horse just purchased that up and dies, a man who cheated at gambling, a new blanket and a sick child—anything. So there's no way of knowing until it's war. Then there's rogues like Charles Wren, the Rustler, stirring the pot with Leschi and the Nisquallys and the Puyallups. There is simply no way of knowing. Hence, we must be prepared." He paused, pointing a finger at William's chest.

"That's why we need more able-bodied men to enlist in the militia. You are the man, Bill Tidd. Charles Eaton's rangers. Eaton's looking for men just like you, capable men who are fearless in the face of adversity, who shrink back at nothing, men of courage and conviction. That's you, isn't it, Bill Tidd?"

William swallowed hard and tried to nod enthusiastically. But no words were coming.

"What's troubling you, son?" said Wiley. "There's noble deeds to be done." Wiley eyed him and nodded slowly. "Bill Tidd, you are your own man. You are not obligated to conform to the low expectations some folks around here may have for you. Because of what your pa done, you can shrivel up like a dried prune, or you can rouse yourself, breathe in a deep draught of clean air, and shake off the stigma. A war like this—it's the opportunity of your lifetime."

"I-I have some commitments," stammered William at last.

"What commitments are more important than defending families throughout the territory?"

"I have a sister," stammered William.

"Cute little blond thing," said Wiley, stroking his chin in thought. "I remember now."

"Junebug, she's sort of special," continued William, "and she's real little."

"And you're thinking that you can do her more good staying home and protecting her, standing betwixt her and any band of hostile Indians that comes calling at your door, is that what you're thinking?"

"I'd do my best," said William. The way the newspaperman put it made it seem sort of ridiculous, one man holding off a mob of Indians bent on killing and burning.

"I'm certain you would, my boy," said Wiley. "I'm certain you would." He paused, eyeing William over his spectacles. "You love her so, you'd be happy to die protecting her. I do believe that." He paused again. "However, you would be dead, and then what? Once you're out of the way, scalp lifted off your skull, there'd be no one betwixt the bloody heathens and your precious little sister Junebug, now would there be?"

William stammered for an answer, but found none.

"But by enlisting with Eaton and the militia," continued Wiley, hiking his glasses up on his nose, "you will strike a blow that will not only keep the Indians from your own door, from harming your own sister, but by signing up and fighting with Eaton's band you'll be protecting all the other sisters and families in the region. Stay and you will die a hero, protecting your sister." The journalist tucked his notepad under an arm and brought his hands together three times in mock applause. "But, dying that way, it's nothing but a fool's courage. And you will have done nothing for the bigger cause—or for Junebug who will have to watch them finish you off and then do her dying on her own, at the hands of the savages."

Wiley grabbled William's threadbare lapels. "Your dead sister, your life and hers ending in a charred huddle, a sincere but pathetic embrace. What is more you will leave other helpless folks, women and children, to the same fate. Can you live with that on your conscience? Can you, Bill Tidd?"

William felt the heat rising in his head as the journalist spoke. He felt he was being played, like there had to be more to the story, but for the life of him, William could not think what other story there could be.

James Wiley suddenly brightened, as if a new angle of argument had just come to him. "You're a literary fellow, now aren't you, William Tidd? I know you are. You read my newspaper. There's this Lowell fellow, a poet from out east. He put it this way:

New occasions teach new duties,
Time makes ancient good uncouth;
They must upward still and onward,
Who would keep abreast of truth.

"I'm thinking this is your poem." The newspaperman nodded, warming enthusiastically at his own argument. "This Indian war breaking on the horizon of your life just now, this is, Bill Tidd, your new occasion, your new duty. Another one of those New England philosophers—your pa was fond of reading him, as I recollect—he put it this way: 'Immortality will come to such as are fit for it; and he who would be a great soul in the future must be a great soul now.'"

James Wiley took William by the shoulders, firmly but with tenderness, like a father ought to. "Bill Tidd, now's your time, time for you to be a great soul."

22

STORM RISING

Summer ended abruptly, not that there had been a great deal of what folks out east or back in Kentucky would call hot summer weather. Precious little of that in Puget Sound country. But at summer's end, the rain got colder, more drenching, and lasted longer, with interminable stretches of gray and drizzle in between.

Just as in the transition from winter to spring, there was a puerile wildness and flouncing unpredictability about autumn weather. It might be comfortable one day, the sunshine glistening off the triple summit of Mount Rainier, and shining golden and russet on the crisp oak leaves and yellow alder leaves rattling above. And then, *wham blam,* it would hit. On gloriously sunny days a body might even be lured into thinking that it will always be this way, the sunshine and warm weather. Who needs a coat and hat, better yet, a tight-woven, cedar-bark cape and head covering? Then, all of a sudden, things turn wild and nasty.

Scowling up at the sky, William hitched his collar up against the breeze and the splashy driblets of rain that had the relentless ability to find their way through his coat and the holes in his felt hat and then to trickle down his neck and back. He wondered about the weather in these parts; wasn't sure if he'd ever get used to it.

As darkness fell, the breeze turned itself into wind, the real kind. Wind tearing at the high branches of Douglas fir, their branches swaying and bending, straining and swirling as the October storm readied itself to tear its way through the forest.

When the Tidd family had first collapsed with their meager belongings and begun the task of wresting some order out of the wilderness, Pa had set to clearing away the trees immediately around the cabin. Pa had always said the big timber was both a blessing and a curse; a blessing as raw material for making a cabin and a barn, but a twofold curse: In a storm, the timber left standing might uproot or snap and fall on your cabin or barn. And a curse for covering the soil, blocking the light, and making for so much work to farm the land in the first place.

There were patches of wide grasslands hereabouts—prairies some called them—but they were low-hanging fruit, snatched up for farmland by the first wave of giddy settlers and by the company. What was left was grueling work. Most of the Americans had to bust their backs felling trees and clearing space for the times when the sun could manage to make its way through the perpetual iron-gray cloud cover and nourish their crops.

High above William's head came an elongated creaking, ominous and slow, like the moaning of a slumbering dragon: two Douglas fir trunks entwined and yawing in the wind, grinding against each other. A tingle trotted down William's neck, and he wiped his brow. He didn't much like thinking about chopping down trees—the instant of hesitation when the chopping was done, the leaning, the accelerating descent, the rush of air like lungs emptying in a scream, the spine-numbing shudder and thud of the downed tree crashing onto the forest floor—especially terrifying were the big ones, the more so when the wind was up.

That last evening, William did his best to make light of the storm to Junebug, pretending it was the trees in the forest playing musical instruments in a wilderness orchestra.

"There's the bass viols," said William. "Do you hear them, Junebug, and there's them big lumbering kettle drums."

Junebug laughed. "Rumbling like thunder. Oh, and that gust sounded like flutes trilling the high notes—*Whoo, whoo!*"

"Flutes and violins, but the violins sound kind of screechy to my ear," said William. "I think they need more practice."

Junebug laughed again. "Maybe they're still just warming up. Yikes! That burst sounded like a large woman singing the really high notes—like opera singing." Junebug hopped on a stool, extended an arm dramatically, threw back her head, and launched a high quavering gush of sound.

"Or the steam signal horn on the *Beaver,*" laughed William. *"Hoot, toot, hoot, toot!"*

They laughed together.

When it was bedtime, Junebug fell asleep without a care, so it seemed, a faint smile on her lips and easy regular breathing. His diversion had worked. For Junebug. William's stomach felt like it was being wrung in the vise-like grip of a Sasquatch. He slept little and ill that night.

Shivering, he pulled the threadbare quilt up tightly about his chin. The wind sounded like a living creature, something wild and terrifying, as it rent its way through the high branches of the firs, low and moaning at first, rising to a screeching that clamped down on William's heart like a beaver trap. He ground his teeth together to keep them from chattering.

Meanwhile, Junebug in the low trundle bed turned and smacked her lips. With a sigh she rolled onto her left side and resumed breathing softly, gently as if nothing were amiss. Junebug was like that. Nothing seemed to trouble her, not this storm hurling itself at the forest and at their tiny cabin, not the bigger storms that had assailed them while coming west—since coming west. Not even Indians and all the talk of war.

For months now, he had been tormented by a recurring dream. Dream? Shucks, he didn't even need to be asleep in bed for this dream to rear its head at him. It was worse with so many noises outside. No way of telling if there were other sounds. Like Indians stalking in the forest, creeping in close, closer. Never hear them in this weather. He'd read a story about a lone child who had somehow survived a night raid, though no one else in the poor kid's family breathed when it was over.

Then his dream would take over. It started innocent enough: the soft hooting of an owl, the nervous whinny of a horse, the low growl of the family dog—then painted savages splintering the door with their tomahawks, whooping, burning, plundering, pillaging, scalping, killing, screams of terror—womenfolk and children hauled off as prisoners, as slaves to be used at the savages' whims.

Clunk! William's heart nearly stopped beating. When he managed to persuade it to start up again, he reassured himself. "It's only a branch." It was a big one—but only a branch torn free by the wind and clunking onto the split shake roof of the cabin. Only that and nothing more. Then the rain began its work on the shakes, dribbling at first and then shying until it sounded like it would come right through into the room, drenching everything. He wondered how Junebug could sleep through all this racket.

He knew he had to tell her. Next morning at breakfast he would do so, tell her what he had done. At the first gray slivers of light visible alongside the shutters of the cabin, William swung his feet over the side of his cot. Scratching Wally's big head, he slipped into his moccasins and grabbed his coat and hat.

Lifting the door to avoid any creaking that might wake Junebug, William stepped outside to survey how much damage the storm had inflicted. It was far from over, by the look of things. The giant fir trees wagged in the stiff breeze like stalks of bunch grass on the prairie. And a crow, riding on the wind overhead, was dipping and bobbing to maintain its place just over the doorway of the cabin. William shuddered. It was as if the black creature was hovering there, waiting for something or someone to die so that it could peck out the eyes and tear at the remainders. Cawing, cawing, cawing ominously, the bird seemed to be taunting him, waiting for him to leave—daring him to leave.

"If I had a gun," said William, eyes narrowed at the crow, "I'd shoot. No more caw-cawing from that foul beak of yours. I'd shoot you dead. If I had a gun."

But he had no gun. When Charles Eaton had inquired about weapons. William had looked at the ground, nudging a clod of horse manure under the boardwalk. "Ain't got no gun," he had said.

"Join up with me and my rangers," said Eaton, "and we'll see what can be done about that."

So William had taken up the pen, hoping Eaton and the others peering over his shoulder couldn't see his hand trembling, and set his name down. There, he was now officially a volunteer in Eaton's Rangers, as the territorial militia was calling itself.

Had he a clearer notion of the perils that lay ahead William might have felt more keenly than ever before his lack of inner courage.

23

MILITIA ON THE MOVE

Two weeks after the storm, October 24, 1855, word arrived from Olympia. Captain Charles Eaton had orders from the governor, a first mission for the territorial militia. Word spread throughout the region like a prairie fire in August. William saddled up Prophet, trying to make it appear—to himself as much as to his sister—that he was just going for a routine ride in the forest, nothing to fear.

Noclas had known. William had told him nearly a week ago, but he was pretty sure the old black man already knew. Telling Junebug had not been easy. She took it easy, though, easier than William. He was satisfied that Noclas would do everything in his power to care for her. But it weren't the things in his power that worried him; it was all the things outside of Noclas's power that gnawed away on William's insides like rats on a chicken carcass. He'd given out his instructions many times before, but couldn't help himself.

"Off to Fort Nisqually at the first hint of trouble," said William. "Don't wait till they're here." He dropped his voice and looked over his shoulder toward where Junebug was ladling food scraps into Wally's dinner bowl. "Don't wait till they've surrounded the cabin. At the first hint that something's not right, hightail it to the fort. They know you'll be bringing her. I made arrangements." It was the best he could do, though it didn't seem like much.

"You know I won't stop at nothing to keep the little thing safe from harm," said Noclas, placing a big hand reassuringly on William's shoulder. "You know I won't. But, come what may, we's in the Lord's hands. And, William, so is you, in the Lord's hands. One way or the other, whether you thinks you like it or not, you's in the Lord's hands."

Junebug packed as much food as she could cram into Prophet's saddlebags: cornmeal, dried apples, dried peas, dried plums, oats for porridge, sweet potatoes, smoked salmon, and a skin of White-Man's-Foot tea, ready to drink on the march, and a sack of dried leaves for making more tea, or for making poultices if someone were to go and get themselves injured or wounded.

Two hours of riding later, William reined in Prophet on the muddy intersection of Third and Main Street in Olympia. "Whoa, big feller." Though it was an iron gray Puget Sound morning with a dank drizzle seeping into the seams of his coat, William's mouth felt like he'd just galloped through a cloud of mosquitoes—with his mouth wide open.

Nineteen men. If his counting wasn't off. Stifling a cough with the back of his hand, William stood up on his stirrups, looking nervously down the street toward the log structure that served as territorial capital; surely there had to be more. He swallowed hard as the realization settled in. Nineteen men. That was it.

Eaton's Rangers, high-sounding title for a tiny band of local farmers commissioned to keep the fierce Yakama tribe from crossing the mountains and joining with the Nisquallys and Puyallups—a combined Indian alliance estimated by some to be as many as several thousand warriors. Against nineteen local farmers—newly formed, poorly trained at best, hugely outnumbered, ill-equipped—calling themselves militia.

"What in the Sam Hill are we doing here?" Prophet's ear twitched as William whispered the words to his horse.

Acting-Governor Mason had mobilized the small band of militia on a mission to hunt down and take into custody the man seen as the principal agitator of the Indian uprising—Chief Leschi of the Nisquallys. Leschi was a big man among the coastal tribes, wealthy in horses and in wives, and he was esteemed by the Yakamas as well, his mother being from that tribe. Few Indians were as highly regarded in the entire territory as Leschi, and there was probably none more able to forge an alliance across such a wide range of tribes. All of which meant more Indians, more horses, more warriors to fight.

"And we're supposed to stop all that," said William to his horse, "with nineteen men." He reined Prophet in a circle, sizing up the other men; two of them were Indians themselves, and if rumor squared with bloodline, one of them was a cousin of Leschi himself. "And you and me with no gun," he murmured bitterly to his mount.

The only thing that kept William from burying his heels in Prophet's flanks and making for home was Charles Eaton himself. Word was that "Packwood Charlie," as some of the locals called him, had come to Puget Sound when there had been few American settlers courageous enough or crazy enough to traverse the continent and settle in the northwest wilderness. He was one of the first. He was tall; strong of limb; rode with confidence and ease; and, unlike the run-of-the-mill frontiersmen, he was self-controlled. Chief among his character qualities, he had the gift of command; he could lead men, and men would follow. Though he could not quantify or measure this quality in the man, nevertheless, William felt it beyond a doubt.

William still remembered the horse race when Eaton gave up his newly won trade musket—to Charlie Salitat.

William looked around, his brow furrowed. Charlie was nowhere to be seen. There were two other Indians among the rangers, but no Charlie. That didn't necessarily mean he had joined up with Leschi, William reassured himself. He spoke English, not just Chinook Jargon, and so the US Army at Fort Steilacoom may have signed Charlie on as a scout or a courier. And there was word of other militia forming in the region; maybe Charlie was part of one of these.

"I'm mighty proud to ride out with you, Bill Tidd." It was James Wiley spurring his mount alongside William. The newspaperman wiped his brow with his handkerchief then corralled his spectacles back up onto his nose with his knuckle, as if in salute.

William looked surprised. "*With* me?" he said. "I had no idea you were enlisting?" Wiley had not seemed the militia type. Fact is, in many respects he didn't fit as a man of the frontier at all.

Wiley smiled and wiped his glasses. "I have every expectation that there will be newsworthy events unfolding in the days ahead, maybe even in the weeks ahead. And brave deeds to be witnessed and reported in the local newspapers—maybe your own heroic deeds, Bill Tidd—here, and out east in the big papers. The whole continent is watching, and I aim to record every significant detail down for the sake of posterity, and for the sake of the news."

They set out from Olympia, women in hoop skirts lining the frontier street, boys and girls and dogs squealing and barking, running along beside their trotting mounts. It was like a parade or a festival. Though none of the men had done anything worthy toward the cause, the townsfolk were, nevertheless, treating the men like heroes. Though William knew deep down that marching out with all his limbs in their place wasn't the same thing as coming home in one piece, yet he felt a surging of entirely undeserved pride at the shouts and well-wishes.

On the edge of town, Charles Eaton, leading his band of new recruits, raised a gloved hand, apparently meaning to halt. But William figured Eaton was just waving his farewells to a family member in the crowd. Others must have reckoned the same. What followed was an awkward moment of disorder that, looking back on it, may have served as a prophetic foreshadowing of coming events. It reminded William of what happens on the Nisqually River in the springtime when the snow pack melts and the water level overflows its banks. Sticks, branches, stumps, whole trees get uprooted and clog up the river. Sometimes the floating debris makes its own dam, and the upstream forest debris plows into the jammed up place, the new debris going cockeyed and splaying out every which way. That's what happened on the edge of town, in front of everybody. Eaton was the logjam and the rest of the rangers were the forest debris tumbling into him and his horse.

Clouds formed on Acting-Governor Mason's brow as he surveyed the disordered band of militia. Stroking his neatly trimmed beard and adjusting a wing of his gold-rimmed spectacles, he cleared his throat and said, "As per your orders, Captain Eaton. Proceed to Muck Creek and invite Leschi and his tyee brother to come unarmed to Olympia. Remind him of what we agreed upon but two days ago. There's no need for war. Tell him to come talk to me as he has agreed—he's two days overdue. Remind him of that. Then invite—or if need be, compel—him to keep his word and come unarmed to Olympia. Now then, be on your way, and Godspeed."

Charles Eaton saluted the Acting-Governor and turned in his saddle to survey his men. What was he thinking? William wondered if it were possible for the grit and integrity of one man to make up for all the lack of it in others. Now that the time had come, the time for Eaton to lead his militia into hostile Indian territory, was he, like William, fearful of how it would end? If he was, Eaton did not betray it in his countenance. He held his hand aloft, and gave the signal to advance. "Move out, men!"

Pressing firmly with his heels on Prophet's flanks, William urged his mount forward. *It begins,* thought William, glancing apprehensively at the men whose future was now entwined irrevocably with his own.

William had fallen in at the rear of the company—not entirely because he felt himself to belong there—it just happened that way. But it gave him a good vantage point on his fellow rangers. Though it appeared that more than half of them were armed—with something that passed for a firearm—few of the men looked like what William thought Indian fighting soldiers ought to look: tough, alert, quick of hand and eye. Eaton was like that, and he'd read about fighters who were like that in books. Few of his fellow rangers appeared anything like that.

There was one. Irish-born bachelor Michael Connell. Word was he had served in the US Army at Fort Steilacoom some years back, but had given up on soldiering and taken to farming, staking a claim on a large chunk of land on a prairie above the river valley east of the Puyallup River, for some time now called Connell Prairie by the locals. Maybe it was Connell's squared shoulders and broad back, but William sensed more than knew for a certainty that this man was different. He was riding out with the small band of rangers not so much as a soldier, a recruit, but as something else. What else, William was not entirely certain. Maybe he was to be a scout or a guide. Farming the uplands, no man would know better the territory into which they headed—and he had been a soldier. Other than Charles Eaton himself, and the two Indians, William had no knowledge of any of the other men being fighting men—himself included.

William's stomach began its midmorning growling as the band neared the Nisqually village along Muck Creek. Maybe the rumbling in his innards was hunger; maybe it was the stench as they drew near the Indian village; maybe it was something else.

The hair on William's neck grew stiff, prickling against the upturned collar of his shirt. It felt like bedbugs clawing for the best position on his spine on a cold night. William had done this before, approached Indian villages, dozens of times. This was different. Rounding a bend in the creek, there it was. But something wasn't right. Half a dozen cedar longhouses, a handful of cattle, a mob of a dozen or more sturdy horses in a corral just south of the village. But it was too quiet.

"Not a living soul," said James McAllister, lieutenant to Eaton. "Blamed inconsiderate of them, I'd say."

"Cows and some fine-looking horseflesh," said Connell. "But no Leschi—no Indians at all, not a squaw, not so much as a papoose."

"How we going to have a proper Injun war," said James McAllister, slapping his thigh in disgust, "if there ain't no Injuns willing to stand and fight?"

"Abandoned," said another. "Look at the plow, standing idle mid-furrow."

"Fixing to plant wheat," said McAllister, "not fixing to fight."

"Smoke still seeping through the cedar planks on the longhouses," said Andrew Laws. "Ain't been long since they done hightailed it."

"They've gone and headed for the hills," agreed McAllister. "Just as I reckoned. This war'll be over before it even has a chance to get itself a good head of steam."

The men had ridden into the common area surrounded by the longhouses. Charles Eaton reined his horse around, and looked at each man in turn. Bringing up the rear, William was on the outside edge of the band of men, closest to the forest that rimmed the village.

"They knew we were coming," said Eaton. He paused, surveying the men deliberately. He continued, measuring each word. "I would very much like to know how they knew we were coming."

William looked at the two Indians, but mostly at the one they called Stahi, Leschi's cousin. Not a flicker; Stahi's face was as unemotional as the chiseled image on a totem pole. The tingling up and down William's spine now felt more like someone was scratching his back with the claw of a hammer. Prophet whinnied. The horse pawed the ground, and his ears twitched.

"What if they ain't gone?" said Andrew Laws, his eyes wide, scanning the dark stand of Douglas fir that encircled the village. He drew his musket, fumbling for a powder cartridge. "W-what if it's a trap?"

24

IF ALIVE

"What if it's a trap?" When Andrew Laws said those words, Captain Charles Eaton seemed to have already anticipated this eventuality. Like a flash, he ordered the men off their horses.

"Take cover!" he shouted. "Follow me!"

The last thing William wanted to do was dismount, leave Prophet. But he followed orders. Hunkered in the longhouse, peering through gaps in the thick cedar planks, all eyes wide, they waited. William's eyes smarted at the smoke. He held his breath in anticipation. Would there be the thundering of hooves—the Nisquallys had no equal in horsemanship—the whooping and war cries, the drums?

But a quarter of an hour passed. William was used to the smell of sweat and hard work, but he realized in those minutes that men in anticipation of danger emit something far stronger than ordinary working sweat. The air in the longhouse grew more dense. The smells of curing deer hide, dried salmon, wet dog hair, cedar bark, alder smoke, and fish oil swirled with a new ingredient—the raw smell of fear.

But as the minutes ticked past, everything outside remained as it had been: cows mooed, horses whinnied, a flock of geese honked as they passed overhead, the wind shied in the fir trees, Muck Creek gurgled mockingly as it flowed toward Puget Sound. Everything stayed as if frozen in an instant of time. No drums, no war whooping. No Indians broke cover and descended on them from the forest.

When it became embarrassingly obvious that they were cowering inside one of Leschi's longhouses for nothing, that there were no Indians about, that it was not a trap, Eaton ordered the men to bring along the best of the abandoned horses, to mount up and fulfill their orders, pursue the Nisqually tribe and apprehend Leschi and their leaders.

"If we do this right, men," said Eaton, "there won't need to be war with the Indians."

For three days the band of rangers searched the Puyallup valley, making their way farther east and toward the upland country, the treacherous foothills leading to the craggy summits and glaciers of the Cascade Mountains. If Leschi had successfully forged an alliance with his relatives, the warlike Yakama tribe, that's where he would be headed. Every tread east brought them closer to a convergence with the hostile Indians.

But as the hours turned into days and still no Indians, not so much as a feather, the raw tingling in William's spine settled into only an occasional flutter of anxiety. A snap of a branch in the forest might set it off. A sudden flurry of starlings bolting from the treetops might set it off. The *whoo-whooing* of an owl call might do it. The *rat-ta-tat-tatting* of a red-bellied sapsucker, or the sharp snapping of a beaver tail might set it off. But still no Indians.

Meanwhile, it was not possible for William to be riding patrol, making camp, cooking and eating, sleeping, standing watch, breaking camp, and scouting for Indians without getting more familiar with the men who had ridden out with Charles Eaton.

William learned that James McAllister and two other men of local standing had enlisted with the understanding that they would be lieutenants, not mere men of the rank and file but officers. James's son George McAllister, perhaps two years younger than William, rode his horse well and seemed excited to be on the march, almost giddy with eagerness. "Pa says we'll be home in a week. He told Ma to be a-watching for us. Once Leschi and the Nisquallys see us on the march, says Pa, they'll stand down without a fight, they will. That there's what Pa says." William tried hunkering deeper into his coat and saddle. So far it looked like he was right about the Indians—not a cedar cape to be seen anywhere—so far. But William had never met someone who could talk so unceasingly as young George McAllister.

Then there was silent Edward Wallace. Edward seemed always to be listening, but rarely spoke a word. If he wanted a fellow to pass him more jerky or a slab of cornbread, he would nod deliberately toward what he needed and extend a hand until someone gave him what he wanted. Edward was a man who lived by the unspoken rule that if a gesture would do, there was no sense in wasting breath on mere words. But there was another distinguishing quality about Edward: he had the largest ears William had ever seen, that is, on a person. Forced to make his assessment of the man without the advantage of having heard him speak more than two words in three days, William somehow felt safer when he rode next to Edward. It may have had a good deal to do with the fact that Edward was armed; he carried a musket and a revolver, and it appeared he knew very much what to do with them.

Then there was cocky Andrew Laws, a young man maybe two years older than William, as near as he could guess. It more than mildly annoyed William that Laws was always carrying on about his gun, extolling its virtues, expounding on its unique qualities, waxing lyrical about its accuracy at ridiculously exaggerated distances. "Two hundred yards ain't nothing to Belinda," so he had named his musket, sometimes stretching it to "Beautiful Belinda." Laws would sit around the fire in the evening, the trade musket cradled on his knees, caressing its stock, running his palm down its barrel, and fingering the trigger like he couldn't wait to pull it. When he'd hear a sound in the forest, he would whip the musket to his shoulder, squint down the long barrel, and go *Pa-kew-pa-kew!* "Another Injun bites the dust," he would say, his lips curled in derision. "With me and Belinda, the world's a better place." Then he'd laugh.

Then there was the Indian Clipwalen, adopted son of the McAllister's, a former slave from up north, one of the Canadian tribes. James McAllister had purchased Clipwalen from the Nisquallys for the price of a young horse, a trade musket, and a bushel of seed corn. James McAllister treated Clipwalen as a son, but his son George was different. Something about George McAllister's studied indifference toward the Indian gave William the distinct impression that the son resented having to share his status with an Indian.

Maybe it was because Clipwalen spoke English so well, maybe it was because the Indian never complained about anything—whatever needed doing, Clipwalen jumped in and did it—for whatever the reason, William liked him, and though this was supposed to be an Indian war, he couldn't figure out any reason not to trust this Indian.

But Stahi, the second Indian, was another matter altogether. To William, Stahi was a mystery. He appeared to understand no English, and spoke only Chinook Jargon, so there was much less ability to communicate with Stahi. The man claimed to be a relative of Leschi, but only by marriage, a cousin by blood to Leschi's third and youngest wife. Stahi took pains to remind his fellow militia men that his cousin was not happy in her marriage to the big tyee, that Leschi was not always kind to his cousin.

Three or four times he had told them this, adding English words in with ease where Chinook Jargon vocabulary was deficient. William wondered how an Indian who spoke no English could do this. Stahi claimed that he had signed on to act as scout and to act as advisor about the strategies of his fellow Indians because he did not like Leschi. "Leschi hit her with fist," he said, chewing the inside of his left cheek as he groped for the Chinook Jargon words to complete his thought. "He drag her by hair. She afraid he hurt her."

Three days had passed and still no Indians. On the morning of October 27, 1855, that was about to change.

"We're running low on everything," said McAllister after breakfast. "Captain, may I suggest we send a few of our boys back to Olympia for supplies—cornmeal, jerky, dried peas, smoked salmon, potatoes, fresh chicken eggs, maybe some thick slabs of good beef. Shucks, we'll be eating pine cones and crow in a day or two if we don't get more grub."

Eaton didn't immediately reply. Three men were at sentinel duty on the perimeter of the camp; Eaton seemed to be taking stock of his men, tallying each, maybe assessing the particular value that each one had as a soldier.

"We're mighty low on men as it is," he said at last. "And we're closer than ever. Indians can't be far from here, not if they're fixing to join up with the Yakamas. This here's where they'll come."

"If they're coming at all," said McAllister. "If we've got to play soldier and chase after ghost Injuns, let's have full bellies doing it, that's what I say."

"It'd be danged foolish to send men back for supplies now," said Michael Connell. "Leave ourselves shorthanded just as we're closing in on them? Danged foolishness."

"All right, all right," said McAllister. "If you fellers are still thinking the Injuns are going to make a stand, I reckon we can hunt and fish to fill the larder."

Eaton nodded, pouring coffee from the kettle into his mug.

Suddenly, bursting into the clearing of their camp, came George McAllister, one of the three on sentinel duty. "Band of Injuns," he said breathing heavily.

"Where?" said Eaton, setting the coffee pot back onto the iron grating over the fire with a clunk.

"Not far. Due east up river," gasped George.

"What were they doing?" asked Eaton, drawing his Colt, spinning the cylinder, levering the loading ram to check the seating of his loads.

"Fishing, near as I could make out," said George.

"Could you identify them?" asked Eaton.

George shrugged. "Just Injuns."

"We need to know more than that," said Eaton. "My orders are to find Leschi, not hunt down just any Indian we come across. You said they were fishing? Leschi's not in a fishing frame of mind at the moment."

"I'll just saddle up and find out," said McAllister, "with your permission."

"I know this stretch of river," said Connell. "It's close to my farm. Count me in."

"I need two more men," said Eaton.

"I go." It was Stahi.

William looked up with a start. The Indian had said the words in English not Chinook Jargon.

"I know Indians," said Stahi—in English.

"All right, then," said Eaton. He hesitated, then added, "I need one more volunteer."

William glanced over at James Wiley; the journalist was scribbling furiously in his notepad. William swallowed hard. Part of him wanted to shout out, "I'll go." Maybe this was his opportunity to be courageous, to change the course of history, to achieve immortality. Maybe he could atone for things and restore some respectability to the family name. Just as he was about to lift his hand, McAllister turned to his adopted son.

"Clipwalen, you willing to come along, son?" he said.

Clipwalen grinned. Without a word he swung into the saddle of his black-on-white Arabian.

"Be careful, James," said Eaton, as the scouting party prepared to leave. "We're shorthanded as it is. I need you back well before dark, and in one piece."

McAllister laughed and saluted. "We'll be back before dark—if alive."

25

FIRST BLOOD

His face contorted in disgust, William chewed pensively, reflecting on how much better Junebug's cornmeal cakes were than the mealy mush that passed for cornbread on the march. Trying hard to swallow, he finally managed with the aid of a big gulp of White-Man's-Foot tea.

"There's a low spot in the road back yonder," said Eaton, pacing in front of the campfire. He checked his revolver again, closed it with a snap, spun the chamber, and returned it to his holster. "It'll never do having a road like this when it comes time to move more men and supplies up the pass." Eaton spun on his heel and paced back in front of the fire, his brow furrowed.

William set his mug down, studying Eaton. Clearly the man was anxious about something.

"Wiley, saddle up," said Eaton abruptly. "Let's see what can be done about that swampy bit back there."

At the same instant, William, not feeling hungry anymore, rose to his feet.

"Bill Tidd, you come along too," added Eaton, swinging his leg over his horse.

Not ten minutes later, Eaton reined in his horse. "Boggy," he said, crossing his arms on his saddle horn and nodding at the stretch of track in front of them. "Far too boggy for moving men and equipment."

"Could fill it with rocks," suggested Wiley. "Plenty of rocks hereabouts."

Eaton nodded absently, staring through the dense forest of hemlock and alder. William followed his gaze. There was an abandoned longhouse in a clearing and an old barn, but the rest was all trees and underbrush. Eaton's eyes were narrow; he was looking in the direction McAllister and Connell and the Indians had headed less than half an hour before.

"They'll be fine, Charles," said the journalist. "You know, there's this story about a couple of fellows who—"

Blam!

"What in tarnation was that?" said Wiley, his yarn suddenly cut short.

Eaton made no reply. There was none needed. The single shot reechoed through the ancient columns of the forest. There was no mistaking it. It had come from up river, the direction McAllister and Connell had taken.

"We'd best go find out," said Eaton.

Just as William pressed his left knee into Prophet's flank, and as he pulled the reins to his right, *Blam!* another shot thundered in the stillness.

And then there was more. *Blam! Blam! Blam!* Ragged volley fire from half a dozen muskets or more.

"God help us," said Eaton. "Our boys are gone." He spurred his horse into a full gallop.

Riding as close as he dared to Eaton, William glanced over his shoulder at Wiley falling farther behind with every stride. In moments, Eaton reined his horse in back at the camp. Hearing the shots, the men were running around in all directions, shouting and spooking their horses. It reminded William of chickens in a barnyard when a fox was circling the perimeter.

"Boys!" shouted Eaton above the din. "Saddle up your horses, get your baggage in readiness, and above all things—keep cool!"

Then more to himself than to William, Eaton murmured, "We need a place to make our stand."

William hesitated. "The longhouse yonder, Sir," he said. "Might be better than here in the open?"

Eaton looked steadily at William and nodded approvingly. Moments later they arrived at the abandoned longhouse. Eaton ordered half of his men to set up a picket line for the horses, and the other half to assess and fortify the longhouse.

William followed Edward Wallace into the longhouse. Silent as Edward was, he was an efficient man. There were eight or ten large baskets lining a cedar bench on the north side of the interior of the longhouse. Edward lifted the lid of first one basket and then another, nodding to William as he did so.

"Sir, it's well provisioned," reported William to Eaton. "Oats, peas, wheat, and dried salmon berries."

Eaton ordered Wallace to fill a cask with fresh water from the stream. "George, Andrew, William, tear down that shack of a barn," he ordered next.

"What good is tearing down this barn doing?" said Andrew, kicking at the rotting door. "We could be shooting Injuns, and Eaton tells us to tear down an old barn?"

William felt the heat rise on his cheeks. He and George tied a rope to the center post of the barn, and, taking a wrap around a fencepost, they yanked with all their might, Andrew holding his musket and looking on with a scowl. Creaking, the roof timbers and shakes collapsed in splinters. The walls, now unsupported, sagged, teetered for an instant, and with a groan, fell flat.

"It was too close," said William, wiping his brow. "It could have provided cover for the Indians." He nodded toward the open field. "Now they have to shoot from them trees yonder, or cross the clearing in full view of our guns."

Andrew's scowl turned into a grin. He caressed the stock of his musket. "Me and Belinda, we'll be ready for 'em."

When Eaton was satisfied that, should they be attacked, everything was in order, he climbed onto a fencepost and peered across the clearing down the road.

"It's an Injun!" shouted Andrew Laws, sighting eagerly down the barrel of his musket.

"It's Clipwalen!" shouted Eaton. "Do not shoot!"

"Dang!" said Andrew, lowering his gun.

Clipwalen was riding hard, his eyes wide and his features pale. And he carried two muskets across his saddle.

"What news?" said Eaton as the Indian reined his horse to a halt and dismounted.

"James McAllister," he looked at George, "he's dead."

After an instant of stunned silence, there were murmurs of condolences intended to make their way to George.

"And Connell and Stahi?" asked Eaton.

"They shot Michael Connell," said Clipwalen. William handed him his skin of tea. The Indian took a long drink and continued. "Indian shoot from inside hollow stump. Michael shot bad. Much blood. But not killed. He turn horse and go on road. I shout for him to go in woods, safer in woods. He ride on down road, but like this." Clipwalen demonstrated, slumping over, holding his side, his tongue lolling from his mouth. "He leave trail of blood. Much blood."

"And Stahi?" said Eaton.

Clipwalen frowned. "He go with Indians."

"They took Stahi prisoner?" asked James Wiley, his pen poised and notebook at the ready.

Clipwalen shook his head violently. "No! He *go* with Indians."

"Double-crossing scoundrel," growled Wiley.

There was little more to learn from Clipwalen.

"It'll be full dark within the hour," said Eaton. "We must ready ourselves for attack."

26

COMMENCE FIRING!

It was almost full dark.

Inside the longhouse, in the damp and cold, William and what remained of Eaton's Rangers waited. How many Indians were there? William wondered. There were only sixteen rangers left, one of them a journalist ill-suited to fighting Indians, and another a young man who not only did not have a weapon but had never shot one.

Eaton ordered Clipwalen to lend McAllister's musket to William, the only man without his own. William held it awkwardly in his arms.

"I reckon you don't know how to shoot," taunted Andrew Laws with a grin.

William was about to retort, "Doesn't everybody know how to shoot?" when Edward Wallace appeared at his side, clasped a big hand around his arm, and guided him through the longhouse doorway, into the evening light.

"Bill Tidd, you'll have no better teacher," said Eaton, nodding approvingly at Edward Wallace as they passed.

Though William had only heard Edward say a handful of words in the last three days, that was about to end.

Though taciturn by nature, when demonstrating the fine points of firing a musket Edward became positively loquacious. Accompanied at first mostly by grunts and nods, Edward measured out gunpowder from the dead man's flask. "Horn's better for gunpowder," said Edward, scowling at the engraved powder flask; it was the most words William had heard the man say at one time.

"Fancy enough looking, but scrape it against a rock," continued Edward, "and it'll make a hole, moisture'll get in and ruin the powder—or the friction'll ignite it." He paused, letting the implication of his words set firm in William's imagination.

"But that's nothing compared to what happens if there's a spark left in the barrel when you're a-measuring powder for another shot from a fancy metal flask like this one," again he paused for dramatic effect. "Spark meets a fancy metal powder flask like this one—*Ka-plooie!* She makes like a bomb and blows your hand off—or your head."

William swallowed hard. He'd heard this sort of thing about muskets and gunpowder before. Probably the reason he had been so reluctant to learn shooting one.

After methodically demonstrating how to use the ramrod to set a musket ball snug in the barrel ready for firing, Edward held the musket in both hands, the firing mechanism facing William. He then explained in plain language how it worked. Ratcheting back the hammer with his thumb, he said, "Put the percussion cap just here, over the nipple, just there." Patiently, Edward demonstrated twice over, then handed the weapon to William. "Now you do it, but mind you, don't ever go off half-cocked."

When William demonstrated that he understood by going through each of the steps on his own, Edward patted his shoulder approvingly. "Now for shooting it," he said. "Only wish you could have a wee bit more practice, but we'll make do with play acting the shooting part."

Edward showed William how to steady the heavy barrel

on the edge of a stump, or in the crook of a tree branch. "Some fellers thinks it's cheating doing that, but I reckon the thing that matters is accuracy, hitting what you're aiming at. That there's what matters with shooting. Ain't no better way to hit what you're needing to hit than keeping the barrel steady as a rock." Then, pinching his left eye tight shut and sighting down the barrel with the other, he demonstrated how to breathe. "Some fellers don't breathe, but that ain't good, not if you aim to shoot what you're aiming at. Let your air out slow and even like, then squeeze the trigger. Breathe and squeeze."

"Leave off shooting school for now." It was a commanding whisper, Eaton's voice from inside the longhouse. "There's something moving out there. Take cover."

Edward looked levelly at William and smiled. "You'll do fine," he said. "Now let's skedaddle."

Seconds later, peering through a crack in the cedar planking of the longhouse, William saw it too. Movement in the dusk. He narrowed his eyes. What he saw was terrifying. There were three of them—at first. Shafts of moonlight broke through the clouds. He thought he could make out more than three. They had painted their naked skin bright red, gleaming red like smeared blood, all over their faces, chests, arms and legs. Two of them wore a leather half-trouser, the other looked stark-staring naked—except for the paint. Moonlight glimmered off their shiny raven-black hair.

His voice a tense whisper, just loud enough to be heard by all sixteen men, Eaton said, "Do not fire your weapon until I give the order. Is that understood? We let the Indians shoot first."

Suspended in the musty air inside the longhouse was an eerie silence as if no one dared to breathe. In that stillness, to his immediate left, William heard a sound, a sound he now understood, the slow cocking of the hammer of a musket. It was full dark inside the longhouse, but he was sure it was Andrew Laws, readying Belinda's firing mechanism.

"We ain't supposed to shoot," whispered William. Edward Wallace at William's immediate right, returning to his taciturn self, grunted approvingly.

"Hush your mouth, boy," said Andrew. "One hasty lesson in musket firing and the boy thinks he knows all. I reckon me and Belinda knows better when it's time to shoot and when it ain't."

William could tell from the squinty tone of Andrew's voice that he was sighting down the barrel of his musket—and enjoying it.

"Besides," continued Andrew, "you ain't supposed to be talking nuther."

Peering into the ghostly dusk, William could make out the Indians, in full view but crouching low and advancing slowly toward their position in the longhouse. "But Captain Eaton said—" William's words were cut off by the thundering of Andrew Laws' musket.

Blam!

Choking blue smoke from the spent gunpowder caught in William's throat and made his eyes smart. Though the cloud of smoke clogged the air in the longhouse, the field of view across the clearing at the Indians' position was largely unobscured by the smoke. So he could see him: one painted Indian sprawled face down in the bunch grass. The Indian's body convulsed, like it wanted to get away, then it lay still. At the same instant, the other two Indians, leaping for cover into the brush, disappeared.

"What part of my order, 'Don't shoot 'till the Indians shoot first,' did you not understand, Andrew Laws?" It was Charles Eaton's voice the length of a man away on William's right.

"But I got 'im!" cried Andrew, his voice jubilant. "Clean through the head, I got me a naked Injun!"

"Well, don't go and break your arm patting yourself on the back," said James Wiley. "You've gone and fueled the rage of all the rest of them."

Seconds later, as if in fulfillment of the journalist's words, a dozen or more muskets thundered in a ragged volley, lead bullets splintering into the cedar plank walls of the longhouse.

"Choose your Injun." Captain Eaton's voice came through the din as steady as if he were telling us to feed the horses or stir the beans. "And make every shot count. Commence firing!"

Pitch dark as it was inside the longhouse, William felt that something wasn't right. After that initial volley, the man next to him seemed to be leaning hard against him. There was no distinguishable sound coming from the man, but then that was usual from the silent Wallace. Then William felt something warm and wet on his shoulder and sleeve.

"Edward! Are you all right?" he called.

His companion gripped William's arm tight and clung onto him.

"You been hit?" cried William. "Edward's been hit!" he called out to no one in particular. "Talk to me, Edward! Confound it, this ain't the time for silence. I can't see a thing in the dark. You've got to tell me where you've been hit." William's voice was drowned out by the thunder of musket fire on either side of him. It was deafening, and William felt like his eardrums would burst with the eruption. Edward sagged more heavily onto him.

Propping his borrowed musket against the cedar planks, William felt for Edward's armpits, and dragged the man away from the wall. Grunting with effort, William was relieved to feel Edward's heart beating, though weakly, and the wounded man moaned as William laid him down, propping his head up on a saddle.

"Can you show me where you've been hit?" William was forced to shout above the musket fire. Edward groped for William's hand and then held it up to the left side of his head. His hand sticky with warm blood, William called out in alarm and jerked his hand away. He was no nurse, and he had a fleeting thought of Sister Marguerite volunteering to tend the wounded. He wished she were here at the moment. The only thing William could think to do was to try and stop the bleeding. Blood belonged inside the body, not out. Unwinding a scarf Junebug had made him, he wrapped it tightly around Edward's head.

"I wish I could do more for you," he said. "But I can't see a blamed thing. You rest easy till I can get some light."

"No light!" cried Eaton. "Do what you can for him, Bill Tidd, but no light. We'll be fish in a barrel if the Indians see light coming through the slits in the planking. Leave off and start shooting!"

William grabbed up his loaded musket and steadied it on the cedar planking. Blinking back the tears clouding his vision from the smoke, he sighted carefully down the barrel.

"Aim small." Edward's pinched voice came from the darkness behind William. He coughed. "Breathe out, and squeeze the trigger."

Blam!

27

EXPRESS RIDER

It was the longest night William could remember. He thought it would never end. And he feared that when it did end, it would not end well.

The Indians seemed to have no shortage of powder, muskets firing, eruptions of flame and smoke in the blackness for an instant giving away their positions. Now only fifteen men returned fire. Reloading in the pitch darkness, William waited for the next volley from the Indians. He chose a spot in the dark. "Breathe and squeeze," as Edward had taught him. William pulled the trigger. *Blam!*

Every man, hoping they were hitting Indians. Hoping their enemy was not reinforced in the night by dozens more, maybe hundreds, hoping beyond hope that they would survive the night, that the Indians would weary of the battle and disappear in the forest, begging it all to end, hoping when it did—they would yet be alive.

Fewer bursts of flame. A diminishing pattering of light-load musket fire. A hint of pre-dawn grayness. Silence.

William had never felt like this before: exhausted from the long night, his nerves taut and frayed like the strings of a fiddle over-tightened and set on a bench too close to the fire. He wanted to curl up and escape into the oblivion of a dreamless sleep. But he knew he could not sleep. He wondered if he would ever be able to sleep again, to rest.

"They must be gone," said Eaton. Their captain's voice was calm and steady, a studied self-control, as if the calm and steadiness had come with great effort.

"It could be a trap." It was the journalist's voice, raspy and deeper than William had remembered it. William wondered what his voice would sound like. Maybe they were all changed by that night, in more than just their voices.

"Permission, Sir, to ride ahead home to Ma and my sisters?" It sounded like young George McAllister, but there was a halting flatness in his tone, as if he were forming his words one hard wooden block letter at a time. "I was thinking they'd be wanting the news." He sounded tired, as if sleep deprivation, the long night battle, the death of his father, as if all of it had drained the loquacious energy out of him.

Eaton gave the young man an appraising look, then glanced around the circle of grim faces before answering. William had a hunch Eaton was tallying up his losses and weighing out the cost of reducing his force by yet another man.

"Go on, then," said Eaton. "Give my sincerest condolences to your mother and family. And, George, you watch your back, now, you hear me?"

Fifteen men, that is, if they counted Edward Wallace, who was alive, but with his head wrapped in an old shirt, blood seeping through where his right ear had been. Of men capable of putting up any kind of fight, they were down now to a mere fourteen men.

"We must make ready," said Eaton when George was gone. "It's as certain as winter coming on, the Indians ain't finished with us yet. They'll be back."

"I for one don't much care for the odds," said James Wiley under his breath.

"If only we had fresh supplies," said Lieutenant Van Ogle, "more ammunition, and a few more men wouldn't hurt."

"There's more men nearby," said Eaton with more confidence than made sense to William. "About the same day we left Olympia," continued Eaton, "Major Rains at Fort Vancouver ordered Captain Maloney and forty odd Steilacoom men, soldiers, well-equipped and well-trained, to meet up with Major Haller with more than eighty soldiers and a company of volunteers under the command of Captain Gilmore Hays readying themselves to do battle with the Yakamas."

"What's the Yakamas gone and done this time?" asked Van Ogle.

"Killed some settlers working the Colville mines," said Eaton. "Cold-blooded murder it were."

"We done paid 'em back for it last night!" said Andrew Laws.

"If I may point out, however," said Wiley, "Colville's more than a hundred miles from here. These weren't the same Indians who killed the miners in Colville, different tribe, even."

"Don't see as how that makes no never mind," said Laws. "Injuns is Injuns."

"I do hope that danged double-crossing Injun Stahi," said Van Ogle "was one of the ones we done killed last night."

"Amen to that," several of the men agreed.

William swallowed hard. Though he'd managed to discharge dead McAllister's musket several rounds during the battle, black night that it'd been, he had no certain knowledge if he'd hit anything, let alone killed anybody.

"I reckon I killed at least a half dozen my own self," said Laws, "probably a blamed sight more'n that."

Eaton cut him off. "There's no way of knowing. Indians drag off their dead—they always do. So there ain't no telling for sure how many we've killed. So there's no sense in wasting time speculating on it."

Andrew Laws fell into a sulky silence.

Eaton stroked his moustache, surveying what was left of his rangers. "We must meet up with Major Haller and Captains Hays and Maloney. Any one of them would do. And the sooner the better."

"There's no other way over the mountains than this one," said Wiley, nodding at the single track Military Road on which they had been traveling.

"Naches Trail's the only way," agreed Eaton.

"So they have to be nearby," said Wiley.

"And there's Lieutenant Slaughter," continued Eaton, "and his company dispatched from Fort Steilacoom and on patrol somewhere nearby on the White River. We're more likely to meet Slaughter sooner than the rest."

"Well, then help's on its way," said Wiley.

Wiley the journalist must have missed the double meaning in Eaton's words, but William didn't. Being more likely to meet with slaughter did not sound encouraging to William. Looking down at it his hands, and to stop them from trembling, he interlocked his fingers together until his knuckles were white.

Lieutenant Slaughter. William knew that name; hear it once, who wouldn't remember it. Slaughter, the considerate young officer from Fort Steilacoom who had bought shingles from him last winter, paid for in flimsy paper army script.

"Ain't none of 'em any help," said Van Ogle, "if we don't know where they are."

"Slaughter, and Maloney," said Eaton, pacing in a circle around the small fire laid in the longhouse. "They can't be far away. We've got to get word to them, for our security as well as theirs. They need to know it's official: we're in a war zone. They could be a quarter of a mile from here; they could be forty miles from here, but I have got to find them."

Eaton halted. "I need one good man." He looked over the haggard faces of his men, and continued, "A reliable man, one who can ride well, better than average. A man who is, at one and the same time, lucky enough to meet up with one or more of the other troops that are in these woods—and *not* meet up with the hostile Indians lurking hereabouts. We need reinforcements bad. And medical care for our wounded." He said the last with a nod toward Edward Wallace, his voice trailing off. He resumed his pacing.

"But, Sir," said Van Ogle. "There's Injuns lying in wait behind every stump, you can bet your bottom dollar on it. Sheesh! Sending one of us out there alone—it's like saying, 'Shoot me! Shoot me!' Danged craziness. I ain't doing it."

"That kind of talk," said the journalist, hiking his glasses up on his nose with more violence than was usual, "sounds frightfully near to cowardice."

"Fair enough. The man who volunteers," said Eaton, "needs to understand the risks. For my express rider, I am, indeed, asking for a man of unusual courage."

William Tidd had never considered himself a man of courage, leastwise, one of unusual courage. Nevertheless, as if watching a drama unfolding from a gallery high above a stage, he saw himself rise from where he had been poking aimlessly at the fire. And then, though part of him desperately wanted to stop it, he heard himself speaking.

"Me and Prophet," he was saying, "we'll do it, Sir."

28

INDIAN MASSACRE

His heart pounded so hard against his ribcage William was afraid he would give himself away, forget the thudding of Prophet's hooves on the rocky mud of the Naches Trail. Maybe it was lack of sleep, maybe it was the ringing in his ears from the long night of musket fire, maybe it was the aftermath of his first taste of real combat; whatever the cause, around every bend, he felt like he was hearing things.

William *was* hearing things. There are real sounds in a sub-alpine forest in the Cascade Mountains: the groaning of cedar branches rubbing against each other; the rustling of slide maple leaves, brittle with the season, yet clinging to their boughs; the wind moaning out a dirge in the high tops of Douglas fir trees; the scolding of a chipmunk; the barking of coyotes; the spine-tingling howl of a lone wolf echoing off the stony foothills. Several times he abruptly reined in his horse, and halted stalk still, not daring to breathe, craning his neck, his ears accosting every sound.

Along with the cold rain dripping relentlessly through the hole in the crown of William's felt hat, the icy fingers of fear clutching at his insides made the hair on the back of his neck stand upright at tremulous attention. An involuntary shiver seemed to convulse through every nerve in his body. How much of it was caused by wet cold and how much by raw fear William had no way of discerning.

Amidst the pattering of rain on the late-autumn leaves and evergreen boughs of the forest, a great horned owl hooted, the wind prolonging its mournful call, borne up on the rain-soaked boughs of the forest. William shivered again.

This was almost worse than the terrors of the nighttime battle he had just survived. Alone in hostile territory, known to be teeming with painted savages on the warpath, try as he might, no amount of reasoning with himself could allay his premonitions. He felt certain he was being followed. Then again, the forest sounds, and the gurgling of the White River, made it impossible to be certain about much of any sounds.

"Prophet," whispered William. Prophet's left ear twitched and turned toward his voice. "Noclas named you Prophet for a reason. I'm counting on him being right about you, about you knowing things ahead of time. I'd be much obliged if you'd let me know it if you hear something, something I ought to know about ahead of time."

As William neared the west bank of the final bend in the river, the wilderness on either side of the trail gave way to cultivation, a settler's holding. And it appeared to be a prime holding, generously watered by the White River, rich, fertile, and picturesque. Neat rows of cedar-rail fencing enclosed a rolling green pasture with several head of brown and white cattle giving their full attention to the bunch grass. Alongside the pasture was a large cedar-plank enclosure; by all the grunts and snuffling, and by the stench, a pen apparently confining several hogs.

Clearly, whoever the homesteader was, he had been busy. There were dozens of neat rows of fruit trees, a good deal more than a thousand apple, pear, and hazelnut trees, by

William's reckoning, all dropping their leaves, their branches looking like rigid arms attempting to hold back the bone-chilling cold of a subalpine winter hovering around the corner. William's mind flashed back to his holding, and he felt a twinge of jealousy at the prosperity on display before him. Then he smelled it, sharp, hot, and pinching.

Smoke. Not the pleasant mouth-watering smoke of the kitchen and the cooking fire, Junebug's cornbread, or the smoke when Noclas was curing salmon or bacon. Not that kind of smoke. This was the charred, choking blackness of conflagration. Nausea convulsed his insides, and he thought he was about to be sick, though he had little to spew up. When he'd last eaten a meal he could not remember.

He slowed Prophet to a walk. Rounding a low hillside, he saw it. Whoever this family was, or had been, their log cabin, their home, was no more. There were no more flames; though the stench of smoke was strong in the air, there were only exhausted little columns of blackness rising from the charred flattened remains of the home, puffs of smoke caught up heavenward that dissipated into nothingness in the breeze.

William halted Prophet and dismounted. While settlers knew how to build sturdy log cabins, Indians knew how to build fires that could reduce those cabins to blackened rubble. Apparently they had piled up bedding and clothing, anything prone to burning, and then doused it with lantern oil and lard, and set it to flames. Dread in his heart, hoping beyond hope that the inhabitants had escaped before the fire was set, William cast his eyes over the rubble. To his immediate relief, there was no obvious shape that looked like it had once been a living human being.

Then he heard it. Barely audible above the hissing and shying of the breeze, from the yard in front of the cabin, he heard a faint cry. A woman's voice.

Dread pressing in on him, William followed the sound. Partially concealed beneath a buckboard wagon lay a woman. He froze, only with great effort resisting the impulse to turn tail and run as fast and as far from the grim scene before him as he could. She was younger than his mother had been—when it had happened. The woman's eyes locked on his, pleading, begging him.

In spite of his fears, William dropped to his knees beside her. By the drag marks in the dirt and from the blood, it looked like she had crawled as far underneath the wagon as she could manage.

"Where are you hurt?" said William. He heard his own voice but scarcely recognized it. There was so much blood, he did not know where to begin, what to do to help her.

"My babies." The words sounded hollow, a hopeless groan coming from the forsaken outer rim of despair.

From the appearance of her wounds, the Indians had used tomahawks, maybe knives and a rifle butt or two, and there was a bullet hole in her right shoulder. How she remained alive, William could not understand.

"Did the Indians do this?" He knew it was a silly question. "Which Indians did this to you?"

Her eyes were wide and staring, as if she were seeing them up close and terrifying all over again.

"Where are your children?" he asked. "I will find them, and help them—if I can."

"Thomas's," she said faintly.

"Is Thomas your son?"

She managed a movement of her head that William took to mean he had not understood her.

"Thomas's? Who are the Thomas's? Your neighbors?"

With a slight nod of her head, the woman said again, "Thomas's."

"How far?"

A tear made a path through the soot on her cheek. "Too far." Her voice was so faint that William had to bend over her and place his ear near her lips. She took hold of his coat.

"I'm dying," she said. Her hand trembled, and William could feel the tremor through his own body. "My babies," she said again.

"I will do everything in my power to find and care for your children." His mind flashing back to his own log cabin. He had tried to say the words with confidence, but he felt a rising panic in his own innards. What would become of Junebug if Indians were to set upon the Tidd cabin? Noclas would do everything in his power, William was certain of that. But what if it wasn't enough?

"My babies," the woman's voice brought him back to the immediate crisis. William wanted to reassure the dying mother, but he felt certain it was hopeless. How could her children have survived such a brutal attack?

"Pray," said the mother. Her eyes, only inches from William's, were wide and pleading. "Pray." Her grip on his coat collar seemed stronger than it should for a woman in her condition. Her trembling increased. William wanted to tear himself from the convulsing grasp of her bloodstained fingers, anything to stop it.

William swallowed hard. Pray? He remembered what Emerson had written about praying, "Men's prayers are a disease of the will." He felt that this would not be the time to share the transcendentalist's wisdom on praying with the dying woman.

"Pray!" She said it as if her life depended on praying, on William's praying.

"I pray."

William had been so engrossed in the dying woman gripping his coat, he had not heard anyone approaching. His heart felt like a drum circle in a longhouse pounding out the death wail. And he braced himself for a blow to the head from a tomahawk.

"I pray." The voice said again, an Indian voice, but a familiar one.

Though the trembling hand of the woman on his collar was becoming weaker, William felt it was not right to tear himself from her, not when she was dying. He craned his neck sideways toward the voice.

"Charlie Salitat?" cried William.

What was Charlie Salitat doing here, at the site of an Indian massacre, where Indians had burned down the home of settlers, where they had likely killed this woman's husband, her children in all likelihood, too, and she about to breathe her last from wounds they had inflicted?

"Charlie Salitat!" cried William again, his teeth clenched together. "What are *you* doing here?"

29

FRIEND OR FOE

"Woman dying," said Charlie.

"I see that," said William curtly. He stared hard at Charlie. What was he doing here, in hostile territory, close at hand after a bloody massacre of settlers? Too close at hand, it seemed to William.

"Noclas, he teach me to pray," said Charlie.

Prying her fingers from his lapels, William rose and stepped aside. As Charlie propped his trade musket up against the buckboard and knelt beside her, the woman's eyes grew wide with terror and her lips trembled.

"You're scaring her," said William. "You forget yourself, Charlie, you look like an Indian. You *are* an Indian."

Charlie ignored him, took the woman's hand in his own, and bowed his head. Then he prayed.

Sure enough, though William had never heard Charlie do it, they were words like what he reckoned Noclas would be mumbling over a dying woman, so it seemed to William. Words about Jesus and mercy, and forgiveness of trespasses, and walking through the valley of the shadow of death but not fearing any evil while doing it, more about Jesus, the cross, some nonsense about the resurrection, and a good bit about life eternal and the joys of heaven. Scowling deeply, William drew farther off so he wouldn't have to hear the rest.

But not so far off that he couldn't see the dying woman's reaction to Charlie's praying. Though she had been agitated with pain and with fear when he first commenced praying over her, the woman now was calm, her eyes locked on Charlie's lips as he prayed, her lips moving along with his. Then her eyelids closed. There was a clattering sound in her throat, like when a medicine man shakes his gourd rattle over the sick. Then a deflating sigh. And she was gone.

Charlie remained still for a moment. After closing her eyelids and folding her hands together on her chest, he rose from his knees. "More settlers like her," he said, eyes fixed on the dead woman.

"What do you mean?" asked William. "Indians attacked other settlers in the area and killed them off too? Or do you mean more settlers will be attacked in the future? Which is it?"

"It both," said Charlie, his voice low, almost reverent, like how folks talk at a funeral.

"Well, it's no good just standing around here," said William, doing his best to keep his voice steady, matter-of-fact sounding. "We must find her children. I promised her, before you came along, I'd do what I could for them."

"One of her babies, name of Johnny," said Charlie, "Johnny King, he only seven."

"How on earth do you know that?" asked William. If there was ever an Indian for surprises, it was Charlie. "Hopefully he's alive and his older siblings are watching out for him."

"He oldest," said Charlie.

William's heart sank. How a seven-year-old could have survived an Indian attack was beyond him. But two more still younger than seven?

"Sister only four, and baby brother, two years," said Charlie, his voice inflected with sympathy.

"If they survived this," said William glancing over the charred remains of the cabin and their dead mother, "and another band of Indians doesn't finish them off, there's no hope; the coyotes and wolves'll get 'em for sure."

"They safe," said Charlie. "Safe, for now."

William opened his mouth to speak, then snapped it closed. Charlie knew far too much about what was going on around here.

"Johnny King and sister and brother safe with Indian," said Charlie.

"With an Indian?" said William. "Sounds like leaving the fox in charge of the henhouse to me. They're gone for sure then."

"Friendly Indian," said Charlie. "My friend, Tyee Pialse. White folks call him Nelson. Her babies with Nelson, and Tom Vollochet, and Dave. These friendly Indians, my friends. Dead woman's babies, they safe."

"How on earth do you know all this?" said William, looking narrowly at Charlie's red-cedar features, searching for a twitch that might lead to a clue.

Charlie ignored the question. "Why you here?"

William shrugged. He'd been asking himself the same question a hundred times in the last few days. "Captain Eaton, I'm one of his rangers, in the territorial militia." It sounded so much more glamorous saying it than being it. "Acting-Governor Mason commissioned us to find Leschi—say, you haven't seen Leschi about, have you?"

"Leschi not here," said Charlie. "He far from here. What happened next?"

"Just before dark, we was set upon by Indians—hostile ones—a dozen or more miles southwest of here. It were a long night. We lost two men, McAllister and Connell shot and killed, couple others wounded, but not hurt bad though. One of our friendly Indians up and turned coat, brother-in-law of Leschi, a bad-apple traitor by the name of Stahi."

Charlie lifted a hand; he stared hard at William, motionless as if he had been chiseled out of a cedar log.

"How many Indians?" he demanded.

"Shucks, Charlie, it was dark," said William. "There's no way to be sure. But there must have been two or three times as many as we had—thirty maybe. I don't know."

Charlie demanded minute details about these Indians: how they'd been dressed, how they'd been painted, what their hair looked like, how well armed they'd been, how many Indians had been killed, and which direction they were headed when the fighting ended.

"Not Leschi," said Charlie. "He not fight that way. American Army soldiers leave here and go over mountains. They think canoe Indian no fight, only fierce Yakama horse Indian fight."

"Well, these fellers sure did fight," said William. "They fought right here. No need for going over the mountains for fighting. They clean blew the ear off Edward Wallace, poor feller. Looks like he'll survive, though he'll be a bit funny looking with only one ear for the rest of his days."

"What you do now?" asked Charlie.

"I'm supposed to be express rider," said William, "sent by Eaton to find Captain Maloney or Hays, or Lieutenant Slaughter—any white man in arms'll do." William hesitated. "Say, Charlie, you seem to know everything that's going on in these parts. You ain't seen any of these fellers about, have you?"

Charlie nodded, pointing east on the Naches Trail. "Maloney with soldiers near mountain pass."

"How far?" said William, grabbing up Prophet's reins.

"You swift rider," said Charlie. "You swift like Paul Revere."

William managed a faint smile; "fast rider" would have sufficed, but Charlie sometimes liked trying on new words he had heard, and he had to be the only Indian William had ever met who knew about American history and Paul

Revere. The Indian continued. "For you, two hours hard riding to Naches Pass—if nothing go wrong."

William mounted. "And you, what will you do?"

Charlie, engrossed in checking his horse's hooves, made no reply.

Suddenly, a thought occurred to William that made him almost shout out for joy. "Hey, why not come along with me?"

Charlie allowed a faint smile to come across his features. And for an instant William thought he might be the old Charlie Salitat, full of laughter and pranks—and that he actually might join up with him now.

"I cannot come with you," said Charlie, flatly.

"And just why would that be?"

"Duty," said Charlie. "I have duty. To stop this, there is big thing Charlie must do."

With that, Charlie Salitat vaulted onto his horse's back, and without a backward look, reined his horse south toward the Puyallup River valley.

"Wait!" called William after him. "What big thing?" But it was too late, Charlie was gone.

30

ENCOUNTER

It wasn't the time for stealth. William spurred Prophet forward at a reckless gallop, careless of the thundering noise horse and rider were making on the trail. Trusting to raw speed, his fears goading him forward, he was determined to meet up with Captain Maloney's company before coming face to face with more Indians. Speed was his savior, speed and a double portion of good luck.

All went well—at first. But he'd ridden scarcely an hour when Prophet broke ranks with galloping and began acting up. Snorting and shaking his head violently, the big horse tried to ride into the dense underbrush on the forest floor on the high side of the Naches Trail.

"What do you think you're doing!" yelled William, reining in the animal. Prophet strained toward the forest cover, his ears alert and twitching. "Go on, then. Do whatever you want," said William, releasing tension on the reins. "I'm just along for the ride."

With a snort, Prophet bolted off the trail and into the forest. From behind the thick boughs of a hemlock, William sat, straining to hear what his horse had already sensed.

Then he heard it. The sound of approaching horses, five or six. Seconds later, through the forest cover, he saw them approaching, five men riding hard. They were not Indians. William began breathing again. Without any command from William, Prophet lunged back onto the mud and gravel of the road—in full view of the approaching riders. William's heart leapt into his throat.

"Whoa!" cried the man leading the pack, signaling to halt with a gloved hand. Amidst stomping hooves, the five men reined in their mounts.

"And precisely who might you be?" barked one of the men.

It was more of an English sounding voice than an American one, and William recognized it: the man who called himself Dr. Matthew P. Burns.

"Speak up, boy," said another, firmly though not unkindly. "There's a war on. Give us your name and what your business is in these parts. Do it now."

"He don't look Injun," said another. "But you can't always tell till after dark when there's throats being cut."

"Tidd's my name," stammered William. "William Tidd, express rider under orders from Captain Charles Eaton, territorial militia. I'm to report to Captain Maloney and request reinforcements."

After an awkward instant of silence, several of the men glancing knowingly at each other, the man closest to William yanked off a riding glove and extended his hand. "Joseph Miles is my name." William reached over and shook the man's hand. Miles was taller than the others, broader at the shoulders. He seemed to be in charge, though it was not entirely clear. "Tidd, you said? Bill Tidd?" said Miles. "Well, we ain't Captain Maloney, but we're riding express for Maloney. The good Irish captain's back thataway."

"I'm Abraham Benton Moses," said the man next to Miles. "What's Eaton needing reinforcements for? Sounds like trouble."

"Bradley's my name, Andrew." The man touched his thumb and index finger to the brim of his hat. "Stumbled onto some coastal Injuns, did you? Probably just gived you a good fright. They's harmless."

"George Bright's my name," said another, nodding his acknowledgment of William with something between a salute and a wave.

Chin aloft, Dr. Burns looked William over slowly. Scowling, he placed a gloved hand on his hip and turned his back. "Gentlemen, if I may make so bold as to remind you, we have a commission to fulfill. One that does not include chit-chatting with every straggler we encounter on the trail whilst fulfilling it."

Ignoring Burns, Miles asked, "Say, Bill Tidd, when did you last eat and sleep?"

The question caught William off his guard. "I really could not say, Sir. There's not been much time for eating and sleeping."

"Just what happened?" asked Miles. "Give us the report you was bringing to Captain Maloney."

William told them of their mission to invite Leschi back to Olympia, compel him if need be, to find him and dissuade him from war. How they had been ambushed by painted Indians near dusk, Stahi's betrayal, the Indians shooting two of their men; he told of the longhouse in which they had taken cover, the battle lasting through the night. He told of the burned-out homestead and of the dying woman and the children who could be wandering in the forest or taken by Indians. "I have it on the best authority, there's more settlers been set upon by hostile Indians in the White River region. Likely more been killed already, and, if it ain't stopped, there's sure to be more massacre coming."

"That there's a sad tale," said Moses, genuine sympathy in his tone. "It's our job to get reinforcements so as to stop any more of this kind of thing. And what of Eaton's Rangers? How many have you lost?"

"All told, we have two dead, two wounded, one deserter, and one rider—McAllister's son—gone back to Olympia to break the news to his mother and sisters."

"Let's see," said George Bright, blinking rapidly and scowling down at his fingers. "You're only down five men. Sure, five men's bad luck, but, shucks, who needs reinforcements when you're only down five men?"

"George, whoever in tarnation gave you the name of Bright wasn't very bright," said Miles, clapping his companion on the back with a laugh. Holding up fingers as they corresponded with his words, he continued, "*Two* wounded, *two* killed, *one* deserter, and *one* express rider—that don't make five, Mr. Bright. It makes one, two, three, four, five, six."

"Seven," said Miles, "counting Bill Tidd, here, makes seven. The real question is, how many men does that leave in Eaton's militia?"

"All told? Twelve," said William. "We started out with only nineteen."

Miles whistled. "That ain't very many men—and hungry and sleep deprived, like Bill Tidd here. Them's not good odds when there's hostiles of indeterminate number lurking behind every rock and stump."

"That's including Captain Eaton," said William. "And our supplies is near gone. On top of that, Eaton reckoned Captain Maloney ought to know that the war's in full swing right here on Puget Sound. No need to ride over the mountains looking for one."

"Fall in with us, Bill Tidd," said Miles. "Make no mistake, there's war on already over the mountains. Yakamas all painted and riled up for killing. Many hundreds of 'em, more than likely, thousands. Maloney halted at the pass rather than cross over and lead his men to annihilation. We're riding ahead, taking urgent dispatches back to Olympia. There's no time to waste. Looks like everybody in these parts is outgunned and outmanned, needing reinforcements."

31

SNIPER

William was relieved. At least he wasn't riding in these woods—hostile Indians lurking about—all alone. Alone, he had felt dwarfed by the giant stands of Douglas fir, their massive trunks rising like palisades in a natural-grown fortress, or like the colossal legs of giants bestriding the trail, and he running through the towering gauntlet—thick trees providing sure-fire cover for hostile Indians coiled to strike. At least now he wasn't alone. But the forest hadn't changed. Leaning over the narrow track that passed for a road, the mammoth trees glowered down, blocking his view around the next bend in the trail, and casting shadows at midday so gloomy it felt like midnight.

With a shudder, William glanced over his shoulder at the Naches Trail zigzagging behind him. He had fallen in behind the other men as Joseph Miles had ordered him, but being last made him feel vulnerable, almost as bad as being alone. What if Indians were following, biding their time, waiting for a chance to pick him off from behind?

Urging Prophet to greater speed, William followed Miles and the others as they burst out of the dense cover of the forest into a grassy prairie. Though the sky was iron gray with clouds and drizzle, the dense evergreen forest for the moment behind them, the open country seemed almost bright, and somehow safer than the somber forest.

Just as William was breathing a sigh of relief, calming his nerves, reassuring himself, and his horse—Prophet was misbehaving, straining from side to side—they rounded a hillock. Suddenly there were cries of alarm from the men, and snorting and clamoring from the horses. William, riding at the rear of the band, at first did not know why they had halted so abruptly. Straining to see over Prophet's head, he yanked hard on the reins, his horse reeling to the left.

The brittle tension of the next moments William felt sure would take a toll of at least ten years off his life expectancy. Wheeling around and facing the express riders was a band of Indians, more than twice their number. Staring into the dark wide eyes of an Indian, William felt a numbing sensation shooting up his neck and engulfing his face and scalp. He glanced at the other red faces. The Indians looked no less surprised than William felt. His mind raced. Apparently they had been lying in wait expecting white men to be advancing from Puget Sound and Fort Steilacoom, not from the east. The hillock they had used for cover had blocked their view behind them to the east, and the sound of unexpected express riders approaching from the opposite direction.

For a nerve-rending instant, neither side spoke or moved. Faces far whiter than their race warranted stared at red faces also drained of color by so complete a surprise. The Indians, as were the riders, were armed—knives, tomahawks, trade muskets, and several pistols. Now would be a good time for a pistol, thought William: close range, ready to hand, far more easily drawn than trying to pull McAllister's trade musket from its resting place on his saddle. The air seemed charged with electricity. William felt that the first man who breathed, who twitched, who so much as blinked would be setting a match to gunpowder. But it was inevitable. Someone did all these, and more.

"You accursed devils!"

William groaned. It was Dr. Matthew Burns. He could think of no worse a man to break the silence than Burns. A young Indian, no more than a teen, stood closest to where Burns had reined in his horse—right next to William. In his left hand, the Indian held a pistol.

"You're the cause of this petty war!" continued Burns, sliding from his saddle. He squared off in front of the young Indian, a young man so astonished, he stared at Burns as if he were a devil. Burns had chosen his man well. William, as if in a nightmare, watched the dark scene unfolding immediately in front of him. With the lightning speed of a cougar, Burns snatched the pistol from the Indian, and aimed it between the boy's eyes. They were eyes now stretched far wider open than William thought possible for a human.

"The tyee behind it all," sneered Burns. "Fortuitous to apprehend you before you can be the cause of any more trouble."

Miles turned in his saddle. "Burns, you've gone stark raving mad! That's not Leschi!"

Burns cocked the hammer of the pistol.

"You're a danged fool," said Abraham Moses. "Leschi's twice this Indian's age."

"Put down the gun, Burns," said Miles. "You pull that trigger and you'll get us all killed. Put it down!"

Every index finger, white or red, was poised on a trigger. William felt that if someone didn't stop Burns, if the doctor pulled the trigger, it would signal slaughter. They were outnumbered more than two to one. At this close a range, once shooting commenced, it would be over quickly. They might take a few Indians down with them. But it was not possible for himself or any of his fellow express riders to survive the encounter.

Reflecting later on that moment, William had no clear explanation for what happened next. All he knew is that someone had to stop Burns or they would all die. The closest to Burns of his companions, William considered leaping from his saddle and trying to wrestle the pistol from Burns, but that would almost certainly result in the pistol discharging and the death of the Indian boy—and he had little doubt that Burns would have no compunction about putting the next bullet in William's head.

There was only one hope. In the complex regions of his horse instincts, Prophet had somehow managed to realize what that hope was. Lowering his head, in one swift motion, Prophet took a step toward Dr. Burns and reared up on his hind legs, his forward hooves catching Burn's arms from underneath, and knocking him backwards away from the Indian, the pistol hurtling through the air, landing harmlessly with a thud in a clump of munch grass beside the trail. Cursing with oaths William had never heard before, the doctor lay on his back, his legs and arms flaying the air like an upended beetle.

Who started it was never clear to William, but first one, then another; soon they were all at it. Laughter, Indian laughter, *Hyuk, hyuk, hyuk!* Miles got off his horse and helped Dr. Burns to his feet. "Not another word, fool," said Miles in a husky whisper in the doctor's ear, "or you'll get us all killed. Now start laughing, or I'll put a bullet in *your* head."

Hearing the laughter, squaws and Indian children poked their heads up from the long prairie grass and joined in. Tension that had been strained to the breaking point only moments before, now gave way to something bordering on merriment—or was it hysteria?

Hostility suspended, at least for the moment, the two parties exchanged words of civility, even verbal expressions of friendship. One leathery-faced squaw presented moccasins decorated with glass beads and began bargaining for them with the men.

Grinning and stroking Prophet's neck, the young Indian William's horse had saved from Dr. Burn's bullet held out a fillet of smoked salmon. "For you," said the Indian, putting it in William's hands. "Horse no eat salmon. You hungry. You eat." He smiled broadly as William bit into the savory fish. Food had not tasted so good for days.

Joseph Miles and Abraham Moses sat down cross-legged on the prairie grass with several of the more important looking Indians, one wearing a black wool-felt coat and tattered beaver-skin top hat. The first opportunity William had to rest for more than twenty-four hours, he collapsed in the grass and listened in, savoring every bite of the smoked salmon. The Indians claimed to know nothing about the burned out cabin and the dead settlers north on the White River, and they insisted their only reason for being in the area was to find winter grasslands for grazing their stock.

"Why are you carrying weapons, then?" asked Miles, nodding at the muskets, pistols and more traditional Indian weaponry bristling from every man.

"Weapons to protect squaw and children," replied the man in the top hat. Looking unblinking at Miles, the Indian countered, "Why you have weapons?"

Anxious to report to Maloney's superiors in Olympia, and anxious to put distance between themselves and armed Indians they were not entirely sure they could trust, Miles gave the order to mount up and move out. "Moses, you ride point. I'll bring up the rear."

As they rode down the Naches Trail toward Fort Steilacoom, William glanced back over his shoulder, slowing Prophet as he did. A dozen or more of the Indians vaulted onto their horses. As near as William could make out, they were heading southwest cutting across the prairie. He frowned deeply. If their sole purpose being in the area was to find grasslands for feeding their horses, why would they now mount up and leave prime winter feeding grounds.

Maybe he ought to catch up with the others and tell them what he'd just seen.

Lashing more speed from their horses, the men were riding hard. William urged Prophet after them. The road narrowed and turned sharply to the left, bordered now by a swamp tangled with low brush and cottonwood stalks, and dense with alder and cedar trees. William drove his heels into Prophet's flanks. Miles rode just ahead of him in the left wagon-wheel rut of the road. William steered Prophet into the right track of the road, determined to come up alongside Miles and tell him what he had seen, then pass the word to the rest. Prophet's head was alongside Miles's horse's rump.

Just ahead, the forest thickened. Though it was not yet dusk, darkness descended as they entered the trees, the swamp now littered with gnarly branches and downed timber. The hair stood stiffly on the back of William's neck. He strained to see into the gloom of the forest. Something wasn't right. Prophet's ears were turned to the right, and his muscular neck strained at something he had heard or sensed in the forest to the right of the road.

"Miles!" yelled William over the noise of their galloping. "The Indians, a dozen or more, mounted up, moments after we left. They cut across the prairie—in this direction!"

William's words were suddenly lost in a volleying of musket fire erupting from the dense cover of the forest on the right side of the road. The precise details of what happened next would be played over in William's mind for the rest of his days. Miles glanced back over his shoulder at William still a horse length behind him. Flicking his reins, Miles suddenly crossed over the center burr of the road into the right track directly ahead of William, as if cutting him off. Puzzled, William switched to the left rut in the road and came up alongside of Miles.

"Miles!" yelled William. Another volley erupted from the forest, Miles now between the shooting and William. To his horror, William saw Miles deflate like a punctured whale float. The man crumpled in his saddle, slumped forward, and fell from his horse.

"Whoa!" yelled William, reining in hard. Miles's horse kept galloping after the others. Prophet halted, facing the forest. William dropped to his knees beside the motionless body of Joseph Miles. A lead bullet had passed through the right side of the man's neck, the exit wound on the left side gaping and bleeding heavily. William stared wide-eyed, repulsed by the blood and the wound, yet wanting to do something to stop it. What had just happened replayed slowly, ominously, in William's mind, and terror and wonder crept up the back of his neck. Miles knew. He had intentionally placed himself between William and the Indians. If he had not and William had overtaken Miles on the right side instead of on the left, that gaping wound would be in his own neck, not in Miles's. William looked down at his hands. They were trembling.

He had to do something for Miles. For a flashing instant, he wished Sister Marguerite was here, with her skill as nurse; maybe she would know what to do, how to tend such a wound. It was for mending wounds like Miles's that the young nun had volunteered. Marguerite wasn't here; it was up to him. He had heard that applying pressure stopped bleeding. But it was the man's neck. Pressure would suffocate him. The exit hole, it was so big.

"Miles!" cried William. "Can you hear me?"

"I'm done for," gasped Miles.

"Don't die, Miles!"

Another volley of musket fire rattled through the forest. *Whisst!* A lead bullet passed over William's head, splintering into the trunk of an alder tree on the other side of the road.

"I'm done for," repeated Miles, his voice barely audible. With a pale hand he gripped William's jacket. "Bill Tidd, I know 'bout your pa."

Another volley erupted from the brake of alder trees, bullets slicing the air far closer than William liked.

"Take my revolver," said Miles. "You're gonna need it. That's an order."

"I know what you did," said William. "I'm not leaving you."

Whisst! Another bullet, so close it made William's flesh crawl.

"Yes you are," gasped Joseph Miles. "Mount up! That's an order."

32

DEATH AT FINNEL'S CREEK

For a fleeting moment, William wished he knew how to pray. Here was another human being, Joseph Miles, dying right in front of him, and he had nothing to give him, nothing to bring him comfort. He wondered if Emerson had ever seen death like this. William wished Charlie or Noclas had been here.

Driving his heels into Prophet's flanks, he chased after the others. Irregular musket fire thundered from the forest, but William knew that speed was his best defense against getting shot himself. There was no time to think, but William could not help thinking. Why had Miles done it? Another ragged volley came from the forest, on the right. It would all be for nothing if he got himself shot now. He urged Prophet to go faster, desperately hoping his luck was better than Miles's had been.

How much time had he lost? The others had been riding fast, for their lives. Prophet was fast, could close the gap sooner than any horse William knew of, except maybe Charlie's.

Whisst! Another bullet passing near enough to his head for him to hear it clear and terrifying, but no more shots followed. To William's surprise, the thundering hooves and the splaying mud of the men and their horses came into view far sooner than he expected. William quickly overtook them.

"Where's Miles?" yelled George Bright.

William didn't immediately reply.

"Did the Injuns shoot him?" hollered Bradley. "Is he dead?"

William didn't trust his voice. He nodded.

Nodding at William's hip, George stared hard at Miles's revolver. "Colt 1851 break-action .44-Cal.," he said almost reverently. "That were Miles's revolver—the latest thing."

"He gave it to me," said William. "Ordered me to take it. Said I'd be needing it."

"He was right about that," said Bradley.

"Why are we riding so slow?" asked William. "There's Indians still lurking about these woods."

"Moses has gone and got himself shot," said Dr. Burns. "Which I think was dashed inconsiderate of him, under the circumstances. I say we find a comfortable place for him alongside the quiet waters of a nearby stream. Perhaps it will restore his soul."

"Finnel's Creek is just through here," said Bradley.

Moses's face was pale and blanching with pain as they lifted him off of his horse and carried him from the road. Burns examined the wound. "Entered through the back just below the left scapula," he said as if he were describing a deer he had shot, "and exited rather grandly through the chest, near the heart, very near the heart, indeed. And a great deal more blood outside the man than in him. Remarkable fortitude. Frankly, I can offer no medical reason why he yet remains in the land of the living. Since miracles are ceased, my good fellow, I'd say it might be an appropriate time to recollect all you can from the catechism—or your *Torah*, or whatever it is you Jews read."

Chilled to the bone, their teeth chattering with cold and shock, all the men but Burns took off their overcoats and wrapped Abraham Benton Moses in them. William had a vague sense that Moses might be accustomed to yet another kind of praying, but it mattered little.

"You rest easy," said George. "We'll be back for you as soon as we can manage it. Keep your head down and your weapons loaded."

"Boys, if you escape," gasped Moses, his lips pale and his face drawn and sunken, "remember me."

William swallowed the lump in his throat: *if* we escape, he thought. Moses was still alive when the men left him and remounted their horses. William stole one last backward glance at the dying man as they rode away. His wound was too severe. Someone who knew a good deal more than he did about doctoring might have been able to do something. Left alone in the forest, the cold, the wet, hostile Indians behind every stump, it was only a matter of time.

Five minutes elapsed—not a single retort of a musket. Dr. Burns had taken command. He raised a gloved hand, signaling to halt. Silence descended over the forest. It was too silent. Eyes wide, the men held their breath, searching the trees that surrounded them. Heart thundering in his ribcage like a kettledrum, William strained to distinguish the panoply of natural forest sounds from those that were almost certainly Indian war signals.

Two men down. Who would be next? And then next, and finally last?

Burns scanned the terrain. He signaled for the men to follow. Maybe the Indians had wearied of shooting at them, William wondered, as he spurred Prophet forward. A thick blanket of evergreen needles cushioned the forest floor, muffling the sounds of their horses' hooves as the men followed Burns to high ground. No one spoke.

Rounding a bluff above the creek, a nerve-chilling *Yeee-Haaah!* shattered the silence. Suddenly, they were face to face with more Indians, or maybe the same Indians. It mattered little. Their Indian bodies smeared and ghastly with red paint, the savages gave a bloodcurdling scream and charged. Perhaps they had spent all their powder or they had run out of primers for their percussion muskets or they had no more lead ball. Or maybe they preferred the more direct terror of close-encounter fighting. For whatever the reason, this was to be grim hand-to-hand combat, knives, tomahawks, war clubs. Flesh against flesh, hands and fingers clutching bodies, entwining around necks, human sweat and smells, a bloody horror that would play itself over and over in William's nightmares for years to come.

William remembered almost none of the specifics of that fight. It happened too fast, was too desperate and brutal. One thing he did remember was drawing out Miles's revolver, taking aim at the red, naked chest of an Indian who held his tomahawk high above his head, just on the instant of crashing its blade into William's skull. Fire erupted from the barrel of the revolver. It was the first time William had ever pulled the trigger of a revolver. But at that range, a child could not have missed. Blood mingled with the paint; the man fell forward, dead before he hit the fir needles on the forest floor.

During the fight, William must have shot the other five rounds in the revolver—it was empty when the engagement ended—and he must have used it as a club after that—its butt was smeared with blood and bits of black hair. It was over in minutes, ones that seemed like an eternity. When the last of the Indians still standing retreated into the blackness of the forest, some left trails of blood from their wounds behind them. Four Indians lay dead at their feet. Inexplicably, all of the men escaped serious injury.

"You devils incarnate!" screamed Dr. Burns, reloading his revolver. "Cowards! Stand and fight!" He rammed a charge down the barrel of his musket and set a primer in place. "Have it your way, then. I am coming after you. I have had enough of your miserable race. We shall settle this tonight!"

As if crazed by the bloody encounters of the day, Burns plunged into the forest, ignoring the protests of his companions.

"The man's gone daft," said Bradley.

"I've thought so all along," said George Bright. "But we'll not see him again after this night. One man against who knows how many hostile Injuns? He's good as dead."

"There's nothing we can do about Burns," said Bradley.

"Forget Burns," said George. "What do we do about us?"

"I don't know," said Bradley, his voice listless. "Maybe we're as good as dead, too."

"It's more important than ever," said William. His teeth chattered as he said it. "We must get these dispatches to Olympia."

"But it's no use," said George, collapsing onto a stump. "We're surrounded by Injuns. It's cold, cold and wet, and it's going to get colder as night falls. There's miles between us and the fort, miles of wild country filled with Injuns eager to cut our throats."

"We can't just sit down and give up," said William. "We have important information, and if we get it to the right people, the army, the militia, there can be a coordinated plan to halt this war, once and for all. If we sit here, the Indians will continue killing—massacring families. I've seen it. Give up now, and who knows what will become of our families."

"You got a family?" asked Bradley. "'Cause I ain't got one."

William said nothing. His sister, he had his sister. And Noclas, he was like family. There wasn't anything he would not do to keep Junebug safe. He looked at the slumped and dejected men around him. Suddenly William knew what he had to do.

"Get up!" he said. "Check your weapons. We must move out. Whatever happens, I'd rather be on the move doing what we were commissioned to do than sit here and freeze to death or wait for the Indians to scalp us in our sleep. Get up!"

Drizzle turned to a hard rain as night fell, temperatures just above freezing. They went back to where they had left Moses. Eyes blank, gazing without a flutter up into the dark and descending rain, the man's body was cold and stiff. Though William wished there was time to give him a proper burial, if they tried it, he knew in all likelihood they'd be needing to dig more graves than just Moses's.

"He won't be needing these," said George, wrenching his overcoat off the body. "Without 'em, we'll be like he is soon enough."

His skin crawling, William lifted his own overcoat off the body of the dead man; he shuddered as he slipped his arms into its sleeves. "We can't travel on the Military Road," he said, trying to conceal the chattering of his teeth. He knew it would be gruelingly slow breaking their own trail through dense underbrush, tangled slash and downed timber, their horses sinking in the boggy mud. But there was no other way. "We're fish in a barrel on the road. We take to the woods. Stay alert. Let's move out."

Time crept along like it was a specter revolving in nightmarish circles. Fearing to stay put and fearing to be on the march, their teeth chattering with the cold and wet, dog-weary from lack of sleep, their nerves were strung to the breaking point. Nearing the banks of the Puyallup, they heard movement across the river. Halting in a clump of trees, William peered into the darkness. More noise—chattering and clinking sounds. "Hush!" Then he realized what it was. Not only their teeth, the bullets in their leather ammunition pouches were rattling with their uncontrollable shivering.

Dribbles of rain soaking his neck, William turned up his collar and took a deep breath, willing himself to stop trembling. He strained his ears, trying to discern what was making the noises. The slosh of hooves in mud, a coarse whispering of voices, the clink of metal on metal. It could be Indians, he thought. Then again, it could be settlers fleeing for their lives, women and children staying one step ahead of the Indians.

Bradley raised his musket.

"Put it down," ordered William, making his whispered voice as hard edged as he dared. "Shooting blind in the dark is craziness. Them folks may be whites making a break for it. Put your gun up. Even if it is Indians, shoot one of them and the racket of the shooting could bring dozens down on our heads—maybe hundreds. Shucks, it may not even be hostiles. Could be friendly Indians."

"Ain't no such thing," said George. "After what we've been through, a Injun's a Injun. The way I sees it, this here's war. That being the case, it's time to kill or be killed."

32

REPRIEVE

So much happened over those three days of trying to get home without running into a band of Indians on the warpath, William's mind suppressed most of the details.

The first thing William wanted to remember was the warmth. He no longer shivered. Full-body shivering where nerve endings, ragged with the wet and cold, sent chilling spasms up the spine and neck. There were times when the convulsions felt so violent he feared they would rattle his joints apart. And his bones, so saturated with the cold they ached like an old man's, now felt like how bones ought to feel, bones there doing their job, holding things up, but not making you feel every grinding edge of the world as they did it.

All that had ended. He was dry, warm and dry. And the tiredness was gone, gone or deliciously indulged in. He felt like his head was on a pillow, his body lying in a warm bed. And there were new smells, ones that made his stomach contort and grumble.

As he gradually became conscious that he was conscious of these things, suddenly cold hands gripped at his heart. He recalled hearing about men freezing to death, how they entered into a condition where they felt tired, comfortable in their weariness, where they stopped caring, unwilling to face the cruel realities of a harsh world at that moment busy wicking life out of their bodies. Prolonged and penetrating cold played tricks with the mind, made you prefer escaping into oblivion rather than continue enduring the slings and arrows of hunger, freezing, bone-numbing weariness—and unrelenting danger.

"No!" cried William, sitting bolt upright. He looked around in utter bewilderment. It was the Tidd cabin. Warm blaze in the river rock fireplace. His own bed. His own nightshirt. Wally's wet nose nuzzling his hand.

"I've made you yummy supper," said a girl's voice. Junebug. His sister Junebug. Relief washed over him, not like a mere emotion; this was something real, hard and tangible, relief that he could touch and hold in his arms. Junebug, his sister, all he had in the world: she must be alive, or was it all a dream? Wally put his front paws up on the bed and began plowing wet furrows in William's face with his tongue. Not dreaming. William reached out a hand toward his sister and attempted a smile.

"I have never been so glad to see another human being," she said, gripping his hand in both of hers, "as I am to see you, alive and well. Well, alive, anyways. You need some fatting up, a bit a cleaning up too, wouldn't hurt." She laughed. "But first, you need some corn cakes, and boiled potatoes, and baked salmon, lots of butter dribbling over it, just the way you like it, and chicken broth. Noclas says that broth'll cure you of most anything that ails a body."

"That and White-Man's Foot tea," said a man's voice. With a bolt of pain shooting up his spine, William turned. Noclas.

"Junebug's yummy cooking," said Noclas, "Noclas's tea, and heaps of rest, that there's what you's needing, Bill Tidd."

William slumped back onto the straw-filled mattress. "How did I get here?" He wiped a hand across his face and eyes. Blinking rapidly, he tried to remember.

"Prophet brung you back," said Noclas, "like what a good horse'll do."

"But my dispatches," said William, trying to get out of the bed. "I must get them to Olympia. Men's lives depend on it."

"Oh, you already done that," said Noclas with a chuckle. "Then Prophet, he brung you back home to get some rest, some food and rest. You's looking a mite thinner than when you headed off a bit more'n a week ago." Noclas pulled up a three-legged stool close by William's bed, eyeing him soberly.

Had it only been just over a week since he left? So much had happened in so short a time, William felt more like it had been a lifetime; he wished it had been someone else's lifetime. Something in Noclas's eyes made William think that the man knew more than he was letting on. The old black man was looking at him as if he were now looking at a man, not a boy.

"Word's all about the countryside," continued Noclas. "There's been troubles aplenty, and William Tidd's been right in the thick of them troubles, that's what the word is hereabouts. Doing his duty, being courageous, saving some lives."

Not saving enough of them, thought William. And taking some lives. But Noclas seemed to know about that too, by the look in his eye.

"Now you just stay put," said Junebug when William attempted to rise from the bed. "I'm fixing to feed you in bed where you belong. There now, what would you like first?"

"Corn cakes," said William, smiling at her. "I lost sleep dreaming about your corn cakes—them and your pictures. You been making more pictures?"

Smiling, her cheeks flushed with pleasure, Junebug showed William her latest charcoal sketches. There were sketches of Noclas, one of him with a Bowie knife gutting a salmon, another of him dozing in the willow rocker, musket cradled on his knees; another of him splitting firewood, repairing shingles on the roof, shoeing Molly and Polly; another up close, Noclas smiling broadly, cheek to jowl with a young girl, a self-portrait, remarkable in its likeness.

It appeared to William that Noclas had been taking good care of his sister. Wincing, William managed to scoot into a sitting position in the bed. Here was another, a drawing of a young man on a horse, straining forward in the saddle, the front of the man's hat brim turned up with the speed, the horse's hooves suspended above the ground like he was flying. Shaking his head in wonder, William turned slowly to look at his sister. Her cheeks glowed with warmth and pleasure, her eyes sparkling in time with the shimmering of the flames in the fire.

"You look like you've seen a ghost," said Junebug with a laugh. "Leave off them pictures. It's time for supper."

"But wait," said William, cocking his head at another sketch. "Who in tarnation is this?" It was a young woman wearing a heavy full-length black dress, seated, in a willow rocker, in front of a small stone fireplace, in a cabin. Though it was clearly the Tidd cabin, William scowled at the young woman. It looked like she was Marguerite's age, though William wasn't entirely certain what the nun's age was. But it couldn't be the nun. The dress looked like the black teepee robe nuns wore, but there was no wimple covering up her head. Junebug had somehow captured not just the shape but something deeper. Somehow his little sister had managed to sketch the warmth and feel of the firelight, rimming the woman's profile, the curve of her forehead, her delicate nose, her soft lips, slightly parted; and the wavy cascading of her hair down onto her slender shoulders. With effort, William pried his eyes from the sketch, studying his sister's face, searching for the source of such an uncanny ability for one so young.

"Time for yummy supper," sang out Junebug, snatching the sketch from William and sliding it under the bed. "This'll cure you, for sure," she said, raising her eyebrows enticingly, holding a wooden bowl, steamy with broth, stirring the contents with a wooden spoon.

Noclas offered up a heartfelt prayer of thanksgiving for the food and "for the good providence of God a-watching over William here and a-bringing him back all in one piece." The old man's voice broke slightly at his words. "In the blessed name of Jesus, A-men."

While Junebug ladled warm chicken broth into her brother's mouth, Noclas filled William in on what they had learned about the tamer parts of the Indian War, now officially being called a war. Parts of it William knew first hand, other parts he'd heard about. Him turning up at Clover Creek with George Bright and Andrew Bradley, all three of them barely alive with the cold and hunger, wasn't entirely news to him. Though most of it was a dull blur, Noclas's words brought back more bits and pieces of recollection. But it was still like watching the events unfold through a windowpane frosty with condensation on a November morning.

After supper when Junebug went off to bed, Wally on guard at her feet, and only when they were certain she was actually asleep, Noclas filled William in on more of the specifics.

No one knew for sure how many of the 6,000 Indians in the region would actually take up arms and fight against the settlers. But the odds did not look good. Homesteaders, like the Judson and the DeLin families at a place called Tacoma, would pack up what they could carry and flee for their lives to Fort Steilacoom, thinking they would be safe at a US Army fort. But Fort Steilacoom only had 400 rounds of ammunition when the war began and only twenty-five regular soldiers—and no fortification. So every community was forced to build blockhouses to protect their women and children and raise their own militia to fight the Indians, the latest volunteers reporting for duty from Port Gamble and Port Townsend.

Reports of the unrest had reached the US Navy, now sending the sloop-of-war *Decatur* from Hawaii and the US Revenue Cutter *Jefferson Davis* into the region to bring supplies and munitions. Worries that the British and The Hudson Bay Company might take the Indians' side of the war were allayed when the schooner-rigged, single-screw steamer the *Otter,* flying the Union Jack, arrived in Puget Sound from Vancouver Island to the north, heavily armed and ready to join in with the US Navy vessels. Two twelve-pound cannons had been put ashore to protect the townsfolk in Steilacoom.

"Captain Hewitt took a company of men from Seattle," continued Noclas, "to the White River Valley to bury the dead. The charred remains of Mr. Jones and the mangled body of his wife and their hired man Cooper shot through the chest, they buried first. Then on to the Brannon's holding nearby where they found the bodies of Mrs. Brannon and her baby son killed and tossed down the well, Mr. Brannon's body lying nearby all cut up and ghastly from a violent struggle before the Indians ended his life. They found the King family dead, word is, their bodies gnawed on a good bit by cougars or wolves, could be either. George, their young son—there was no sign of the little feller; they fear he's dead, or worse, been taken captive."

William wiped his hand across his face and eyes. But it was no good. The pleading eyes of the dying woman at the White River homestead stared at him. Her trembling, her pleading with him to care for her babies, her begging him to pray, the rattling in her throat as she breathed her last.

Wally whined and placed a wide gray paw up on the worn point blanket. William played absently with the big dog's floppy ear.

33

THE MIDNIGHT RIDE OF CHARLIE SALITAT

William feared to ask but he had to know. "Noclas, tell me. What happened to Johnny King and his two siblings?"

"Now, there's a story to tell," said Noclas. "They turned up in Seattle, safe and sound. Friendly Indians took them in, protected them, and delivered them to white folks in Seattle. Anybody who says Indians is all bad, probably is so himself."

"It was Charlie," said William. "Charlie Salitat, he arranged for them children to get to safety. Them little ones is heaps younger than Junebug." His voice trailed off.

"That ain't all Charlie Salitat done," said Noclas, smiling and shaking his head in wonder. "He done the bravest deed likely to be done in this war. It were on the night of October 29, Charlie Salitat done his midnight ride through Puyallup Valley warning American settlers to flee for their lives. Some speculate that if Charlie had not done that, dozens, maybe hundreds of settlers, families with little ones, they'd have all been killed by Indians, by the hostile ones, that is."

William's mind flashed back to the "big thing" Charlie said he had to do. "Charlie, he turned up," said William in a low whisper. "He just turned up, you know how he does that. She were dying, Johnny King's mother was dying. Been cut and hacked up pretty bad by the Indians. Charlie knelt down in the mud beside her."

"And did what?" asked Noclas.

William hesitated. "Prayed."

Noclas nodded approvingly. "You'll be pleased to know that Captain Eaton and what was left of his rangers made it safe to Olympia. James Wiley writing it all up in his newspaper; some good bits in them papers about an express rider of the name of Tidd, there is."

"Have you heard what became of Miles and Moses?" asked William, his voice low and sober. "I was with them near the end. Miles gived me his revolver, just there." William nodded toward a hook by the door where they had hung his things. "It were a good thing he did. He said where he was heading, he wouldn't be needing it no more, but I would. He sure was right about that." He paused, deep in thought for a moment. "I wanted to do something for them at the end, but there was nothing to do. They was too bad hurt."

"Buried down at Bush's Prairie, the both of them," said Noclas. "Yesterday it was, in the rain, their widows riding behind in a buckboard. Acting-Governor Mason there to give his respects for the fallen."

William tried to picture the dismal scene. He hadn't known either of the men more than a few hours, and now they were both dead. "Facing off with the Indians," said William. "It was no Sunday School picnic."

"I don't expect it was," said Noclas.

William bit his lower lip. Then he told Noclas what Miles had done. "Why would a man do that for another fellow?" asked William. "Putting himself between me and the Indians like he done? It just don't make no sense to me."

"Um-huh," Noclas murmured encouraging sounds as he listened.

William hesitated. "Noclas, just before the end, Miles, he done said something about Pa. Something different than the way other folks go on about it. It don't make no sense, but it seemed like, while he was on his way under, he was trying to give me something. Something far more than his Colt revolver." William trailed off. "It don't make no sense."

"Maybe it do. 'Greater love hath no man than this,'" murmured Noclas, "'than when a feller done goes and lays down his life for his friend.' So says the Good Book."

"That's just it," said William. "I'd only known Miles for a few hours. Oh, I'd seen him around town, and he seemed to know and care about what happened to Pa. But I reckon I hadn't known him half long enough to be a friend." He paused, then murmured, "I feel I owe him so much for what he done." William fell silent, staring with hollow eyes into the shadows of the cabin.

"Um-huh," murmured Noclas encouragingly. He began humming, like what a mother does when rocking her child to sleep. Gradually, imperceptibly, his humming became singing, Noclas's voice rich and deep, filling the walls of the tiny cabin with feeling:

I lay my griefs on Jesus,
My burdens and my cares;
He from them all releases;
He all my sorrows shares.

I rest my soul on Jesus,
This weary soul of mine . . .

Noclas broke off singing and returned to humming. William was dozing. Noclas tucked the comforter up around William's shoulders. After making sure Junebug was covered well against the chill, Noclas stoked the fire and settled into the willow rocking chair. He would stay the night and keep watch over the brother and sister.

But no sooner had Noclas begun to doze himself when he heard William's voice again. "I don't know if I'll ever get clear of it."

"Um-huh," murmured Noclas.

"Red-painted savages a-whooping and a-hollering," continued William, "coming at us fit to kill, and that ain't no metaphor. I see 'em every time I close my eyes. Blood, more blood than I've seen before, man blood, that is. Been around pig blood, and chickens, and the like. This were different. Same color, but different." He paused, looking levelly at Noclas. "Do you reckon Sister Marguerite might have been able to stop it?"

"To stop it?" repeated Noclas.

"The blood. Stop the blood. There was so much of it coming from Miles's neck wound, same for Moses, but his was in the back, back and chest." He hesitated. "Indians, when they get shot, they bleed too, just like white folks. I often wondered if she could have doctored 'em, white folks and Indians—she said she'd do it for both. Stop up their wounds. You know, heal 'em?"

"War or no war," said Noclas, "Miss Marguerite, she's tireless in lovin' on sick folk and the needy, is she. Rich or poor, white or Injun; Catholic, Protestant, or pagan—even black—it makes no never mind to Miss Marguerite."

"Does she look in on Junebug?" asked William.

Noclas nodded. "Most all the time," he said.

William frowned. He could see her sitting just there in her black-teepee nun's get-up, hooding her eyes in William's direction, but talking and laughing with Junebug, and knitting. He wasn't sure if he ought to be content with the nun looking in on his sister so much. What if Junebug got it in her head to become like the nun? He could never allow that to happen.

Scratching the wiry hair between Wally's ears, William felt tired; he said little for the next few minutes. What was there to say? Unlike most men, Noclas had an uncanny ability to know when to speak and when there was healing underway in that balm called silence. The old man nodded encouragingly, waiting for William to talk it out, patting him on the shoulder when he would break off and stare unblinking into the shadows.

"Rest in Jesus," said Noclas after one of William's longer stretches of silence. "He can bear all your griefs, your sorrows, all your cares. All you've seen and done, trying to carry the load yourself—it'll crush you. But Jesus alone can bear your burden and give you rest."

William twisted the bed sheet into a knot around his fist and bit down hard on the wad. "Times I was so scared," he continued, "I wanted to run, get away from it all, put it all behind, leave off and let somebody else fix it."

"But you didn't," said Noclas.

"No, I didn't," agreed William. "Wish I could say it was because I'm a hero, that I done my duty because I'm brave. But truth is, I didn't run from it all because there was no place to run. Injuns was all around us, so it seemed. Leastwise, we didn't know where they were, how many of them there were, that is, until they hurled themselves at us. Then we knew. Oh, we knew then. More than ever we wanted to know."

"There's talk about what you done," said Noclas. "You may not think you's hero material, but there's others thinking you is. Word is from folks and from the newspaper, Bill Tidd's the best express rider in the territory. Regular army fellers, trained officers and soldiers alike, they's saying the same."

William didn't know what to think of this. Noclas was not a man given to exaggeration. With the black man's words, though, there came an ominous flutter in his insides. He was not wounded; none of his blood had been spilt.

Just tuckered out, needing food and rest. If the US Army was saying he's the best express rider in the region, and communication is the key to victory in this or any war, then he would be needed again. The realization settled over him like a clammy December vapor hovering over swampland.

"What are they saying about Charlie?" asked William, changing the subject. "He's the real hero, saving all those lives like he done."

Noclas frowned. He placed another log on the fire, sparks crackling and flying up the chimney, and sat back down. "To white folk Charlie's a great hero, right up there with our Paul Revere. But with Indian folk, not so much. Word is, some of his own folk is calling him a traitor. For what Charlie done, some wants to lynch him, or put a bullet in his head."

34

PITCHED BATTLE

Not a single Indian sighted. It was November 3, 1855, and William had been especially chosen as express rider to accompany some fifty volunteers under the command of Gilmore Hays. Among the buckskinned volunteers were, here and there, familiar faces: Andrew Laws had turned up with Belinda, eager as ever for more killing; and Dr. Matthew Burns appeared like a specter, full of bravado and tall tales, extrapolating with relish about his murderous exploits.

Though they had ridden all day, and not an Indian sighted, with every mile, William felt dread hovering over his head. Captain Hays was leading them right back to the White River, right back to the spot where the massacre had taken place, to the same region of the forest where McAllister, Connell, Miles, and Moses had been shot and killed.

Spinning the cylinder on Miles's revolver, William checked to see that it was loaded, as he had done a dozen or fifteen times in the last three hours. He replaced it in its holster. It may not be as accurate at long range as a musket, but in the space of time it took to reload the musket, he could fire six rounds in rapid succession; with the spare cylinder, in seconds he could reload, and do it all again.

Captain Hays was leading the volunteers as an advance party. Behind them a half mile, give or take, were several dozen army recruits, both regulars and militia under the overall command of Lieutenant Slaughter.

William almost wished he'd been shot, not bad hurt like the men who had died of their wounds, just bad enough to give him more rest. Lying in his bed in the Tidd cabin had been delicious after what he had experienced, and he wasn't ready for it to end. After doing little more than sleeping and eating for two straight days, duty had called. And it didn't seem to matter whether William wanted or was ready to answer that call or not. He was needed. Anxious as he was about facing off with more Indians, there was something good about being needed. But they had been on the move for hours, and not an Indian sighted. Maybe they had all hightailed it over Naches Pass to join the Yakamas. Maybe, before it even got fully started, the war was over. William rechecked his revolver. And maybe not.

Two miles south of where the White River converges with the Green River, William's new commander called the halt. He ordered his men to dismount and make camp—on the soggy leaves and needles of the forest floor.

After supper, William, sighing deeply, his stomach full of beans and bacon, tried to get himself comfortable for the night. Reaching under his blanket, he removed a stone the size of a pheasant egg and tried again. Listening to the rain dripping heavily on the canvas of his tent, he wondered how the Indians slept when on the march. There had been no sign of an Indian all that long day, and he desperately hoped there'd be no sign of them in the night.

There was no denying it; he was worried. It had been a long, wet, and grueling day of riding, but, fearful of what might happen to him while he slept, William tossed and turned. It was some time before the oblivion of sleep at last settled fitfully over him.

William awoke to the shying of the wind in the fir boughs high overhead, and the steady pattering of rain on the underbrush, on the fronds of bracken fern, sliding off the shiny salal leaves onto decomposing cottonwood and alder leaves littering the forest floor.

Sizing up the men, Gilmore Hays said, "I need a man who can chop a tree down faster than any other man in this company."

Several of the men laughed.

"You want Beaver," said a man called Tom Perkins, "Sir, Beaver's a madman with an axe. There ain't nobody in Puget Sound who can chop a tree down faster than Beaver."

"This is a volunteer militia, gentlemen," said Hays. "So I am asking this man called 'Beaver' to step forward and volunteer, if you please."

William smiled as Beaver stepped up to his commander. He was lanky and lean, with broad bony shoulders. Beaver had a chin that joined from his lower lip to down his neck in a way that made it difficult to tell what was chin and what was neck. It almost looked like Beaver had no chin. But his most memorable feature was his front teeth, jutting forward, well, like a beaver's. With the biggest hands William ever remembered seeing, Beaver held a two-bladed axe over his right shoulder and grinned. It appeared that the man always grinned.

"Beaver, I presume," said Captain Hays, "I need a large tree felled near the river bank, felled so that it can be utilized as a bridge to send over a scout or two to the other side. Can you do that, Beaver?"

"Yes, Sir!" said Beaver, spitting on his hands, then windmilling his double-bladed axe on his right side and then on his left.

At Gilmore Hays's orders, the men fed their horses, broke camp, and saddled up, checking and rechecking their weapons. Prophet seemed out of sorts, pawing the ground, shaking his head, cocking his ears toward the river. William felt a crawling up his spine and a gnawing on his insides that he could not account for.

Meanwhile, echoing through the columns and vaults of the forest was Beaver's felling. *Chop! Chop! Chop!*

William had never seen tree felling like what Beaver did that morning. Swinging his axe rhythmically, Beaver did not appear to be doing so faster than the average man. But every stroke went deep. *Chop! Chop! Chop!* Purposefully and with power, Beaver never slowed. In fact, he seemed to warm to his work, loosening up his muscles and joints, smiling broadly with every powerful blow. *Chop! Chop! Chop!*

"When Beaver drops that tree over the river, just there," said Hays, "we'll scout us up some Indians on the other side."

William recollected later that Captain Hays's mouth was open as if he was about to assign men their roles for the day. Abruptly, his words were cut off.

Blam! Blam! Blam! echoed through the forest. Three shots fired.

Men shouted. Horses reared and neighed in terror. Captain Hays hollered for the men to take cover. "Return fire on my signal!" he shouted above the racket.

William became aware of another sound, or the absence of that sound. There was no more chopping. The rhythmic *Chop! Chop! Chop!* of Beaver's axe abruptly halted. He told himself that was natural. When the shooting started, naturally the woodcutter would halt and take cover like the rest of the men. But something didn't seem right.

"Beaver's done bought it!" yelled Tom Perkins. "Clean through the neck."

William shuddered at the news, and his knees nearly buckled under him. Did the Indians aim for men's necks, he wondered, or had it been another lucky shot?

More musket fire, *Blam! Blam! Blam!* echoed through the forest.

Hays ordered his men to tether their horses in the forest, and advance on foot to the south bank of the White River. "Take cover in the driftwood," he shouted, "and commence firing at will!"

After loading McAllister's musket, William replaced the ramrod under the barrel, readying himself to advance toward the river.

"Halt, there, Bill Tidd!" called Hays. "I need you to get word to Lieutenant Slaughter. Tell him we're under heavy fire. Could be Leschi, Quiemuth, maybe Kanasket or Tecumseh. By the sounds of it, there's a good deal more than fifty Injuns across the river. Bring his men up on the double!"

Vaulting onto Prophet's back, William rode toward where he supposed Slaughter to be with his soldiers, trained ones, from Fort Steilacoom, the musket fire fading into a pattering behind him. Relieved as he felt, he was forced to admit to himself that there was always the danger of being ambushed in the forest, an Indian sniper waiting in the concealment of a giant nurse stump, or drawing a bead on his neck from behind a boulder. Driving his heels into Prophet's flanks, he rode faster. Slaughter's company couldn't be far.

Then, with a sinking feeling in the pit of his stomach, he wondered how he would avoid being shot as he approached the US Army. A lone man riding hard in the forest, men jumpy at the echoes of gunfire in the distance behind him, Indians lurking everywhere? Would they shoot first and ask questions later?

"Halt!" The order came from behind a large moss-covered rock on the edge of a clearing just ahead.

"Don't shoot!" yelled William, reining Prophet in and leaping from the saddle.

"Name and commander?" came the voice. A soldier emerged from behind the rock, his rifle steady, the barrel leveled at William's chest.

"William Tidd, express rider for Captain Gilmore Hays," said William, "Washington territorial militia, Sir."

Within moments William found himself standing before Lieutenant Slaughter. William thought he detected a flicker of recognition in the young officer's eyes. "What is the word?"

"We are under fire," said William. "Less than a mile ahead, along the river."

"How many Indians?" asked Slaughter.

"I do not know for sure, Sir," said William. "Captain Hays says more than fifty of them."

"Any casualties?"

"Yes, Sir," said William. And then he told the lieutenant about Beaver. "Captain Hays has requested reinforcements, the sooner the better."

In the next few moments, William learned something of the difference between volunteer militia and trained soldiers. Smartly dressed in military uniforms, the men wore sky-blue trousers, a red strip running down the sides, dark wool jackets, trimmed in the matching blue of their trousers, brass buttons lining the front. Slaughter wore his black wool-felt hat, decorated with brass. Encircling his waist was a red sash.

William smoothed the front of his threadbare jacket with his hands, wiped the toes of his boots on the back of his homespun trousers, and adjusted his tattered felt hat.

Lieutenant Slaughter ordered his men to break camp and ready themselves to move out in five minutes. The bugler gave out the signal, the bright tones echoing throughout the camp and the forest. The drummer, sticks flashing like the wings of a hummingbird, rolled out a corresponding signal. In a crisp flurry, ordered and disciplined, Slaughter had his men mounted and ready to move out in five minutes, maybe less.

As William mounted up and fell in at the rear of the army, he recognized several of the soldiers, ones he had seen at Fort

Steilacoom or about the town. There were faces he had seen on the parade ground that day practicing cavalry maneuvers, and there were the two privates, John Edgar and Addisom Parham, whom he had heard speculating on the Indians, the army's strength, and the impending war. And another soldier, Andrew Burge, he recognized from the streets of Steilacoom, as well as a corporal named Northcraft.

The Stars and Stripes snapping in the breeze, they galloped toward the river, the musket fire increasing in volume and intensity as they drew nearer. Once at the site where the militia's camp had been, Slaughter ordered his men to picket their horses, ready their weapons, and, to the shrill sounds of the bugle, advance toward the Indians and take up their positions.

Slaughter assumed command of both his regular army and Hays's volunteer militia. There was little strategy needed, however. For several hours the Indians fired from their side of the river and the whites returned fire from theirs, neither side certain of the damage done to the other. By nightfall the musket fire tittered off into an uneasy silence.

That night around the campfires, sentinels assigned to guard the little army in shifts throughout the night, men told their stories of the day's fighting.

"Blowed the heel clean off my boot," said Corporal Northcraft, holding up his mangled footwear. He laughed nervously. "But not a drop of blood, not even a scratch."

Two men had sustained flesh wounds, one from Slaughter's company, and the other from Hays's militia. How many Indians they had killed was a topic of great dispute that evening.

"Thirty, not a feather less," insisted Andrew Laws. "I heard Lieutenant Slaughter say the same. I'm sure I did."

"Hays done said the same," said Burge, drawing on his clay pipe and sending a smoke ring oscillating into the dark canopy above the camp. "He said it was great fun, and we done fought like real soldiers today."

"Shucks, he's right about that," said Laws. "Thirty Injuns—a good day's work. And one of them was a squaw."

The clattering of tin plates and mugs halted abruptly. The men stared at Laws in cold silence.

"And just how do you know that?" asked a soldier. William recognized the man's voice; it was Private John Edgar, a scout from Fort Steilacoom.

"Because I done saw her with my own eyes," said Laws. "She was a-leaping out to drag off her man who'd been shot through."

"Which one of us shot a woman," said Andrew Burge. "That ain't right, not in my book."

There was a moment of awkward silence, the fire crackling, and sparks flying into the blackness above.

"Shucks, if a woman Injun decides to put herself in the midst of the fray," whined Laws, defensively, "I say she's fair game for shooting."

"Then you's the one that done it?" said Edgar. "Shot a woman in cold blood?"

"It weren't in cold blood," said Burge. "Not when they started it, shooting Beaver dead this morning, don't forget that, and all the other slaughtering mischief they's been up to lately."

"Now you're talking sense," said Laws. "Shucks, I was the one that done it, me and Belinda, and no apology. I took a bead on her and dropped her where she was a-standing. And I'd do it again. She's only an Injun woman. It ain't the same."

Edgar rose deliberately to his feet. William saw firelight gleaming off the blade of his bowie knife. He'd heard a rumor that Edgar kept an Indian woman for wife. Edgar stood over Laws for an instant, then crammed his knife back in his sheath and disappeared in the shadows.

William had seen and heard enough. He was tired. He'd been kept busy throughout the day running dispatches between Lieutenant Slaughter and Captain Hays, which meant he had had to do little shooting himself. It was more of a day to be shot at than to shoot. He'd heard bullets whistling past his head more than once as he ran back and forth across the improvised driftwood fortification. He pulled off his hat and wiped his brow. Sleep, that's what he needed. Fingering his hat, he felt something odd. He turned it toward the light glowing off the campfire.

Along with sweat stains encircling his hat, there had been plenty of holes, holes from being worn for more years than the average lifetime of a wool-felt hat, hard used in the territories. Battered as it was, William had worn it for nearly three years, and Pa had worn it for an indeterminate number of years before that, till he was done needing it in '52. There were plenty of thin spots and several holes. But this was different.

Feeling a tingle starting between his shoulders, creeping its way up his neck, and clawing onto his scalp, William slipped an index finger through a new hole, one that entered on the right side, and exited on the left.

Blowing a long low whistle, Burge said, "That there's a bullet hole, Bill Tidd, gone clean through your hat."

"A whisker lower," said Laws, "and you'd be lying in the cold, wet ground tonight with Beaver. Don't go all wide-eyed and 'fraidy-cat looking like that. You wouldn't be feeling a thing, top of your head blowed off like that, not a thing."

35

LONE GUNMAN

November 5, 1855, a drenching rain fell. Across the river, not an Indian in sight. Yesterday there had been dozens of them—eighty in all by the estimation of several men. Today they had vanished into the dark shadows of the forest. All that remained was a drenching silence, rain pelting down in sheets, the shying of the river, but not a sight or sound of Indians.

"Don't be fooled, men," said Lieutenant Slaughter after breaking camp and mounting up. Rain water dribbled from the brim of his hat and off the folds of his officer's cape. "This is not yet over. Today we shall begin to find our enemy and subdue them. Patience wins wars. And we, therefore, must be patient, for we will win this war. We will defeat the savages of Puget Sound, mark my words. Keep alert. Keep your weapons and ammunition dry and at the ready. Move out!"

Musing on his new commander, William felt that same vague sense he had when he had first met him. Slaughter was ambitious, eager to make a name for himself, but there was something missing. For all the violence of his name,

Slaughter lacked the gift of command. Perhaps it was to his credit that he was deficient in the brutal hard edge, the most accessible counterfeit manner for tough leaders of men. On the other hand, his men generally seemed to like him, if not sufficiently fear him. They had good reason. He was gentlemanly toward his men, respected them, and was liked in return by them, but he did not instill in his men the unflinching determination to follow their commander to the ends of the earth and back. In the absence of the brutal demeanor of a hardened military titan, Slaughter was a benevolent leader, an amiable commander.

William ruminated on these things as he rode out to fulfill his commission to find William H. Wallace, a Steilacoom lawyer who was also commander of Company D of the First Washington Territorial Volunteer Infantry. He was supposed to be *en route* from Steilacoom with more volunteers, farmers, sailors, carpenters, hatters, clerks, and a blacksmith—none of them trained soldiers. At last William intercepted them and led Wallace and his volunteers to a rendezvous with Lieutenant Slaughter's company before noon.

The rain had not let up. Determined to find the band of Indians that had attacked yesterday, Slaughter was scouting for a way to cross the river. His task was made more difficult as the river was overrunning its banks, churning with white water and forest debris caused by the torrential rainfall. William had experienced rain like this many times before. Weather like this always felt as if it would rain forever, as if life would be gray, wet, and dreary; and he would shiver, and his teeth would chatter—forever. But now, with two more holes in his hat, rain was worse than ever.

After ordering the felling of more trees, Slaughter and Hays put able men in charge of engineering a makeshift bridge from the downed trees. Still the rain fell and the river rose higher. As the first men crossed, several lost their footing, and more than one man lost his musket in the rushing water. "Danged waste of perfectly good muskets, that is," said Andrew Laws in disgust.

Cautious of his footing on the wet log bridge, William dismounted and led Prophet across the river. He then stationed himself downstream and readied himself with a coil of rope.

Lieutenant Slaughter brought up the rear. As the man rode out onto the log bridge, William was about to shout a warning to him, but checked himself. Who was he to tell his commander that it was not prudent to ride his horse across a soaking wet, narrow, slippery, makeshift bridge over a river running as high and turbulent as this river?

Eyes wide, straining at the bit, Slaughter's horse seemed to share William's worries. Without warning, the animal's left front hoof slipped. It fell to its knees. Instantly, with an angry shake of its head, the horse regained his footing. Slaughter hurtled head-over-heels into the river. The lieutenant, caught in the raging green water, his cape swirling about him, was being dragged under.

It happened so fast, William could not recollect consciously planning to do anything. It just happened. Wrapping his right arm around the branch of a slide maple tree angling over the river, William reached for the young officer. The water was racing by swiftly. There would be no second chance. Slaughter saw William's hand. He reached out as far as he could. Their hands locked. For an instant, William was afraid the current, the weight of the lieutenant, his equipment, his drenched cape alone must weigh as much as a musket—he felt himself being pulled in, his right arm feeling like it was about to pop apart at the shoulder socket.

Somehow, William managed to hold on, and Slaughter was soon crawling onto the bank. Drenched to the bone and breathing heavily, he staggered to his feet. "I am deeply in your debt," he said through teeth clenched to keep them from chattering, the look of frustrated ambition stronger than ever in his eyes.

William, not sure what to say, and hesitant to make eye contact with a man brought to such an extremity of humiliation in front of his men, murmured, "It is an honor, Sir."

There was an awkward silence throughout the ranks of Slaughter's men. But to the young lieutenant's credit, he shook himself, rung out his cape, checked his weapons and ammunition, collected his horse, mounted, and resumed command.

After crossing Muckleshoot Prairie, they mounted a bluff overlooking the Green River Valley. William was riding just behind Slaughter, and next to the lieutenant rode Andrew Burge who was, for his knowledge of the territory, acting as guide. At the high point of the bluff stood a giant hollow cedar stump. It must have once been a massive tree, and was one of the largest stumps William had seen in the territory, bigger than three men could encompass with their hands locked.

As they came up alongside the stump, suddenly a war cry rose from inside the stump. Out leapt a tall Indian, his body painted red, his black hair decorated with feathers. Eyes wide and terrifying, the warrior aimed a trade musket at Burge's leg and pulled the trigger. At point-blank range, he could not have missed. Burge screamed in agony, clutching at his right knee.

What the Indian did next was the most astonishing thing William had ever witnessed. With a final war whoop, he ran to the edge of the bluff and leapt off. All this happened so suddenly, and they were taken so completely by surprise, not a single man returned fire. In the split seconds that transpired, there was no time to react before the Indian disappeared over the brow of the hill, and no sane man dared follow the Indian in his desperate leap from the bluff. Landing on the sloping floor of the forest, the Indian tumbled over several times, sprang to his feet, and turned back toward the men. *Eeeuow!* In a final whoop of defiance, he bolted into the forest and disappeared.

"He's not alone!" shouted Slaughter. "Form ranks. We hold the high ground. Hays, right flank your boys. On the double!"

Captain Hays hesitated. The ominous thudding of war drums came from below, and they could just make out through the trees a longhouse. To form ranks on the right flank meant descending the bluff, closing in on the longhouse, the drums, and where the crazed warrior had rejoined the other Indians. It wasn't only Hays who hesitated.

"Flank!" yelled Lieutenant Slaughter. "That's an order! Do it now, or we'll all be killed!"

For the next two hours musket fire rumbled from both sides, bullets flying thick and hot overhead. Back and forth came the staccato of discharging gunfire, stray bullets severing boughs and small branches of fir trees overhead. Most of the lead went wide or high, and there were remarkably few injuries for all the chaos of noise. The only Indian shot with any certainty was an old man pounding on a drum on top of the longhouse. Andrew Laws gleefully took credit. "Me and Belinda! We done it again!"

Rain continued. As darkness fell, the Indians stopped shooting. It got colder. Soon it was snowing. Wolf howls surrounded the men, and owl calls drifted hauntingly from the shadows of the forest that encircled them.

"I wish them was wolves," said Burge, between gritted teeth. "We'd stand a better chance with wolves than these savages."

William dressed Burge's wound, his stomach lurching at the blood and mangled tissue. Burge, his face blanching and pale, took a long pull from a flask given him by Edgar.

"Men, I hate to give this order, cold as it is," said Slaughter. "No fires. Not so much as striking a light for smoking your pipes. Indians see a flicker of light, and they'll shoot you dead. Make yourselves as comfortable as you can till morning—but not so much as a spark."

36

ONE BULLET

It was the longest, coldest night William had ever survived. He groaned at the dim gray dawn showing early next morning. Shaking off a layer of wet snow from his point blanket, he rose stiffly to his feet. He checked Burge's wound. The bleeding had stopped. That was good. Now if they could just get him to a doctor, someone who could keep the wound from festering, going green. Burge had remarkable resilience. He looked healthier than William felt.

After a hasty breakfast of corn meal dumped in a pot of cold beans and handed from man to man, the snow frittered into a haze of near-freezing rain. William couldn't stop thinking about a mug of Noclas's White-Man's-Foot tea, hot and steaming, warming his insides and chasing off contagion; a poultice of the stuff would be just what Burge's wound needed.

"They're out there," said Tom Perkins. "Injuns surrounding us, lurking about, shadowing us like wolves stalking a herd of elk. They're just waiting."

"And we're running low on ammunition," said Edgar. "Heard Slaughter say so himself."

"And low on victuals," groaned Parham, up-ending an empty pot.

Eyes narrowed, Tom Perkins scanned the terrain slowly. "Humph. I just may have an idea."

Before anyone could stop him, Tom climbed into the high branches of a Douglas fir and started shouting.

"Has he gone daft?" said Addisom Parham, his voice going higher like a girl's. "I-I can't understand a word he's saying."

"He's talking Chinook Jargon, genius," said Dr. Burns. "Naturally, as you are entirely ignorant of Chinook Jargon—among many other things—hence, you understand not a word Perkins is saying. I, on the other hand, understand it perfectly."

Burns stepped to the base of the tree and called up to Tom. "Tell them the Great White Father in the District of Columbia feels benevolently toward his red subjects."

"That's a good one," said Tom. He hollered in Chinook at the Indians. They hollered back. Tom shouting a reply.

"W-what's he saying?" asked Parham.

"He's invited them to send over three Indians to talk peace," said Burns, "so we can all go home. A ridiculous notion, indeed. There's only one way to end this."

The spokesman for the Indians was shouting something. Burns cocked his ear, straining to catch the man's words.

"What's Tom y-yammering about now?" asked Parham.

"Words that prove my point precisely," said Burns. "The Indians called you Bostons a pack of cowards, says the whites had stolen their women, their land, their fishing rights and hunting grounds. He swears the Indians will drive the whites from their land and promises Indian vengeance as they do it. And he flatly refuses to send over men to talk peace with Bostons. There you have it. Now then, I say we do it my way."

Burns cupped his hand around his mouth and called up to Tom. "Tell them that since they're not man enough to come themselves and talk peace, tell them to send over three of their squaws to do it instead."

Tom hesitated. "Now, that there's stirring the pot, and it's sure to rile 'em up fit to kill, don't you reckon?"

"Tell them!" shouted Burns. "Now men, prepare yourselves. Perhaps now we can finish this business once and for all."

Tom Perkins delivered the message, but William thought he sounded reluctant. No sooner had he spoken, and the Indians, whooping with rage, let loose with a ragged volley of musket fire.

"Reckon they didn't much like that," yelled John Edgar, diving behind a downed log covered with moss. "Hey, Tom! You danged fool. Get yourself down here 'fore they make a screen door out of your hide."

"Take cover, men," ordered Slaughter. "But don't return fire. We hold the high ground at the moment. Let them wear themselves out and spend their powder and shot." Under his breath, William heard him add, "*We* certainly can't afford to waste a single cartridge."

For a quarter of an hour bursts of flame erupted from dozens of discharging muskets in the forest below, and bullets collided with tree trunks, rocks, and mounds of forest debris. But for the moment, not so much as a fragment of lead hit any of Slaughter's men. Along with the others, William took pains to keep his head down—and his hat. He could ill afford more holes in it.

But it didn't last long. After a quarter of an hour, the rumbling staccato of musket fire dwindled into a disordered pattering. And then all went silent.

From where he crouched behind a tree, Slaughter placed his hat on the end of his rifle and cautiously held it in full view. Nothing. From behind rocks, trees, stumps, and mounds, other men did the same. William decided his hat could ill afford more holes and studied the result to other men's hats. Nothing.

It was a hopeful sign. Maybe the Indians had used up their powder, cartridges, or percussion caps. Then again, freezing rain falls on whites and Indians alike, William mused. Or maybe they'd spent their rage and, weary of the fight, they were itching for the comforts of their smoky longhouses.

"Saddle up!" ordered Slaughter. Captain Hays repeated the order to his volunteer company. Among a flurry of other commands, Slaughter ordered his scout, John Edgar, to advance with a handful of men in support, including Private Addisom Parham, never far from Edgar's side.

At Lieutenant Slaughter's orders, William was never far from the young commander's side; if Slaughter needed to get strategic word to Captain Hays or Captain Wallace, he needed his express rider ready to hand; if he needed to send an urgent word to other companies rumored to be on patrol in the region, he needed to have William close, ready to ride on the instant.

After shaking water from the brim, William fingered the new hole in his hat, then crammed it back on his head. Dangerous as his duty was, and foul as the weather was for doing it in, it was good to be needed.

It was hard to stay alert hunkered in the saddle against the elements, the frigid shying of rain obscuring all other sounds, and isolating every man from every other in his misery, a misery so potent under the stern scowl of the elements that it even made fear of the Indians recede. William wondered which was worse, dying of raw exposure, or getting his head split open with a tomahawk. A stronger momentary shower of rain pounded his threadbare coat; the tomahawk would be quicker.

They slogged on through the muck and drenching forest, without sight or sound of Indians, for more than two uneventful and despondent hours. Heads bowed, the men and horses passed like phantoms beneath endless columns of Douglas fir trees, their bark black with moisture, their boughs saturated with rain. As if the men were not sufficiently wet to the bone already, moaning in the forest canopy high above them, the wind kicked up, flicking still more concentrated showers down on the miserable troop. William did his best to control the spasms of shivering that jerked at every nerve in his body.

"Injuns got the same," said Andrew Burge, philosophically.

"Looks like they's smarter than we are, though," said Tom Perkins. "Ain't seen a one of 'em for hours."

"Feet up, warming their toes in their longhouses," said Burge.

"Like I says, smarter than we are," said Tom.

"Wish I were with 'em," said Burge through clenched teeth.

"Well, I wish they was here," said Andrew Laws. "Me and Belinda, we'd know what to do if they was."

"Silence," said Slaughter. "In all likelihood, they are here."

No sooner had he said the words than a burst of flame came from a dense patch of salal visible through the driving rain across the river. More shooting followed. *Blam! Blam! Blam!*

"Tell Captain Hays to circle around to the left!" yelled Slaughter. "We'll trap them in the middle."

Bent low, William drove his heels into Prophet's flanks, bullets whizzing close as he rode. Moments later, after delivering orders to Hays, William saw Slaughter advancing toward the Indians' position. In his wake lay two men, one on top of the other. William reined in and leapt from his saddle.

He would never forget what he saw. By the army uniform, it was clearly soldiers not militia. An Indian had shot the first man square in the chest—William's hands trembled as he inspected their wounds. The bullet had exited through the man's back, and lodged in the chest of the man directly behind him. Two men down—with one bullet.

37

HORSE THIEVES

The two men shot with one Indian bullet were John Edgar and Addisom Parham. Timorous Parham had never let Edgar out of his sight, shadowed him like he had been his guardian angel. So close were they, it had only taken one bullet to finish them off. Three more men were badly wounded in that dismal skirmish near the Carbon River. They buried John Edgar November 21, 1855; the rain halted, but in its place a clammy fog settled over the bowed heads of the sober company giving their last respects.

As November drizzled into December, more men spilt their blood and expelled their last breath under the vault of the dense forests of Puget Sound—white and Indian. Fiercely determined to keep what was theirs, the Indians were showing more fight than anyone figured they would.

Major General John Wool, aging commander-in-chief of all US military on the west coast of North America, from his headquarters far away in sunny California was largely unconvinced of the seriousness of the bloody drama unfolding in Washington Territory. Desperate to defend themselves, ordinary settlers—farmers and trappers, husbands and fathers—formed themselves into militias, drilling in the mud of every fledgling town and settlement in the region. Small, determined bands of unofficial militia took it upon themselves to rid the territory of hostile Indians.

More than thirty fortified blockhouses were hastily built from felled trees throughout the region, and refugee settlers abandoned their homesteads and fled for their lives to many of them. The town of Steilacoom converted Reverend John DeVore's two-story log home into a refugee center, and into a makeshift field hospital for tending the wounded. Folks from Olympia feverishly worked at erecting a stout fortification where Third and Main Streets intersected. Residents of Seattle built a defensive wall to protect the cluster of thirty cabins, sawmills, and claptrap structures that made up their town. Under Captain Hewitt's guidance, Seattle dwellers worked around the clock, building two parallel walls of sturdy lumber milled at the Alki Mill, set eighteen inches apart, the gap filled with packed sawdust and gravel to make it bulletproof. Similar preparations sprang up all along the towns and settlements of Puget Sound.

After the death of Edgar and the casualties inflicted on other men under his command, Lieutenant Slaughter issued a new order. "There's no telling the good ones from the bad. Shoot any Indian who breathes."

William could not help being troubled by such an order. What would happen if one of them came across Charlie Salitat? And there were others like Charlie. At Slaughter's order, men like Dr. Burns and Andrew Laws readied their weapons with glee.

"What I've been saying all along," said Laws.

"Let us commence," said Burns with a sniff, "and be done with them."

"It's like hunting deer," said volunteer David Hall. "Leave your gun in the cabin, you'll see dozens. Have it loaded and at the ready—you ain't going to see nothing."

William had to agree. They could ride for days and not see a single Indian, and then all of a sudden, when they least expected it, another ambush, more blood, more death. More wilderness funerals.

Today was one of the dull, slogging days, not a sign of an Indian from first light to dusk, not a whoop, not a feather. On days like this, William began daydreaming—that was that. It was all over. The Indians had shrunk back into their cluttered little longhouse villages at the mouths of the rivers, content to gather and eat the plentiful harvests of sea and land. He kept reassuring himself of this hope that afternoon when Slaughter ordered William and Prophet to ride north, meet up with Captain Hewitt's troop, joining them from Seattle, and arrange a rendezvous for the next day. His hopes were high; nevertheless, William kept his eyes peeled, his revolver loaded, and his head low—but not an Indian in sight.

As dusk fell, Lieutenant Slaughter called the halt. That's when something began feeling wrong to William. With so many dangers encircling them, he was learning not always to trust his intuitions. A premonition of danger could turn up groundless—nothing gained, nothing lost. So, in a moment of apparent safety, they could be, in a flash, assaulted by the enemy—everything lost.

Nevertheless, William felt that something was not right. Prophet seemed to feel the same. William studied the terrain: a shot-up longhouse, dense forest, remains of a rotten barn, small clearing. He knew this place. Slaughter had given the order to make camp on precisely the same spot where McAllister and Connell were shot only a month ago. William wished he'd picked almost any other place in the territory—except anywhere nearby where Miles and Moses had been shot.

"This here's bad luck," murmured Tom Perkins, scowling at the terrain. "They say Leschi done the killing."

"Who says that?" asked William, heaving Prophet's saddle off.

"Everybody knows it's Leschi," said Tom.

"Well, everybody's wrong then," said William. "Leschi weren't anywheres near here."

"And just how can Bill Tidd be so certain sure about that?" asked Tom, dropping his saddlebags on the ground and eyeing him suspiciously.

William started to reply, then clamped his mouth shut. If he said he learned it from Charlie Salitat, from an Indian, it would look like he'd be fraternizing with the enemy. Slaughter had made it clear what they were now to do when they met an Indian—*any* Indian.

"I ride express," said William, "me and Prophet do. We learn things. Leschi weren't here, not when Miles and Moses went under. That's a fact."

"Stop your yammering and make camp!"

William couldn't be sure whose voice it was, but it was an order. When a commander orders his company to make camp, good soldiers do what they're told. There were many things to do when making a temporary military camp: collecting fresh water, assessing food supplies and cooking, pitching tents or finding shelter, drying out clothes, cleaning weapons. But of central importance was the care of horses. Men on the march generally took good care of their horses. So much depended on them. A lame horse, or a sick one, was as good as not having one. And in this hostile wilderness, not having a horse was a death sentence. As far as William was concerned, Noclas was right: There was no better horse than Prophet. He'd proved it time and again.

"You'll be fine, Prophet," said William just before crawling into the sack for the night. "Here you are. I've saved out your favorite." William smiled as the velvety lips of the animal nibbled at the lump sugar in his palm, then nuzzled in his pockets for more, sniffing loudly. "Naw, that's all I got. You get some rest, now. I'll see you in the morning."

It was during David Hall's guard duty that the alarm came. William had just drifted off into a troubled doze, when he was suddenly wide awake, his heart thundering against his ribs. Hall was screaming like doomsday had come and gone. "The Injuns! They're after the horses!"

William bolted to his feet, grabbed up his pistol, and plunged into the darkness and dense fog in the direction of the picket line, where they had tethered their horses for the night. Judging by the stumbling and cursing all around him, the other men were doing the same.

But they were too late. More than two dozen horses—gone. Stolen from under their noses while they slept. At least the Indians had not succeeded in stealing all of them. He could hear the remaining horses snorting and stamping their hooves. William was frantic. Was Prophet one of them? It was so dark he couldn't see his hand in front of his face.

"A light! Does anyone have a match?" cried William.

"No light!" It was Slaughter's voice. When he spoke like that it was not necessary to see his face to know who was doing the speaking; it was an order not to be disobeyed. "They're near to hand. Strike a light and an Indian sniper will put a hole in you. Losing horses is bad enough. We can ill afford to lose more men."

William slept little that night. If Prophet had been stolen by the Indians, he was ruined. Without his horse—Noclas's horse—he was worthless to the army.

38

WITHOUT PROPHET

Next morning, it was confirmed, and it was worse than they feared. The Indians had stolen thirty-two horses. Prophet was one of them. It was one of the darkest days of William Tidd's life. What good was an express rider without a horse? And Prophet was not just any horse. What would he tell Noclas? "Your one-of-a-kind, best horse on the continent—I done lost her to thieving Indians."

For Lieutenant Slaughter, it was a devastating blow. How would he explain this to his superiors? His hopes of success, of a military triumph, one that would reflect well on his leadership, at this unfortuitous turn of events, were smashed. Dangerous as this operation had been, the real peril to life was increased substantially by the loss of so many of his men's horses. He could not make half of his men march on foot through rugged territory teeming with hostile Indians. It was suicide.

William felt like he had lost his only link to his home. He was flooded with unwanted emotions at the loss, and angry with himself for them. It struck him like lightning to the tallest tree on a hilltop: Prophet was more than a horse to him. The animal had been his protector, his link to Noclas, to the old man's wisdom, and in some hard-to-define way, a link to his sister—to everything that mattered to him. It was asking a lot of horse. And on top of all, he had been his friend.

While Slaughter, Hays, and Wallace conferred together in the lieutenant's tent, a small contingent of militia rode into camp. This was not altogether uncommon, reports and dispatches arriving from Steilacoom, Olympia, and Seattle. This band had come from Steilacoom and appeared to be led by a man who called himself Elijah Price. Slaughter called the man into the tent.

William observed what was going on around him as if in a trance. He had no idea what to do next, how to go on without Prophet. William had thrown Prophet's saddle over a downed log last night. He scowled at it. The Indians had only stolen the horses, not the saddles and bridles. William walked over to the log and swung his leg over the vacant saddle. With his bowie knife, he slashed off a low branch of a cedar tree and began viciously carving it into a point. Carving helped him think, and he had need of thinking just then. The mound of wood shavings between his feet grew higher.

When the new militiaman Elijah Price came from Slaughter's tent, he halted and looked around at the dejected men. "Hey, anybody here by the name of Tidd?"

William halted, his bowie knife poised over the dwindling remains of a chunk of wood.

"I was asked to give this here package to a feller answering to the name of Bill Tidd." The man laughed. "Tidd's kinfolk gived it to me—big feller, face like the inside of a chimney, craggy as the hills, and old as the hills. And a little white girl, and a fine looking young woman, fine figure of a woman, she was, if you're asking me. But a jumbled-up confused excuse for kinfolk, that is, if you're asking me. But they done sent this along for Bill Tidd. Unless he's done got himself killed. I reckon it's fair game for the rest of us if he's dead."

William snatched the package from Price's grip, mumbled his thanks, and headed off to be by himself, something there was not nearly enough of in the militia. Today he felt it more keenly than ever before. Carrying water last night, he'd noticed a depression formed by an outcrop of rock jutting over the hollow where the spring flowed. It would be a dry place to read his mail.

A fine time to receive a package, he thought as he cut through the string and tore it open. It contained several items. The first one he picked up was from Junebug. She had made him a corn cake, "baked hard so it'll hold up in all weathers," and she'd sent along a little pot of honey. Noclas had included a cloth sack stuffed full with tea, and he had written a short scrawly letter, hoping the White-Man's-Foot tea would do him good, and assuring William of his prayers. And Junebug had been at her sketching. Though the charcoal was smudged from rough handling, this time there could be no doubt about who it was. Sister Marguerite, but not looking like any nun William had ever seen. Junebug had written in neat cursive at the bottom of the drawing. "I wish you could see how she does it, tending the wounded like she does. That's why she has not got on her wimple. She used it for bandaging up a volunteer's head at the DeVore blockhouse. When she came by for supper like that, I just had to draw her picture for you. Don't she look nice without her head covered all over like that? Noclas got you a newspaper, knowing how you like to read and keep up on what's going on in the world."

There was more, but William would save it for later. Unfolding the *Courier,* it was like hearing James Wiley talking as he read. Reading that paper under cover of the rocky outcrop, rain drip-dripping off the lip of the rock, William could see the journalist. Though it was Wiley who had gotten him into this war, William, in spite of himself, couldn't help smiling as he pictured the journalist hiking his spectacles up on his nose in salute.

Wiley wrote about a fellow in Steilacoom, Lemuel Bills, who had advertised in the *Courier* for a wife. Just as the war broke out, Ellen Brooks answered the advertisement, and Wiley began printing the correspondence of their budding romance. "Where are you Lemuel, during these times that try the pluck of men and the souls of women? Now's the time to immortalize your name. Oh Lemuel, that you could become great. Oh that one feather might be plucked from the tail of that venerable bird the American eagle, for the purpose of inscribing upon the annals of fame the name of—"

William looked up. The rain had stopped and there was a momentary sun break, a shaft of light illuminating a gravelly bar along the edge of the spring. He heard boots squelching in the mud, then clonking on stones. Someone was approaching. Leaning forward he peered out, rainwater still dripping off the rock outcrop above his head. It was the new volunteer, Elijah Price, swinging an empty water bucket and whistling.

Pressing his back hard against the shallow cave, William hoped he would not be seen. Price's boots crunched on the gravel, and he squatted down as he filled the bucket at the spring. Out of the corner of his eye, William caught sight of a glint in the dense salal twenty yards on the other side of the spring, the sun reflecting off something shiny. Salal leaves were shiny when wet. William scowled, studying the underbrush. But this was shinier, like metal. Suddenly, William was at full alert, his heart pumping his blood so loudly he was afraid it would give away his position.

"Take cover!" he yelled at Price.

At the same instant, a single musket shot thundered from the clump of salal. Price, in the act of lifting the full bucket of water from the spring, lost his grip, spun on his heel in the gravel, and slumped to the ground.

William's shout and the musket shot brought more men from the camp. Yanking his revolver from his holster, William fired into the clump of underbrush. Other men did the same. But the Indian was gone, a lone sniper, so it seemed. There was no return fire.

"I reckon it were Leschi," said Tom Perkins. "It's his way, you know."

"Did anyone see him?" asked Slaughter.

William told what he saw. "But I did not see Leschi, only a reflection off a knife blade or something shiny. Didn't actually see any Indian."

"Well, we know what he done," said Tom, "murdering savages."

"What did he say his name was?" asked David Hall.

"Price," said William. "Elijah Price."

"He just arrived today," said Hall, "and shot dead clean through his vitals. Now that's what I call bad luck."

Slaughter looked worried. "We can't stay here. Saddle up. We head north in a quarter of an hour."

"Saddle up, Sir?" said William.

Slaughter blinked rapidly. "Those who can, saddle up. The rest will march. We are going to recover these horses. Every last one of them."

39

SHOT IN THE DARK

After three miserable and fruitless days of scouring the forest for the Indians that stole their horses, Slaughter ordered his discouraged and exhausted band of men to halt and make camp at Brannon's Prairie, Captain Hewitt and his Seattle militia having joined them.

"This here's where it happened," said Laws.

"Where what happened?" asked Tom Perkins.

"Indians cut up Mr. and Mrs. Brannon real bad," said Laws. "This being their homestead, right here where our lieutenant has ordered us to make camp, their ghosts hovering up there in them trees, no doubt, a-watching over all. Chopped up the missus and her baby and dumped their bodies down the well, yonder." Laws indicated the well with a casual toss of his head, pointing with his thumb over his shoulder. "Just there. Indian agent's report says they done it with a sharpened sawmill file."

William shuddered from more than the cold. He wondered how Laws could be so uncaring about the suffering of others, Indian or white, and how it was he knew anything about an official territorial report about anything.

"Indeed, the savages' close-quarter weapon of choice," said Dr. Burns.

"That's a fact," said Laws. "Watch your guts when they draw one of them."

"Our commander lodges tonight in luxury," said Burns, feigning a bow. "If you call the deceased family's root house luxury."

"In these parts, that there *is* luxury," said Tom. "Whatever else there was the Injuns done burned to the ground weeks ago."

"Captain Hewitt don't look happy," said Laws. "Something's up."

William strolled over to the root house to be on hand in case Slaughter wanted him for any reason, and to find out, if he could, what was the matter. The door to the root house had been wrenched off its hinges, and he couldn't help overhearing the men inside through the opening.

"I don't like it." It was Hewitt's voice. "Danged Injuns everywhere. It maybe don't at West Point, but lightning do strike twice around here."

"We're the ones poised to strike," said Slaughter.

"We are?" said Hewitt. "I reckon the Injuns are doing most of the striking in these parts."

"Captain Wallace and his militia hold the Puyallup River, here." It was Slaughter's voice, and it sounded like the men were poring over a map. "And Hays and his men are covering Muck Creek and the Nisqually, here, and here. Our job is to corner the Indians here, between the White and Green Rivers. Brannon Prairie's the perfect staging ground."

"I respectfully disagree, Sir," said Hewitt. "There's a fortified camp a few miles up the White River, heaps more protection than here in this exposed hollow. Think what happened to the Brannon family in this very spot, Sir."

There was silence for a moment, then William heard Slaughter heave a deep sigh. "The fact is, my men are spent, exhausted. Half of them have lost their horses to the Indians. Even my express rider has no horse. All of them are footsore and done in, and that's a fact. Captain Hewitt, I don't believe my men could march another step if the Devil were at their heels. Besides, it's almost dark. We camp here for the night. That's final."

Slaughter came to the open door. He saw William standing nearby. "Bill Tidd, gather up some firewood. This root house is colder than outdoors. Good for potatoes. Not so good for men."

"Sir?" said William. "A fire?"

"Yes, a fire," said Slaughter, fingering the row of brass buttons up the front of his uniform, a hint of irritation in his voice. "You need not worry, Bill Tidd. Captain Hewitt here is doing more than his share of that. Get us some wood and strike a fire. It's perfectly safe."

Over the last six weeks of Indians and soldiers skulking after each other, back and forth, through the area, the Brannon's firewood had been plundered until there wasn't a sliver left. The Indians had torched the cabin and outbuildings after the massacre so there was no scavenging dry wood from them. William checked his revolver and strolled into the forest. There were always strips of cedar bark and chunks of Douglas fir bark on the forest floor, kept more or less dry by the heavy canopy of fir boughs above. Once bark caught hold, it burned long, glowing and hot.

Light drizzle fell, nothing more than a heavy mist, as William walked into the trees. Though it was dusk, a lingering layer of gray light in the clouds to the west, in the forest it was full dark, like midnight when there's no moon or stars out—which was most of the time in December.

Feeling his way to the wide trunk of an old cedar tree, William bent over and began feeling around for bark. Snatching it up with his right hand, he made a crook of his left to pile it on. Then he heard it, a scuffling in the underbrush, maybe a muskrat in the salal—probably a raccoon. Moving cautiously in the dark, William felt his way to the base of another tree, gathering more bark. Moments later as he rose to his feet, another sound made him catch his breath. An owl hoot-hooting high overhead, or was it that high? It seemed to come from his left, due north and east, and coming closer.

William felt the pile of bark in his left arm. If he could grab up a few more dry chunks in his right, he'd be able to make a nice roaring fire inside the root house for Lieutenant Slaughter.

Just as he bent over, William felt his spine tingling, the hair rising on the back of his neck, and his scalp going numb. He was not alone. There was no scientific way to explain things like this, which troubled William, but he knew he was not alone.

Suddenly, something plopped against the brim of his hat; it felt like a fir cone. William swallowed the lump forming in his throat. This was a forest, with fir trees, with cones in them; maybe it just fell on its own from the boughs overhead. But he knew it wasn't so.

"Make no sound," hissed a voice, so close William could smell the boiled camas bulb on his breath.

Frantic, William realized how utterly exposed he was. His arms loaded with firewood, there was no chance of drawing his Colt, not without making a racket dropping the wood. By then there could be a sawmill file, sharpened to a razor's edge, in his ribs.

"I not hurt Bill Tidd," said the voice.

"You know me?" said William, his voice dry and pinched sounding to his ears.

The man gave off a soft, *Hyuk-hyuk!* a whispered laugh.

"Charlie? Charlie Salitat? Is that you? What are you doing here?"

A wave of relief flooded over William, and he suddenly wanted to sit down with the Indian and tell him everything that had happened. "I lost Prophet. Gone, stolen by the Indians about three nights ago. It's the worst thing that's happened. Well, there's been worse troubles I reckon for other folks, but for me, losing Prophet was like losing my life. What will the Indians do to him?"

"Indians like horses," said Charlie. "Take good care of Prophet."

"How do you know?"

"I Indian," said Charlie, "and Prophet horse."

And then William heard Charlie in the dark next to him suppressing little hiccups of laughter.

"Charlie? Stop clowning. What are you up to?"

"I bring you gifts," said Charlie. "First, a warning. Brannon Prairie, not good place for you tonight. Tell big white chief, not good place for white man tonight."

It's what Hewitt had been saying to Lieutenant Slaughter an hour ago. How did Charlie know these things? William wondered.

"Leschi and Tecumseh," said Charlie, "they have plan to destroy Seattle. With two bands of warriors, they attack one hour after bedtime. When guns stand behind doors, as Indians say." He paused.

"What is the plan?" asked William afraid to hear the answer.

"Tecumseh walk into Seattle," said Charlie, "claim he is friendly Indian. Leschi with one thousand warriors prepare attack from woods on hill east of town."

"Then what?" asked William.

"Kill white settlers, kill all white settlers," said Charlie. "Then with canoes, Indians board ships anchored in bay, *Decatur* and *Active*. Kill crew and steal gunpowder and supplies."

"They must be stopped," said William.

"Yes."

"But how?"

"Bill Tidd, he stop them," said Charlie. "Ride swiftly to Seattle, warn Lieutenant Phelps and Captain Gansevoort of *Decatur*."

It was William's turn to laugh. "Charlie, you ain't been listening to what I was telling you," he said bitterly. "Ride swiftly, you say. Look at me. All I gots is my shanks and my feet. I ain't got no horse to ride swiftly on."

Charlie did not reply, and William heard the Indian taking steps back into the forest.

"Charlie, don't you run off now!" hissed William at the darkness.

Then he heard Charlie's faint steps coming back toward him. But he wasn't alone. He was leading something heavy behind him.

William knew that smell, that sound, that aura emanating from a large body mass, bigger than any man. Inhaling deeply, William knew. Charlie was leading a horse.

"Charlie," said William, a warning lilt in his voice. "I don't want just any horse, and I sure ain't going to take yours."

More of Charlie's soft *Hyuk-hyuk!* chuckling. And then something came over William. Pitch dark though it was, a mysterious sense, less measurable than the everyday ones, enveloped him. It was a horse, but not just any horse. Prophet. He knew it was Prophet.

"I-I don't understand," he said, running his hands over the familiar contours of the creature's neck and face. In the darkness, he could only touch the horse, and feel Prophet's hard muscles, his soft hide, his velvety nose, now nibbling at William's hat. "H-how did you do it?"

"It better I not tell," said Charlie. "But remember warning. White man not safe here tonight. And every man, woman, and child in Seattle dies if Bill Tidd does not ride swiftly." Then Charlie gave William detailed information about the best way for him to get into Seattle undetected by the Indians. "Not Indian trail from lake. Enter town by narrow sand-spit south of the marsh. It low tide by midnight. You safe then. Go now."

William knew he should act on Charlie's warning immediately, but he lingered. "I heard what you done for the white folks in the Puyallup Valley, after the massacre, after you prayed with Johnny King's dying mother, and we parted ways. I heard what you done. Folks is calling you 'Paul Revere of Puget Sound,' they are, warning people and saving their lives, like you done. Has a nice ring to it, don't it, 'Paul Revere of Puget Sound'? Charlie Salitat, you's going to be in books for what you done for folks."

William had been stroking the soft hair on Prophet's forehead, Charlie not saying a word at his side. And then William knew, Charlie was no longer at his side. Opening his eyes wider, trying to see into the blackness of the forest, William searched for the big Indian. He knew it was no use. Charlie was gone, vanished, like a dream.

Moments later, back at camp, William tethered Prophet in the shadows. Ducking under the low doorway of the root house, William entered with his armload of bark. There Hewitt and Slaughter were, studying the map by candlelight. He had to tell them, but just as he opened his mouth—

"Get us a fire roaring, Bill Tidd," said Slaughter, blinking rapidly. "I'm chilled to the bone and hungry as a horse."

"Sir?" said William.

"Not now, Tidd. You can see we're busy."

In moments William—down low on his knees, his mind whirling in torment—had coaxed the bark into a warm smoky glow; moments later, with steady blowing, bright yellow flames, ablaze with light, lapped at the dry bark. With the butt of his musket, a private busted through the cedar shakes to make a hole in the low roof for the smoke.

Avoiding the black opening of the doorway, William held his hands up to the flames. He had to tell Lieutenant Slaughter what Charlie had said, but how? He remembered

Charles "The Rustler" Wren, playing false with Indians and whites, stirring up trouble on both sides for his own profit. Things like that cause wars. And playing double is like spying. Was that what Charlie was, a spy? Either way, it did not look good. Meeting up with an Indian—any Indian—in the dark woods, talking with him, being on friendly terms, accepting a horse from him? In time of war, a fellow could get himself hanged for less.

"Potatoes, Sir," said Private Callum, coming in the doorway and plopping down a large knobby gunnysack; opening the sack, he began arranging potatoes around William's fire.

As William watched, another thought occurred to him, more troubling still. How was he going to explain to Lieutenant Slaughter that his express rider now had his stolen horse back? An Indian had met him in the forest and given it back to him, just like that. Feeling his neck, William gazed into the flames, swallowing the lump forming in his throat. Slaughter was a spit-and-polish military man; he did things by the book. From what he'd heard, the military had only one course of action for a man caught consorting with the enemy.

William rose and stepped through the doorway, leaving the warmth and light behind him, the cold and wet hitting him full in the face. Covering the dozen yards back to his horse, he wondered if maybe he needed to hide Prophet, disguise him in some way, but how? "We may just have an enormous problem on our hands, old boy," he said, stroking the horse's neck. Turning his collar up at the chill, William looked back toward the root house, a warm glow of light coming from the open doorway.

It was as if time suddenly slowed to a crawl, every detail of movement imprinting itself on William's memory. He watched as the lieutenant rose from his chair at the table in the root house, and walked to the doorway. Now backlit by the fire William had laid, every detail of Slaughter's lean figure was visible in silhouette, the doorframe outlining and enlarging him against the blackness of the night.

"Bill Tidd!" he called. "Where on earth did you find your—"

Blam! His words were cut off by the crack of a musket firing in the night.

40

IMMEDIATE ACTION

With a single bullet, an Indian sniper, at close range, lurking in the black shadows of the nearby woods, shot Lieutenant William Slaughter clean through the heart. He was dead before he hit the packed-earth floor of the root house, now stained with blood.

Whether the shot was luck or skill, it mattered not a whisker to the young lieutenant. But the shot acted as a signal. An instant after the young officer fell dead, a clattering of musket fire burst from the darkness and bullets tore through the encampment. Inside the root house, Private Callum collapsed in a heap, potatoes scattering, his blood pooling and hissing in the fire. At the same instant, Captain Hewitt clutched at the left side of his face; William later learned that it was only a flesh wound, one that plowed a path through his whiskers, doing more damage to facial hair than flesh and blood; ever after a shiny trough of scar tissue in which no hair would grow adorned his cheek. The Indians shot well that night, and several other privates and a corporal fell to their deaths. It was a daring barrage, and it worked.

In the chaos that followed, men returning fire at dark phantoms in the night, Slaughter now dead, Captain Hewitt took firm command. "Douse your fires! Every danged one of 'em!" Air filling with smoke and foul smells, men dumped coffee, squash soup, baked beans, anything liquid they had on their campfires.

"Take cover and commence firing!" ordered Hewitt.

"Bill Tidd!" he yelled.

At the sound of his own name, William's heart lurched into his throat.

"Mount up, on the double! How good's that horse of your'n? Wait, didn't the Injuns steal—never mind. Get word to Seattle. We're pinned down, 'bout to be massacred."

William vaulted into the saddle, a torrent of emotions pummeling him from every side. If only he had not delayed. If only he had spoken up to Lieutenant Slaughter, told him what he knew, told him everything.

"After you get word to Seattle," yelled Hewitt, "hightail it to Olympia. Get word to Acting-Governor Mason—and deliver the unhappy news to Mrs. Slaughter, with my deepest condolences—"

A fresh volley of musket fire drowned the rest of his words. Bent low in the saddle, William buried his heels in Prophet's flanks. "We got to get to Seattle, Prophet, and swiftly!" There was no time to lose. Deeply troubled at the blood and thundering he was leaving behind him, William and Prophet hurtled into the darkness toward Seattle.

How many times in the next hour and a half he ought to have fallen in a ditch, Prophet's legs broken in a rabbit hole, or on any other of dozens of hazards invisible in the night, or how many bands of Indians on the warpath Prophet managed to sense, steer clear, and avoid, William would never know.

At the convergence of the White River and the Cedar River, the wagon road improved, the rain let up, and William urged Prophet to go faster still. As he rode the final miles to Seattle that dark night, he began thinking more clearly about the ambush and the shooting of Lieutenant Slaughter. Out of the chaos and noise of battle, he began asking himself some questions. Who had done it? Angry at himself for even thinking it, William wondered. Charlie had been there, only moments before the killing. He was better than most Indians with his musket. Shaking his head violently, William refused to believe it; it felt like betrayal even to form the thought in his mind. Besides, if Charlie did it, why would he warn William to tell his commander that it wasn't a safe place to camp? It made no sense. And why would he send William to warn Seattle against an Indian attack? No, it was simply out of the question that Charlie had anything to do with it. His being right there—that was just circumstantial evidence. Surely Charlie being Indian, and being there at the time of the shooting would not be enough to condemn him, not in a just court of law, if it came to that.

"It won't be long now," William said in Prophet's ear. "Seattle's just there. Wood chips, mud, and saltwater—I can smell it."

Seattle's cluster of log cabins and some milled-lumber buildings, dozens of windows twinkling cheerily with candlelight, lay unsuspecting before him. Anchored in Elliot Bay were the sloop-of-war *Decatur* and the well-armed *Active,* just as Charlie had said they would be, their cabin lights glowing yellow from portholes and shimmering on the sea water. William peered up at the dark ridge of Douglas fir trees lining the hill just above the town. If Charlie was right, Leschi and a thousand painted warriors lay ready to pounce, awaiting the signal to fall on defenseless fathers and mothers tucking their little ones in bed for the night. He had to hurry. It sounded like an owl reunion, so much hooting was echoing from the ridge north and east of the town.

Rehearsing Charlie's instructions, William oriented himself to the lay of the settlement. "Follow the narrow stream south of the settlement, and you'll find the way into

Seattle on a narrow sand-spit." The tide was low. Moments later, breathing in the piney scent of fresh-sawn lumber at Yesler's mill, he nudged Prophet into a gallop, mud splattering on the main thoroughfare of Seattle.

He hesitated, doubts flooding his mind. Here he was doing what Paul Revere had done in 1775. Doing what Charlie had done saving dozens of families in the Puyallup Valley two months ago. But what if they didn't believe him? Prophet snorted, shaking his head and pawing the mud and wood chips in the street.

Not certain what to say, William cleared his throat and yelled, "To arms! To arms!"

"I say you'd best put your own danged arms up," growled a voice, "afore I blow your head off."

William halted, men accosting him with questions. Who was he? How had he acquired his information? How many Indians? How did he know they weren't friendly ones?

"There's no time to waste." shouted William over the crowd. "Snuff your fires—all lights must be extinguished! Who is in charge here? I have urgent news. I must speak to Lieutenant Phelps."

"You are doing it, son," said a tall man, stepping from the shadows, dressed much as Lieutenant Slaughter had been dressed. "Tell me everything you know."

William had never spoken so rapidly in all his life. When he told them of Tecumseh's plan to infiltrate Seattle, to lie in readiness to fall on the townsfolk when they were all asleep, Phelps cut him off.

"Tecumseh's already in town. Claims he's a friendly. I questioned him just this afternoon. Didn't care much for his answers then, and I care less for them now."

"He and a band of their kind are holed up at Tom Pepper's place," shouted a voice from the crowd. "Up to no good, for sure."

Phelps took command. After ordering a dozen of his soldiers to surround Tom Pepper's house, he ordered everyone to douse any light. "Load your muskets, men! Make ready to defend your families. Women and children to the blockhouses. If this here express rider, Bill Tidd, is right about half of this, there's no time to lose!"

Turning to William, Lieutenant Phelps looked levelly at him and said, "Bill Tidd, I need you to get word to Captain Gansevoort on the *Decatur*. Tell him the whole story, and tell him it is my urgent recommendation that he and Captain Morris ready their cannons for immediate action."

41

THE BATTLE OF SEATTLE

Lieutenant Phelps handed William a hastily drafted but detailed dispatch for him to deliver to Captain Gansevoort. After that he assigned a young man named Milton Holgate to accompany William and a private named Carson to the shore, with orders to arrange for a boat to transport Carson and William out to the *Decatur,* without delay.

"Follow me," drawled Holgate. William decided that they were about the same age. "My people were the first settlers in these parts. I know every rathole and molehill in this county."

When they reached the beach, the cloud cover thinned, and the moon cast a silvery illumination over the town, the shoreline, and the ships. In a flurry of shouting and running, men carried children and led their wives into several sturdy blockhouses. A fire glowed on the east edge of the settlement.

"Injuns must have attacked already," said Holgate with a shrug. Their boots crunching on the gravel shore, Holgate halted at a dugout canoe.

He spun on his heel and frowned at Prophet. "You know you can't take your horse?"

William, leading Prophet by the reins, halted abruptly. Somehow he had not reckoned with leaving Prophet on shore.

"Don't worry about a thing. I'll look after him for you," said Holgate, reaching for the reins. "I'll stable him at Yesler's mill. Phelps has been using it for army headquarters anyway. Ain't nothing to worry about."

After losing Prophet and only hours ago getting him back, William's grip on Prophet's reins was like a blacksmith's vice on a chunk of iron.

Holgate whistled. "You've got some grip, there. Ain't nothing going to happen to your horse, not while he's in Milton Holgate's care." Nodding at the reins, Holgate continued. "I reckon there's lives depending on them dispatches you're carrying to the ship—*sans cheval*. That there's the Frenchies' way of saying 'without your danged horse,' case you didn't know."

Without a word, William handed over the reins. He caressed Prophet's neck, turned, snatched up a paddle, and stepped into the canoe.

"I ain't much good at paddling," said Private Carson as he clambered after William into the canoe.

"Stay low, and follow my lead," said William, burying his paddle in the water. The sooner they got out to the *Decatur*, the sooner this would all be over, and he could get Prophet back again.

Just as William glanced back over his shoulder, hoping to catch a last glimpse of Prophet, a single musket shot rent the air, echoing eerily over the water. A man who had been standing in the doorway of one of the blockhouses, his figure framed by lantern light within, crumpled to the ground.

"Ain't nothing we can do for that feller," said Carson. William, numb with recollection of Slaughter's death in much the same fashion, knew the soldier was right. The battle had begun. Reaching forward, he buried his paddle in the water and pulled with all his might.

With every stroke, *Decatur* grew larger. William began to be worried. They were paddling a dugout canoe, like what Indians paddle. It was dark out. What if a trigger-happy marine thought they *were* Indians? All he could do was hope for the best, though Charlie, no doubt, would tell him to do some praying. It occurred suddenly to William that Charlie, knowing what he had sent William to do, likely *was* praying.

"Halt! Who goes there?" barked a marine.

William heard the ominous click of a musket hammer. "Tell him!" hissed William to the private.

"Private Richard Carson, Third Division, under command of Lieutenant Phelps, Sir! We have urgent news for Captain Gansevoort. Urgent news! Permission to come aboard?"

"And who's that with you?" growled the marine. "Let me hear him speak for hisself."

"William Tidd, Washington Territorial Militia, express rider, on urgent business for Captain Hewitt and Lieutenant Phelps, Sir. Permission to come aboard?"

"Permission granted," said the marine. "But keep your hands where I can see 'em."

Captain Gansevoort listened to William's story. To William's relief, Gansevoort, unblinking eyes appraising him, asked not a single clarifying question, nor did he ask where William had learned his information. He turned to his executive officer. "Let us show them of what stuff the navy is made."

"Beat to quarters!" The schooner was suddenly alive with activity, bosun's whistle tweeting, first mate shouting orders, the clank and chink of weapons passing from man to man. Signal flags gave word to *Active* anchored two hundred yards away.

"Ready the guns!" yelled the mate.

William positioned himself on the port quarter rail. Here he was clear of the gun crews manning their cannons, and it gave him a decent vantage point on the battle. Grateful for the reprieve in the clouds and rain, William gazed out over Seattle and her coastline, shimmering lovely and clear in the filtered moonlight. Struck by the momentary beauty of the scene, he felt like the battle about to unfold, the intractable hostility, the certainty of violent death about to be played on the wilderness stage before his eyes was all a bad dream.

Phelps had given detailed instruction to the captain of the *Decatur* about where to concentrate his cannons. Ringing clearly over the water, William heard the energizing staccato of the bugle call to arms. Phelps's division was advancing into position to defend the town against the attacking Indians from the ridge. It was more of a local joke to call Phelps's soldiers a division. William had picked up enough military jargon in the last months to know that a division was supposed to be thousands of men, not Phelps's dozens—eighty-five, maybe a hundred soldiers. The Indians, on the other hand, appeared to have closer to a thousand.

William was not prepared for what happened next.

"Fire!" yelled the mate.

The deafening roar of nine twelve-pounders erupted simultaneously. When that first volley of cannons fired, the terrifying thundering in his ears, magnified by the water, made William feel like major organs inside his body had come unstuck from their intended places. His eyes burned with smoke, and his lungs groped for clean air. He had clamped his hands over his ears, but a split second too late; he feared his eardrums might have burst.

William had never been on anything larger than a canoe, leastwise on board a warship. Though *Decatur* was by no means the largest vessel in the US Navy, it was a sturdy sloop-of-war, equipped with eighteen twelve-pounder Napoleon gun-howitzer cannons, capable of firing exploding shells enormous distances with terrifying accuracy. In the next hour, he came to have a deep respect for the able command of Captain Gansevoort and the skill of the men who obeyed those orders like well-fitted cogs in a machine. And he couldn't help feeling sorry for the Indians; their zeal was no match for the firepower arrayed against them.

As near as William could tell, the damage of that first well-aimed barrage was significant, and wholly unexpected by the Indians; returning musket fire from their guns was wholly disproportionate. The house where Tecumseh and his "friendly" Indians had waited to break out and commence slaughtering the townsfolk took a direct hit from Gansevoort's guns, a geyser of smoke and splintered wood shooting into the sky where Tom Pepper's house had stood.

As if mad with rage, the Indians erupted in a blood-chilling war cry from the ridge above the settlement, followed by hundreds of bursts of musket fire flashing from the dark ridge. Then, like a red tide, Indians descended on the cabins and shacks that made up the town. As if cheering the warriors on to fight manfully, Indian squaws raised a frantic, eerie cry that sent a chill up the back of William's neck.

More precise bugle signals echoed across the water. Lieutenant Phelps led his Third Division troops up the hill east of Yesler's mill, repulsing the Indian charge. When the Indians retreated, another bugle call signaled a recall. To be clear of the coming barrage, Phelps's division drew back. As planned, Gansevoort was ready. Another thundering volley from the *Decatur,* followed by the same from the *Active,* and Phelps's division again charged the hill. As the smoke settled, only a smattering of musket fire came from the ridge where the Indians had been.

Though driven back, the Indians were not to be so easily defeated. It was only a lull in hostilities. As dawn shone gray in the east, men sculled barges carrying women and children out to *Active* and *Decatur*. Gansevoort placed a twelve-pound field gun and fourteen well-armed marines on one of the barges with orders to return to Seattle and set up a defensive position near the wharf and engage the enemy at the first sign of movement.

While this operation was in motion, an odd scene played out on the beach, visible to all on both ships. An Indian called Curley by locals, a man who assured everyone who would listen that he was a friendly Indian, dressed himself in red paint and feathers, and holding an antique bow in one hand and a trade musket in the other, danced about on the mud and sawdust, screeching like a demented soul.

Perhaps it was intended to be a diversion to benefit the Indians, or maybe Curley did his primitive dance to show solidarity with his white friends. Either way, when he had wearied of it, the Indians had prepared a surprise. From an advance position near the shore, dozens of feathered warriors sent a volley of musket fire at the *Decatur*. By stealth, they had managed to flank the town and set up a position behind large drift logs on the shoreline, less than 200 yards from the sloop-of-war. Indian light-load smoothbore musket fire, against weapon technology from another world—the twelve-pounder Napoleon gun-howitzer, firing exploding projectiles, accurate at great distances.

There was a pattering of lead sloshing into the water, as bullets fell short of the ship. From muskets aimed by Indians who had used a slightly heavier charge of powder, a handful of lead balls thudded against the hull, barely nicking the paint, then plopped with a sploosh and a hiss into the water.

"Shaking in our boots, ain't we?" yelled a seaman, pausing with a cartridge shell in the load position at his gun-howitzer.

"A wee bit out of range, red man!" hollered another.

"Like a bumblebee taking on a herd of buffalo," chimed in another.

To the uproarious amusement of his mates, a seaman jumped up on the rail, wrenched open his tunic, and scrawled a big X with a soot-blackened finger on his bare white chest. "See if you can hit this 'ere!" he shouted at the Indians. "I'll hold real still, honest Injun, I will!"

Still more laughter from the seamen. Several others bared their chests and joined in the taunting.

"Man your guns!" yelled the mate. "Danged fools! Never underestimate your enemy!"

Meanwhile, there was movement from the ridge above and east of the town. William sucked in his breath. It had been a ruse. Leschi and his warriors were bearing down on Phelps's Third Division once again. Though outnumbered, bugles trilling, Phelps's men held their position, repulsing once again the Indian charge.

"Ready your guns!" yelled the mate.

"Fire!"

Again William thought his insides had exploded. His eyes burned from the smoke. A blue cloud enveloped the starboard side of the sloop, obscuring his sight of the effect of that barrage. William glanced around him. If only he could see over the smoke. Grabbing hold of the tarred ratlines, he scrambled up several rope rungs of the ladder. This was better. He turned, squinting toward shore.

Another volley erupted from behind the driftwood on the beach, rippling echoes sounding across the water, whistling through the damp air. Then it was less of a volley of musket lead hurtling toward the ship. William became aware of a lone bullet outdistancing the rest, coming closer, closer.

Suddenly, there was a sharp sting in his shoulder. Just a sting. The roar of the battle receded into a muted haze of confused sights and sounds. A sting like a large wasp. Blinking rapidly to clear his vision, William steadied himself on the ratlines. Wincing, he lowered himself down onto the quarterdeck. Maybe it was a stray fragment of hot lead from the latest barrage. Maybe it was nothing, lack of sleep, the euphoria of the battle, hunger.

"They're done for," drawled a voice out of the cacophony. "The Battle of Seattle is over. It weren't even close."

The crew, the marines, midshipman, and officers up the ranks joined in the *Hurrah! Hurrah!* at *Decatur*'s victory. William heard a croaking coming from his parched throat as he tried to join in.

Roused by the jubilation, William's head cleared. He had to get to shore and find Prophet. Holgate had promised he'd take care of his horse, stable it at Yesler's Mill, so he'd said.

Captain Gansevoort looked hazy and his features were distorted like the mirrors William had once seen at a circus when he was a boy back in Kentucky. "Permission to return to shore?" William heard himself say.

Gansevoort leaned toward William and frowned. "You're looking more pale-faced than you ought to. You sure you're all right, son?"

William assured the captain that he was under orders of Captain Hewitt to carry important dispatches to Fort Steilacoom and Olympia. "I must get to shore and find Prophet," he concluded.

"Profit?" Gansevoort frowned. "You fixing to plunder the town?"

"Prophet, my horse. An express rider needs his horse, and Prophet's the best there is."

"Wait, let me get this straight, young man," said Gansevoort. "You think you're going ashore and getting on your horse and riding from Seattle to Olympia?"

"Yes, Sir. That's my orders."

"Young man, I'm not sure you're thinking real straight," said the sea captain. "There's several thousand painted savages out there, scattered far and wide, licking their wounds, and madder than Hades at all white men. And you plan to hop on your horse and ride to Steilacoom and then on to Olympia, tipping your hat and saying 'Howdy' to them as you ride by? Are you sure you didn't hit your head during the battle, son?"

The circus mirror began doing its work on Captain Gansevoort's face again. William felt confused and a bit nauseous. "But I got to get to my horse." He swallowed hard at the gurgling and lurching in his stomach. It would not do to empty its meager contents on the captain's boots and on the deck of his ship.

Gansevoort took charge. To a midshipman at his elbow he said, "Take this man ashore. Find his horse. Load him on the barge." Turning back to William, he said, "The tide turns in one hour. You be back here with your horse by then—that's an order."

"Sir?"

"It'd take you two full days to ride to Olympia—that's in the unlikely event that you didn't lose your scalp in the first ten minutes. I've got a fair wind and favorable current for the next six hours. We're sailing to Steilacoom—with Bill Tidd and your horse."

42

NARROW ESCAPE

Once on shore, William and the midshipmen began searching for Holgate; accosting the first person they met at the wharf, they asked if he knew where the young man was.

"Blamed if I know. Check at Yesler's mill yonderways. They've set up a morgue there. Might do you should check there."

At Yesler's mill they found Holgate. Dead. The man shot in the doorway of the blockhouse. Though he was dead, true to his word, Holgate had brought Prophet to the mill. Rather Prophet had brought Holgate. Folks had put his body over Prophet's back who then carried him to the makeshift morgue. Phelps's livery, thinking he had a fine buckskin horse for the US Army, had placed the animal in a stall for safe keeping.

William felt like a mother hen when the crew of the *Decatur* rigged a sling and brought Prophet on board. He wished his head would stop spinning. There was nothing he could do but talk encouragingly to Prophet. Once on board, his horse munching oats in the hold, William watched as the crew readied the sloop-of-war for sea.

Captain Gansevoort meant business, and his crew knew it. At his orders, the anchor chain clattered as men raised the ship's iron ground tackle, and men chanted as they heaved on the halyards. Canvas snapping in the freshening breeze, captain and crew soon had sails trimmed and the *Decatur* heeling down Puget Sound Channel toward Commencement Bay.

A midshipman made sure William had something to eat: hardtack and corned beef washed down with a mug of cider. Sitting cross-legged in the straw, he dined down in the hold with Prophet. His shoulder felt stiff and sticky. He tried to ignore it. Stretching out in the straw, William tried to remember when he had last slept; his mind felt like a lump of last week's oatmeal; every time he tried to calculate when it was, he got confused, had to start over. His belly full, and with the easy motion of the vessel, the wind humming in the rigging, the water shying against the hull, Prophet munching contentedly beside him, he was soon asleep.

He awoke with a start. It was pitch dark in the hold. Drifting off into sleep, he had felt like he could sleep for a week. What had awakened him? Prophet was nickering softly, nudging his shoulder and nibbling at his hat. Drawing in a deep breath, William checked his Colt, got up, and headed toward the companionway ladder. Pain shot through his shoulder, and his head felt light; he was forced to steady himself against the bulkhead. In the crew's quarters, two dozen canvas hammocks, bulging with their contents, hung from the deck beams, rocking gently with the motion of the sloop. It smelled of tar and rope, but mostly of man smells and sweat, the pungent sweat men emit when under extreme stress or fear. Weary from battle, a chorus of snoring hovered over the sleeping seamen and marines. It reminded William of opossums hanging by their tails from a branch of a maple tree—and smelled about as bad.

Once on deck, William oriented himself to their position. He knew the territory well, but far more so from the land than from the sea. As near as he could calculate, they had doubled Point Defiance and were sailing on a broad reach, south into the narrow passage of sea aptly named The Narrows. Dark as it was, there were thin patches in the clouds; William could see the dense forests of Douglas fir lining the tops of the cliffs on either side. William shivered; oddly, he felt both hot and cold. Black and deep looking, the sea caught occasional flashes of moonlight on whitecaps hissing from their wake.

Without taking his eyes from the horizon, his feet planted wide, hands easy on the spokes of the wheel, the helmsmen nodded wordlessly at William. Four or five seamen on watch did the same. The sloop was in blackout, not so much as a running light showing, and Captain Gansevoort must have ordered silence; not a man spoke a word.

All seemed ordered and under control, almost tranquil, as if it was another world, one not rending itself apart with war. Something Noclas had read flashed back into William's mind, something about breaking down walls of hostility, establishing peace. On a perfect night like this one, sailing up The Narrows, the wind, the ship, the sea, the current, men resting peacefully in their quarters—everything in balance, for the moment, it almost felt like peace had come. But why had Prophet roused him from sleep?

Though William's intuitions and fears often played tricks on him, Prophet's never seemed to. Something must be amiss. Maybe he should tell the officer of the watch. Forewarned is forearmed. But there was the blackout and silence. Besides, they would think he had come unstrung if he said, "My horse just woke me up. Something isn't right. My horse told me so." There would be knowing looks, a wink of amusement, a good jest to tell at the saloon, but surely not a man would take him seriously. Maybe Prophet was restless; it was not every day that he was slung by the belly into a sloop-of-war, and he'd never been sailing before. Just restless, that was all.

As William ruminated, leaning on the starboard rail, he spotted a black shape in the water—no, two black shapes. Probably drift logs. There were often logs and branches, sometimes whole trees, floating on the Sound, especially in winter after heavy rainfall. Probably just logs. Steadying himself on the standing rigging, he walked over to the portside and gazed into the dark forest. The mainsail billowing taut blocking the wind made it warmer on this side of the vessel. Wiping sweat from his forehead on his sleeve, William tried moving his shoulder. Pain shot through the left side of his body, and there was that sticky feeling again. Better head below and get some more sleep.

Pausing at the companionway, his foot on the first rung, William decided to take one last look off the starboard rail. Steadying himself on the ratlines, he looked off at the tree-covered bluff, his eyes following the contours down to the shoreline, as near as he could tell; it was so dark. The drift logs were nowhere in sight. Which was odd, because it had been only moments ago when he had seen them. Drift logs just drift, and with the incoming current they would be more likely to appear to stay closer to their position. Well, it was dark. How could he expect to spot them again—black logs, on a black sea, on a black night? He yawned, wincing at the pain in his shoulder.

Turning to go below, he saw them. Close to the hull, end-to-end along the length of the boat, and bigger than they had seemed when he first saw them. Something was moving on the logs. Not infrequently when William was paddling Charlie's canoe on the Sound, he would see whole flocks of cormorants parked on drift logs, drying out the pits under their wings, maybe these were—.

His heart stopped. They had feathers, but these were no cormorants. And they weren't logs. They were war canoes.

"Indians!" screamed William, drawing his revolver. "Boarding on the starboard! Two canoes, full of 'em!"

At the same instant the Indians let loose with their wild war cry, *Eeu-oww!* clamoring up the hull of the sloop-of-war.

The men on watch immediately began clubbing at the black shadows of hands and arms and heads, as Indian after Indian attempted to grapple onboard the sloop.

"To quarters! To quarters!" yelled the officer of the watch. There was a wild staccato of drumsticks signaling men to man their battle stations. "Repel boarders!"

Men who had been in the oblivion of much-earned sleep an instant before, were now on deck, barefooted, moving like pale ghosts in their long underwear, hacking and clubbing at the boarders, desperate to defend their ship.

Officers drew their swords and slashed away at dark shadows, at arms and hands and fingers. William found that, under the circumstances, his Colt worked best as a club. Holding the barrel, he brought the butt down on a set of Indian knuckles made white by gripping the rail. With a yowl of pain, the Indian let go and fell with a clunk back into the dugout canoe. Next to him, a midshipman swung away with a hatchet at hands and fingers.

It was over as rapidly as it had begun. Captain Gansevoort, deciding it was futile to give chase, ordered his men to fire a volley after the black retreating shapes of two canoes, disappearing into the night.

Later William learned that in the morning the crew of *Decatur* discovered—amidst the hack marks of axes, swords, pistol and musket butts—a quantity of blood, and four severed fingers littering the starboard rail.

When at last Gansevoort and his officers restored order, reset the sloop's course, doubled the watch, and sent the rest of the men below to try and get more rest, William steadied himself with his right hand on the rail. His left hand didn't seem to want to do what it was supposed to.

A racket of sounds came at William from all sides: husky whispered orders, clomping feet, clanking weapons. Rubbing his eyes, blinking rapidly; his eyes refused to focus. He felt lightheaded, like it had all been a nightmare, but one from which he was unable to awaken himself. He felt it coming, but couldn't stop it. His knees buckled. He was collapsing on the deck. William wasn't sure if this was sleep or delirium—or something worse. He wasn't sure if it mattered. Nothing mattered.

43

GUILTY

The next conscious memories William had seemed to be in a court room. He was sitting in the witness stand, and Charlie Salitat sat where the defendant sat, ramrod straight, dignified but not haughty, staring up at William, his eyes boring into his heart.

"William Tidd," said the bailiff, "do you promise to tell the truth, the whole truth, and nothing but the truth, so help you God?"

"Y-yes, I swear it," said William. He winced as he said it; his shoulder felt like it was on fire.

"Charlie Salitat, known Indian, as you can see, and known Indian sympathizer in these our recent troubles, and in all likelihood, a spy for Leschi," said the prosecuting attorney. "Is hereby accused of the heinous deed of shooting through the heart and killing, in cold blood, on the night of December 4, 1855, an officer of the US Army, Lieutenant William Slaughter."

William felt the sweat breaking on his forehead, his shirt and trousers clammy and sticking to his skin. What he had feared, here it was, coming down upon him, unfolding before his very eyes. But they had it all wrong. Why wasn't Charles the Rustler sitting in the dock up there? Foul-smelling, thieving Charles Wren, he was more responsible than any other human being for this war, the fighting and killing—stirring up Indians one day, stirring up whites the next. They had it all wrong.

Though William was certain Charlie Salitat hadn't shot Slaughter and any evidence was purely circumstantial, he had feared all along that he couldn't prove that his friend had not done it. And, what's more, the circumstantial evidence against Charlie was so compelling, there were times when even William had wondered if Charlie might not be a foe instead of a friend. If he could think that way about his friend, how much more would a judge or jury made up of men who had buried family killed by Indians in the war, made up of folks who distrusted all Indians, how much more would they look askance at the evidence, convict him, and sentence him to hang for it.

And here he was, as he had feared, sitting in the witness stand, to testify against Charlie Salitat, his friend.

"Where were you on the night of December 4, 1855?" The prosecutor was addressing William. He tried to focus, to concentrate, to choose his words more carefully than ever before he had thought necessary.

"Give it lip, man," said the prosecutor. "You swore to tell the whole truth and nothing but the truth, so help you God. The Almighty's doing his part. Now's the time to do yours!"

"I-I was at Brannon's Prairie, sir," stammered William.

"Under whose command?"

"Washington Territorial Militia, under the overall command of Lieutenant Slaughter—the late Lieutenant William Slaughter."

"And your role under his command?"

"Express rider," said William.

"Explain to the court how an express rider employs his time."

"I carry dispatches from one officer to another," said William.

"Alone?"

"Well, me and my horse," said William.

A titter of laughter rippled throughout the courtroom. A set to his jaw, the prosecutor scowled down at William.

Blam! "Order in the court!" said the judge, rapping his gavel.

"So you ride out alone—on your horse—and carry secret messages. Did you, and your horse, in the execution of any of your duties, ever come in contact with the accused, Charlie Salitat?"

William bit his lower lip until he tasted blood.

"Bill Tidd, may I remind you that you are under oath," said the judge, scowling down at William, the man's eyebrows looking like they were transplanted from the back of a porcupine.

"Y-yes," said William.

"Yes, what?" said the prosecutor, strolling in front of the jury, his hands clasped behind his back like a general inspecting his troops.

"Yes, I did encounter him," said William, his voice barely above a whisper.

"More than once?"

William swallowed. "Yes."

"And was not the first of these meetings immediately after the White River Massacre?"

"I-it was," stammered William.

"The bodies were not yet cold, and Charlie Salitat—the accused—was there. How do you know that he did not participate in the wanton and barbaric massacre of innocent men, women, and children? How do you know that he did not?"

William felt like a rabbit, cornered by a coyote. He looked up at the judge. Did he have to answer a question worded like that? Why didn't the defense attorney for Charlie stand up and object?

"I can see from the eloquence of your silence," said the prosecutor, his back to William, standing now in front of the jury, rocking from his heels up onto his toes, "I can see that you are not absolutely certain Charlie did not participate in the killing."

"He did not do it!" shouted William. "I know he couldn't have done it. Charlie helped the children, and he rode through the night warning—"

"Calm down, my boy. You are merely to answer the questions, not retell every episode of our late and tragic war. You seem far too touchy for being trustworthy. Let me redirect my examination. Is it not also true that you met with the accused, Charlie Salitat, on the night of December 4, 1855, in the forest only yards away from the root house in which Slaughter would be cut down, and only moments before the killing? Is this not true?"

Frantic, William considered bolting for the plank door of the rustic courtroom. Wasn't there some kind of amendment to the Constitution that he could appeal to so as not to have to answer a question that would be so incriminating to his friend—maybe to himself?

"Did you meet with him or did you not?" said the prosecutor. "It is a simple question, requiring a simple yes or no. But may I remind you—"

"Yes, I did meet with him."

"Let me get this straight," said the prosecutor, blinking rapidly and feigning bewilderment. "In the very center of full-scale Indian hostilities and massacre, Bill Tidd, here, leaves his duties and sneaks into the forest to meet with an Indian—in the midst of a war with *Indians*—retrieves his horse he claims was stolen (forgive me for failing to mention the little matter of the horse the accused gave to Bill Tidd that night, perhaps as an exchange for information? Evidence for a different trial), and moments later a US Army officer is shot through the heart by an Indian sniper, one who had to be in close range." He stood before the jury, his hands turned palms up, waggling his head as if to say, "What else could any reasonable man conclude?"

Spinning on his heel, his eyes boring into William, the prosecutor continued. "Bill Tidd, you have confessed that the defendant Charlie Salitat was there, within range of the killing—and I have it on good authority that the defendant is considerably above average in his ability to shoot with accuracy. Here is my question to you, Bill Tidd. Was there any other Indian, of which you were personally aware, in the immediate vicinity before the killing?"

Again William felt panic rising inside him. How he replied to this question could put the final nail in Charlie's coffin—if he even got a coffin. "Judging from musket fire boring down on our encampment right after Slaughter fell, there must have been dozens of Indians in the vicinity."

"—Aha, but you have failed to answer my question, a clever deflection," said the prosecutor, tilting his head and narrowing his eyes knowingly at the jury. "My question was very precise. Were you personally aware of any other Indians in the vicinity *before* the shooting? Please answer that question for the court."

"No."

"There, now," said the prosecutor. "That weren't so painful, now, was it?" About to turn toward the judge, he hesitated in his theatrical manner. "I must warn you, Bill Tidd, there are matters of your involvement in all this that are deeply troubling. But that's for another day, perhaps another trial."

He broke off, turning to face the bench. "Your honor," said the prosecutor, shrugging his shoulders in a gesture of feigned humility. "I see no reason to presume any further on the patience of this court. I rest my case."

The jurors filed toward the deliberation chamber, passing before William like specters in a dream, nightmarish figures drifting into the dark cavernous doorway at the side of the judge's bench. With every minute the jury remained behind closed doors in their deliberation, William felt the heat rising in his face, sweat dribbling off his nose and chin, haze quavering before his eyes like a mirage.

He was in despair. It was all his fault. William knew that his testimony, far from helping to clear Charlie, would be used instead to convict the Indian of a crime he did not commit. William was sure of it. But he was equally sure that in the aftermath of the Indian war, Charlie was guilty in the minds of those who sat in judgment on him. How could a jury, manipulated so cleverly by the theatrics of the prosecutor, how could they do anything but find Charlie guilty as charged? As inevitable as icefall on a glacier in August, white man's justice was about to put a noose around his neck and draw it tight.

And then, like the glacial clutches of death itself, a still more troubling thought began to work in William's head. Noclas had said that some Indians were none too pleased with Charlie for warning settlers to flee for their lives from another Indian massacre. If somehow Charlie was acquitted by the white man jury wrangling in the back room of the courthouse, what then? What would Indian justice do to him? William shivered feverishly at the thought. Caught between the white man's world and the Indian one, Charlie was a condemned man. And it was William's testimony that did it.

Suddenly the jury door opened. William felt like he was being strangled. He couldn't breathe. He searched the faces of the jurors as they past. What had they decided? What would be Charlie's sentence? The sheriff escorted Charlie back into the courtroom. William looked at his friend, pleading for him with his eyes. Charlie winked at William and broke into a wide grin. William was afraid he would begin his ridiculous laughing, what he done when he was being white, when he was happy, when he was contented and at peace.

"All rise!" called the bailiff.

Shrouded in a wide black robe, the judge entered the courtroom. After scanning the courtroom with a frown, he turned on Charlie, his eyes boring holes in him, so it seemed to William.

"Foreman, have you reached a verdict?" growled the judge.

"Your Honor, we the jury find the accused, Charlie Salitat—" the foreman hesitated, or was he pausing for dramatic effect? "We find the accused—guilty, as charged."

Blam! crashed the judge's gavel. "Order in the court!"

44

PEACE FEAST

B*lam!* William felt like his head was being split open with a tomahawk. Could be a musket firing, or was it the judge's gavel? He found himself flailing from side to side, his teeth clenched tight on a wad of red point blanket.

"Clumsy ole me! Look what I've done. Dropped the fry pan and woke him up. William, you all right?"

It was Junebug's voice. Through the haze, William saw her face; it was definitely Junebug, his sister, leaning close, her eyes sparkling with moisture, looking wide and anxious. And at her side was Noclas, his black polished features shimmering in the warm glow of candlelight. And a shaggy gray-haired face, long snout, one ear flopped over, panting and tongue lolling, big teeth, walleyed. William wondered if this was dreaming or hallucinating. Or maybe this was his home, back in the Tidd cabin. But how did he get here?

Swelling and shrinking, the room pulsed before him, candlelight quavering into a fuzzy halo, pulsing gradually back into a pinpoint of light, then back again into a wide halo. William's stomach lurched with nausea. He tried sitting up, having a better look. Pain shot through his left shoulder.

"You must rest," said a young woman's voice on his left. He tried to turn.

Wincing at the pain, he managed to say, "What happened to me?"

"You were shot," said the woman's voice. "In the shoulder."

Lying back on the pillow, William tried to reconstruct what had happened. "How did I get here?"

Noclas smiled, his broad teeth looking whiter than William had remembered.

"Prophet done brung you home," said Junebug. "A good thing he done it when he did. You'd been leaking pretty bad, were weak as kitten. But you're looking better already. Marguerite, she's been doctoring of you. That's what done it."

William turned to his left. He blinked and frowned. Marguerite pretended to be absorbed in checking the wound in his shoulder. "Noclas made the poultice and the tea," she said, narrowing her eyes critically at the wound.

"Well, it were The Almighty who made the ingredients for the poultice and the tea," said Noclas.

"And Junebug's chicken broth," added Marguerite. "I believe the broth has done far more good than the best of my efforts."

"William Tidd, you being alive and mending here after all these troubles," said Noclas. "It's answer to a good deal of praying that's been going on in this here cabin. I sure do bless the Lord seeing you awake and being better." The black man gently patted William's good shoulder as he spoke.

"I aim to fat you up, Brother," said Junebug. "Now, you open your mouth."

Slurping down spoonful after spoonful of Junebug's broth, warmth radiated throughout every joint of William's body. Grinning at him, his sister wiped the dribbles from his chin. "Time for you to get some shut-eye now."

How long he slept, William did not know. Save for the heavy breathing of Wally, the cabin was silent. It must be middle of the night. A soft glow of light came from the coals in the fireplace. William wiped his forehead. It was neither cold nor hot, and the sweating and shivering were gone. He breathed a deep sigh. He had survived, when so many hadn't. But why?

There was movement at the rocking chair. Noclas peered around the bent-willow frame. "You's awake," he said, rising softly to his feet and bringing a stool up close by the bedside. "You be needing anything?"

Staring at the underside of the cedar shakes above, William felt there was a great deal he needed, but where to begin? It was as if the war had intensified everything, his whole life, especially the unhappy bits, the ones that—try as he might—he could make neither head nor tail of; it was all passing before him as if for inspection, as if he were supposed to do something, fix something. But what?

He turned and looked at the old black man's understanding face. Yes, he felt very much like he needed something. And at just that moment, he felt certain that more than anybody else, it was Noclas who might be able to make head or tails out of it all.

"It don't make no sense," he said, staring back at the rough beams and shakes above. "So many died. I seen it. They was alive one minute, spitting and swearing some of 'em, then they was dead, bullet through the heart or the neck. But dead. And here I am, scratched up a bit by a musket ball, but alive and mending. It don't make no sense."

Noclas nodded encouragingly but said nothing.

Several minutes passed. "Death and dying. It don't make no sense." He turned and looked full on at Noclas. "Why did Ma have to do it?" he said. "Die? Her and her little one. Why?"

Noclas said not a word. Patting William's forearm, he just gave off more of his little encouraging grunts and murmurs.

William would never forget it, his baby brother falling ill and dying in '52. They had a name for it; child paralysis, it was being called. Word was it was a virus that struck all over the continent, like a plague from the Dark Ages, sweeping away little children by the thousands. It made no sense to him. And he would never forget how his mother had taken sick in the wagon, coughing and shivering. Lots of womenfolk and children got sick on the trail west. Some died, but some shook it off and recovered.

"Ma held out for more than a year—a long, painful year it was," continued William. "Then it struck her too; she never recovered." After another stretch of silence, he continued. "Neither did Pa. Setting right there in that chair, reading about nonconformity, being one with nature, self-reliance, and the green-apple theory, how folks and society are supposed to be ripening to perfection. Day in, day out, and the more he read the worse he got. Pa weren't ripening; he was rotting. Then he was gone." His voice trailed off.

Noclas said nothing for several minutes; at last he murmured, "How your Pa ended his life—I'm thinking all that's a bit too heavy for lifting. It'll crush you like a rock crushing an ant. A feller knows when a log or boulder's too heavy for lifting—knows it'll kill him if he relies on himself. So a real man, he finds himself something stronger, an ox or mule, to heft it for him."

William felt hemmed in, nowhere else to turn. Noclas's words were accompanied by the wind moaning in the fir boughs outside, the rain spattering on the cedar shakes, Wally sighing contentedly in his sleep, and the fire hissing softly on the grate. It was like an orchestra, Noclas's resonant voice singing the solo part.

"There ain't no other way," continued Noclas. "You need someone stronger than Bill Tidd, someone who can heft all them griefs, all them sorrows, all them cares for you. On your own it'll crush you—like a bug under a boot heel. There ain't no other way, but *the Way*. Jesus alone can bear your burden, carry off your sins, wash away your guilt, and give you peace."

William eased himself into a sitting position. "But it just don't make no sense."

"There ain't no other way to make sense of it all, no other way to find peace," said Noclas. "Peace in here," he patted William's chest with his calloused fingers, "and peace in the midst of all these troubles, peace for white men, peace for Injuns, even peace for an old black feller the likes of me—it don't come nowhere else but at the cross where the Prince of Peace done laid down his life for his friends—white friends, red friends, black friends. You've seen how them other ways turn out, with trouble, war, death, and killing. You're right, Bill Tidd. There ain't no sense to be found in them other ways."

William did a good deal of sleeping and eating in the next week—and musing on Noclas's words. Then one morning he awoke, and he knew that things had changed. It was as if a new world was blossoming outside. Cold and wet as winter was in the Puget Sound, warmer breezes would blow soon enough and drive it away. Outside, William heard a flock of dozens of starlings, giddy with the new life the change of seasons promised, fluttering and twittering frantically from the shake roof of the Tidd cabin, to the rail fence bordering the cornfield, to the boughs of fir trees, to the hitching post, and back again.

After William had eaten two heaping platefuls of bacon, eggs, and fried sweet potatoes, Noclas came by with a pouch full of a new supply of White-Man's-Foot tea. Shortly thereafter, Marguerite stopped in to change the poultice on William's shoulder.

"Mending nicely, so it would appear," she said, smiling with satisfaction as she examined the wound and prepared a clean strip of cloth for a dressing.

The stronger William felt the more awkward he felt having the close ministrations of a young woman, working salve into his skin with her soft white hands, leaning in close to inspect the progress of healing in his wound.

"Don't know why there's so much fuss," he said. It was too gruff, not how he wanted it to sound. "That is, I mean—thank you." William tried slipping his arm back in the sleeve of his shirt, but his fingers got hung up in a fraying hole in the elbow.

"Allow me," said Marguerite, untangling the sleeve. "The buttons, on your shirt. Shall I help with them?"

"No!" said William. "I mean, I can manage." After an uncomfortable silence, he asked, "Junebug, she sent me a picture, a sketch she'd made—of you. Now I seen it with my own eyes. Reckon I might ask what happened to your nun's get-up; you know, the black teepee dress, and the thingamajig that used to cover up your head? That is, if you don't mind me asking?"

Twirling a lock of her auburn hair around a finger, the color rose on Marguerite's cheeks. With a quick shrug of her shoulders, she looked at William and smiled. "Noclas showed me things in his book."

"Now, Miss Marguerite," said Noclas, a gentle rebuke in his tone. "One of them things I've been trying to show you is it *ain't* my book. It's God's book."

Marguerite smiled. "And Charlie Salitat," she continued, her voiced hushed, almost reverent. "Remember in the canoe, after the tyee died at the longhouse?"

William nodded.

"Charlie's questions—I had no real answers to them," she said, again looking at William.

He couldn't help noticing that there was no more hooding of her eyes when she looked his way. Irritated with himself for it, William couldn't stop the quickening of his pulse when she entered the cabin, when she leaned in close to check his wound. What is more, he couldn't help noticing how well she matched up with the sketch of her that Junebug had sent him.

"While you were gone," continued Marguerite, "fighting in the war, every time I stopped to see how Junebug was getting along, Noclas always would read to us. At first, I persisted in listening only to my questions. I thought my questions were more clever than God's answers."

"Yes, I s'pose you did," said Noclas. "But you was being changed. We could see it, ain't that right, Junebug?"

"We sure could," agreed Junebug.

"Something was changing me," continued Marguerite. "I cannot fully explain it. But gradually I stopped listening to my questions and began listening to God's answers—in his book. That's when things began to make sense."

"Is that why you gave up calling yourself Sister Marguerite?" asked William.

Pulling out a ball of yarn and her knitting needles, Marguerite nodded. "'Sister Marguerite' was my given name, given me by the Mother Superior at the convent. Noclas is the one who dropped 'Sister' and started calling me 'Miss Marguerite.'"

"Does that mean," asked William, trying to make his voice sound as indifferent as asking what's for supper, "you're not a nun anymore?"

For a moment Marguerite's knitting seemed to demand her complete concentration. Then she looked up, and, almost imperceptibly, shook her head. "I am not," she said softly.

Junebug looked up, a charcoal smudge on her chin from the sketch she had been working on. "What is your real name, the one your ma and pa gave you when you was born?"

"I was very young," said Marguerite. "I do not know."

"If 'Sister Marguerite' ain't your real name, anyhow," said Junebug, "could be you need a new one. I like 'Marguerite,' mind you, but what about 'Maggie'? 'Maggie' sounds more like we're on real friendly terms with you." Junebug grinned. "Which we are."

"It's a right pretty name," said Noclas, "that is, if Miss Marguerite takes a fancy to being called by it."

Her knitting needles halting midstitch, Marguerite looked into the rafters, her lips moving slowly, repeating the name as if she were trying it on. She looked steadily at Junebug. "What is it about 'Maggie' that makes you like it so much?"

"I like both names," said Junebug. "But there is something about 'Maggie.' It sounds more familiar, like we know you real good, like we're family."

Marguerite smiled. "'Maggie' it is, then," she said. "At least that's what my family will call me. Now I must be off. There's more than one fellow in the territory right now needing doctoring."

"Wait," said William. "What's for supper, Junebug?"

"Well, first I think we'll have salmon prepared the way Charlie's folks do it—there's another thing I like about Indians—then we'll have some yummy baked sweet potatoes, and—"

"That sounds good," said William. Turning to Maggie, he hesitated. "You'll come around at suppertime, won't you? Check on my shoulder?"

Maggie didn't immediately reply.

"You got to eat," said William.

"I will if I am invited," said Maggie.

William sat up. Clearing his throat, he said, "Would you do us the honor, Maggie, of joining us for supper?"

"I will," she said, with a smile.

Later that morning, William got out of bed, washed up, and dressed. He walked slowly around the cabin; he'd been doing it for several days now, more turns around the cabin with each day. His shoulder was still a bit stiff, but the pain was mostly gone, and he felt new strength returning to his limbs. Wally loping at his side, William went outdoors to inspect his cabin, his fences, and his fields. There were repairs to be made, some cedar shakes had blown off during winter storms, and a fence rail here and there needed replacing, and there was spring plowing and planting just around the corner. The sooner his shoulder healed up the better.

"What you going to do now the war's over?" asked Junebug, later that afternoon.

"Reckon I'll set me down in that there rocking chair," said William.

"And after that?" she asked.

"After a good long spell," said William, "I just might think about doing me some rocking."

Junebug searched his features, trying to figure it out. William broke into a broad grin. Though his face was not used to doing it, it felt good. "I'm just foxing you."

Junebug gave him a whack, and the cabin rang with laughter. Wally joined in, barking and planting his paws on William's chest. "But before that," said William, scratching the beast behind the ears, "I say we need to have ourselves a feast."

"A yummy thanksgiving feast, like the Pilgrims had," said Junebug. "And they done had it with the Indians. Wait! Ours could be a war-over, *peace* feast! We could invite the Indians too—leastwise, Charlie, and of course we'll have Noclas and Maggie."

Charlie Salitat. William's grin disappeared. Junebug's voice, drifting into the background of his thoughts, continued listing off other folks she would invite.

After the courtroom trial that had troubled him in his delirium, William thought often about his friend Charlie Salitat. He tried allaying his fears by telling himself it was just a dream, but still he worried. More than a week had passed and no sign of Charlie appearing out of the drizzle. Maybe when the hostilities were fully ended, peace fully restored. Maybe when William least expected it, a fir cone lobbed out of nowhere would hit him on the hat, or Charlie's *Hyuk-hyuk-ing* would come from behind a bunch of salal in the forest, and then mingle warmly with other happy sounds filling the Tidd cabin.

There was no stopping Junebug now. She was in a frenzy of excited planning for the feast. Snatching up a scrap of paper and some charcoal, she sketched as she continued. "Then we'll have roasted venison, sweet potatoes baked just to the point when the skin splits, codfish swimming in butter and herbs, turkeys baked till the skin is crispy and brown with cranberry sauce dribbled all over it, acorn squash halves with heaps of cinnamon and honey in the bowl, and alder-smoked salmon, roasted apples, pumpkin pies with whipped cream swirling on top—just like the Pilgrims."

"A peace feast," mused William, savoring the words. "Do you reckon the Pilgrims ate corn cakes baked to golden perfection and dribbling with melting butter and honey?"

"I reckon they did!" laughed Junebug.

William took a playful tug on his sister's ponytail. "Bet they weren't near so yummy as somebody else's I know."

THE END

EPILOGUE

After the war, William Tidd became a carpenter in Steilacoom; he never did see Charlie Salitat again. Charlie Salitat, "The Paul Revere of Puget Sound," for his midnight ride October 29, 1855 warning the settlers in the Puyallup Valley of impending massacre, was later killed by Indians who believed he had betrayed the Indian cause. In 1858, Chief Leschi was betrayed by his nephew Sluggia, arrested and tried for the murder of Abraham Moses and Joseph Miles. After being first acquitted, he was later retried, condemned, and hanged February 19 near Fort Steilacoom. The US Army would not allow the trial or the hanging to take place at the fort because it was believed that Leschi was not guilty of the charges. Leschi repeatedly denied committing the murders, even offering to have a hand cut off to prove his innocence. "I deny that I had any part in the killing . . . . As God sees me, this is the truth," insisted Leschi. Charles Grainger, territorial hangman, agreed. "I felt then I was hanging an innocent man, and I believe it yet."

TIMELINE

1818	Joint Occupation Agreement between British and American governments for joint use of land in the Oregon Territory.
1825	Hudson Bay Company establishes Fort Vancouver on the Columbia River.
1826	James Fenimore Cooper's *The Last of the Mohicans* published.
1830s	Sam Hill's Mercantile in Prescott, Arizona, the origin of the expression, "What in the Sam Hill is that?"
1833	Hudson Bay Company establishes Fort Nisqually for fur trading on Puget Sound.
1840	Chloe Clark arrives at Fort Nisqually as first female Christian missionary teacher in Puget Sound.
1841	American Captain Charles Wilkes arrives in Puget Sound, making American territorial claims near Hudson Bay lands.

1841	Ralph Waldo Emerson's essay *Self-Reliance* published.
1843	Fort Nisqually moved up Sequalitchew Creek to a knoll at present-day Dupont, Washington (in the 1930s two original fort buildings were moved to Point Defiance Park, Tacoma, and the fort reconstructed within walking distance of the author's home).
1843–1844	Publication of *Songs for the Wilderness,* Scottish poet Horatius Bonar's widely circulated hymn collection. It includes the hymn Noclas sings to William, "I Lay My Sins on Jesus."
1844	African American settler George Bush (Noclas) arrives in Puget Sound and begins farming near present-day Olympia, Washington.
1844	Indian skirmish with Hudson Bay Company at Fort Nisqually.
1846	Oregon Treaty.
1846	Smithsonian Institute established by Congress.
1847	Francis Blanchet brings twenty-one priests and nuns from Europe to Catholic missions in the Northwest.
1847	Protestant missionary Marcus Whitman and others massacred by Cayuse Indians in Eastern Washington.
1848	Karl Marx's *Communist Manifesto* published.
1848	Seneca Falls Convention, women's rights activist Elizabeth Cady Stanton presents her *Declaration of Sentiments*.
1849	California Gold Rush; first recorded use of the word shenanigan.

1849	Captain Bennet Hill rents the Joseph Heath farm and establishes the first US Army base in the region at Fort Steilacoom.
1850	Nathanael Hawthorne's *Scarlet Letter* published.
1851	Charles Hodge begins his tenure at Princeton Theological Seminary.
1852	African American settler George Washington arrives in Puget Sound region and begins farming.
1852	Thomas Chambers builds a sawmill on Chambers Creek near present-day Steilacoom, Washington, within a few hundred yards of where the author's father Douglas Elwood Bond is buried.
1852	Child paralysis epidemic mysteriously kills thousands of children across the continent.
1852	Harriet Beecher Stowe's *Uncle Tom's Cabin* published.
1853	John Howie's *The Scots Worthies* published; popular book owned and read by Hudson Bay Company employees and Scots settlers.
1853	Colonel William Wallace's house built in Steilacoom, Washington.
1854	Snohomish Indians murder Alki sawmill engineer; Seattle sheriff and deputies attacked by Indians, three wounded, one killed; in return fire, nine Indians are killed, two taken, tried, executed.
1854	December 25: New Territorial Governor Isaac Stevens drafts Medicine Creek Treaty; Nisqually tribal leader, Leschi, disgruntled with treaty.

1855	January: Rumors of horse Indians and canoe Indians forming war alliance; Chief Seattle signs Elliot Point Treaty; US Navy sloop-of-war *Decatur* arrives from Hawaii in Puget Sound to quell Indian uprising.
	February: Judson and DeLin families warned by friendly Indian Scarface Charlie and abandon their farms at Commencement Bay, near the author's home in present-day Tacoma, Washington, and flee to Fort Steilacoom.
	February 8: Abraham Lincoln elected to the US Senate for Illinois.
	April: Walt Whitman's *Leaves of Grass* published.
	September: American settlers construct blockades and organize militia.
	October: White River settlers, including children, killed by Indians; Charles Eaton (Eaton's Rangers) sent out with nineteen militia volunteers from Olympia; American settlers James McAllister and Michael Connell shot and killed.
	October 29: Puyallup Indian Charlie Salitat becomes the Paul Revere of Puget Sound; for warning dozens of American white settlers of imminent Indian attack, Salitat is accused of betrayal and later killed by fellow tribesmen; young William Tidd of Steilacoom becomes tireless courier of military dispatches.
	November: Joseph Miles and Abram Benton Moses (former sheriff of Thurston County) shot and killed while on patrol; Leschi accused of murdering them.

	December: Lieutenant William Slaughter and three other US Army soldiers killed near present day Auburn, Washington.
1856	January: several hundred Indians attack Seattle, repelled by bombardment from the sloop-of-war *Decatur* anchored in Elliot Bay; Indians retreat, burning and pillaging the houses and farms of local settlers.
	February–March: US Army soldiers and volunteer militia hunt down Indian leaders; several are tried, convicted, and executed.
	Spring: American settlers leave blockades in Steilacoom, Seattle, Olympia and cautiously return to plant their crops under army and militia protection.
1858	Leschi betrayed by his nephew Sluggia, arrested and after a mistrial, retried, condemned, and hanged February 19 near Fort Steilacoom.
1859	Charles Darwin's *Origin of Species* published.
1860–1865	American Civil War or War of Northern Aggression.
1864	Job Carr, founder of Tacoma, Washington, builds a log cabin in Old Town on the shores of Puget Sound, a few blocks from the present-day home of the author.
1871	Tacoma becomes the western terminus of the Northern Pacific Railroad.
1885	Mark Twain's *The Adventures of Huckleberry Finn* published.
1889	Washington Territory becomes Washington State.

GLOSSARY OF TERMS

Capots: long, hooded outer garments made from wool blankets.

Clairvoyant: having the supposed ability to know things beyond the five senses.

Coke: hot-burning coal used by blacksmiths.

Gunkhole: a shallow, often muddy body of water, such as a creek or marsh; to *gunkhole* is to sail through the same.

Howitzer: originally a fifteenth-century Czech name for a cannon, by 1855 a gun-howitzer shooting exploding cartridges. Indians were demoralized by long-range ordnance that would explode when it hit, erupting with deadly lead balls that could kill many of them in one explosion; they believed it was the work of evil spirits who were warring with the whites against them.

Laissez-faire: free-market economics, where the government leaves individuals and business alone to create wealth by providing goods and services that their neighbors want, need, and are willing to buy without coercion.

Moulinet: a circular cut with a saber sometimes including a defending parry with the blade; cavalry term derived from the French word for reel (as in fishing reel) or winch.

Murder: the name for a group of crows, a murder of crows, as in a flock of geese.

Papoose: generic Indian name for infant or young child.

Potlatch: a ceremonial feast where Northwest Indians would try to outgive gifts to each other to gain status.

Shaman: Indian medicine man claiming to be the physical and spiritual healer for the tribe.

Travois: a wooden framework dragged behind a horse or a dog for carrying cargo.